THE RIGHT WRONG THING

Also by Ellen Kirschman

Fiction: Dot Meyerhoff Series
Burying Ben

Nonfiction:

*Counseling Cops: What Clinicians Need to Know
(with Mark Kamena and Joel Fay, 2014)*

*I Love a Cop: What Police Families Need to Know
(first edition 1997, revised edition 2007)*

I Love a Fire Fighter: What The Family Needs to Know (2004)

THE RIGHT WRONG THING

A Dot Meyerhoff Mystery

ELLEN KIRSCHMAN

Oceanview Publishing
Longboat Key, Florida

ISBN: 978-1-60809-154-6

Published in the United States of America by Oceanview Publishing Longboat Key, Florida

www.oceanviewpub.com

10 9 8 7 6 5 4 3 2 1

PRINTED IN THE UNITED STATES OF AMERICA

To the men and women of law enforcement
Thank you for your service

ACKNOWLEDGMENTS

I was a police psychologist long before I started writing mysteries. Police work is a tough calling. I have counseled cops who feel guilty for something they've done and cops who feel guilty for something they didn't do. I'm indebted to every one of them for sharing their stories and inspiring me to write.

I am grateful to have so many friends, cops, and colleagues to cheer me on. Special thanks go to Sheriff's Deputy Harriet Fox, police psychologists Phil Trompetter, Joel Fay, and Mark Kamena, my colleagues at the Psychological Services Section of the International Association of Chiefs of Police, and the dedicated staff at the First Responder Support Network (FRSN). FRSN is truly a haven for first responders with post-traumatic stress injuries.

My agent, Cynthia Zigmund of Second City Publishing, has been a calm and reassuring presence. Without her keen eye and writerly guidance, this book would still be looking for a home. Pat and Bob Gussin of Oceanview Publishing have welcomed me with enthusiasm. I know I am in good hands. My husband, Steve Johnson, reads my work and manages my life. Without him, there would be no laughter, no laundry, and no lunch.

THE RIGHT WRONG THING

PROLOGUE

Randy Alderson Spelling looks more like a girl than a woman. So tiny she's nearly lost in the cushions of my office couch. Her legs jut out over the floor until she scoots forward and places her feet squarely on the ground, leaving a foot of space behind her. She waits for me to start, all the while pulling on her fingers, cracking each tiny knuckle. I'm the last hurdle between her and the job she covets—police officer for the Kenilworth Police Department. She's aced the entire gamut of challenges: a background check that combed over all twenty-four years of her life; a medical examination; tests of reading, writing, and judgment; officer interviews; agility tests; and an interview with Acting Chief Jay Pence. Now she's down to me, the department psychologist. I'm looking into the nooks and crannies of her emotional stability now that she's received a conditional offer of employment from Pence; conditional, that is, upon my finding her free of any psychological conditions that would prevent her from fulfilling the role of police officer.

Pence wants this woman on the force. He's made that clear with his slightly overreaching and out-of-character enthusiasm. The truth is, women officers haven't done well at KPD. None of the four women who were hired before my time worked out. One got pregnant and never returned from maternity leave. Another woman's husband was promoted and the family moved to New York. A third decided to go to law school, and the fourth was flushed out of the field-training program after she totaled a police car. Pence needs women on the force. KPD is the only department in the county with no female officers, something the female-majority city council finds unacceptable. And since he's in contention for the chief's job, making nice with the city council is not just preferable, it's a necessity.

All of which is his problem, not mine. My job is to make sure this candidate has what it takes, psychologically, to be a cop, and given the results of her psych tests, she seems to fill the bill. All she needs now is to complete my interview and she's on her way to the police academy. At this point, it would be rare for her or any applicant to flunk the interview process, but it happens. The person and the paper avatar are sometimes not the same, which is why state law requires me to do interviews and not just rely on the results of the candidate's written tests.

When Randy showed up a week ago to take the battery of tests I administer, she had long silky hair. Today her hair is cut into a short spiky cap, pixie style with little points and wisps. No fuss, no muss, nothing for a bad guy to grab. I take this new hair-style as an expression of her confidence that I'm going to give her a green light. And, as far as I can see, she's probably right. She seems like an excellent candidate. Psychologically stable, good im-pulse control, no problems with anger, not excessively vulnerable to stress or substance abuse, extraverted, and optimistic. Born into a law enforcement family, she was a star athlete in high school, completed college with a 3.0 and recently married her high school sweetheart who is a sheriff's deputy.

We go through the usual questions about why she wants to be a cop, and I get the usual answers—to make a difference in her community and to help people.

"And your family? How do they feel about you being a police officer?"

"They're all in law enforcement, except my mom. She wor-ries about me, of course. But growing up with my brothers, she knows I can take care of myself."

"Tough being the little sister?" I ask.

"A little."

I take her candor as a sign that she isn't afraid to admit to some weakness which suggests that she might be willing to get help if she ever needs it and—being a cop—it's fairly certain that she will. Sometime, somewhere, she'll run into something or someone that will give her nightmares. The sooner she talks about it, the better off she'll be.

"You know what they say, good things come in little packages, so does poison." She smiles and then winces when she realizes that I'm as short as she is, and I'm not laughing. "What I mean is I gave it back as good as they gave it, which is why I know I can handle a bad guy. Not that I'd be aggressive, hit somebody for no reason or anything like that." I let her trip over her own words for another minute to see where this leads and when she stops digging herself into a hole I move to my next question.

"Your husband is a deputy sheriff. How does he feel about you becoming a cop?"

She looks to the ceiling, gathering her thoughts, careful to take this question more seriously. She's worried that I've taken offense at her spontaneous little joke. To the contrary, I'm finding her rather delightful, although I can't show it.

"We talked about it for a long time. He knows it's what I've wanted to do forever. I mean, my father and brothers are all in law enforcement. How could I not be? What we agreed was that we wouldn't work in the same department, that we'd try to work similar shifts so we could see each other more, and that we wouldn't bring work home. Think that makes sense, Doc?"

I'm tempted to dig deeper, probe the concern behind her question. Police marriages are complicated—too many variables. It works well for some and for others it's double trouble, two overly stressed people living life in a fishbowl.

Anyhow, this isn't therapy, this is a pre-employment screening interview, and I have strict guidelines to follow. Any conversation beyond the purpose of determining her stability is strictly off limits.

"I think we'll be okay. I know we will. Rich and I have known each other since high school. We read each other like books. I helped him study when he was going through the academy: I made flash cards, tested him on his ten codes. I even let him put me in handcuffs." A pink flush brightens her face. Some association between handcuffs and sex or domestic abuse. She shifts a little further forward. "Now he can help me. We're a team."

Mark and I were a team once. We studied together, wrote together, taught together, and practiced together. The only thing he did without me was fall in love with his psychology intern. And then he divorced me, married her, and had the child he never wanted us to have together. I shake my head to loosen the clutch of old memories.

"We're just about through. Do you have any questions for me?"

"Did I pass?"

"I'll have my report in forty-eight hours. As you know, I have no decision-making authority—all I do is recommend, thumbs up or thumbs down. The final decision belongs to Acting Chief Pence." Her shoulders sag a little at yet another impediment. "But you'll be relieved to know that I'm going to give you a thumbs up. Congratulations."

"Really?"

"Yes, really."

She closes her fist, pumps her arm in the air and whispers "yes" dragging the esses out in a long hiss. I imagine she'd rather jump up and shout, but given the formality of the situation she shows admirable restraint and an appropriate reading of the social context.

I stand. She stands. We shake hands. "You have no idea how much this means to me. I've wanted this all my life. Being a cop is my dream come true." She shakes my hand again. "Thanks, Doctor," she says, "I promise. You won't be sorry."

CHAPTER ONE

"The trouble with women in policing is men." Jacqueline Reagon says this without a trace of animus in her voice. "I've had to compete with men at every rank right up to chief. Men only have to be as good as each other. I've had to be better." The men on the city council look uncomfortable. The women are beaming. "If you select me as chief, I can assure you that the Kenilworth Police Department will be a place where competent women can succeed without hindrance or harassment. I've moved two organizations from cowboy cultures to community policing by rewarding interpersonal skills and problem solving, as much, if not more, than acts of physical prowess or daring, which, until I became chief, were the only activities that counted." She speaks in a low, slow monotone, letting the impact of her words settle over the room. Even sitting down, she is taller than Jay Pence. And certainly less handsome. I wince at my own sexism, how easy it is to judge a woman on her looks, not her competence.

"Thank you, Chief Reagon," the mayor says. "Now we'll have a chance to hear from Acting Chief Pence about his plans for hiring women." The mayor smiles warmly at everyone as though hosting a party. He owns an insurance agency and, like the other men on the council, his service to the city is motivated by his business interests. The newly elected councilwomen are a different matter. They mean business and are determined to move Kenilworth out of its coddled, self-congratulatory existence into the real world, half of whom are women.

Jay Pence walks to the front of the room as the streetlights come on, lighting the windows behind the council members' seats. We've been in special session for more than two hours putting these final two candidates through their paces. It's taken months to winnow down the list of applicants to replace former Chief Bob Baxter, the perfect narcissist cum sociopath who's off somewhere in the Middle East making tons of money providing executive security to Arab oil magnates, unmoved by the lives he wrecked, or nearly wrecked, including mine.

Jay Pence coughs and smiles. His teeth are unnaturally white and even. "I've done a great deal to rectify the embarrassment caused by my predecessor, especially in the area of bringing women into the department. I'm proud, very proud, of the fact that I hired Officer Randy Alderson Spelling. She is, as I predicted, literally sailing through field training and is almost finished with probation."

I went to Randy's badge-pinning ceremony. Rich, her husband, was all thumbs trying to pin her badge on straight and she was all smiles. Same for field training: nothing but smiles and high marks from her trainers. "I love this job so much I'd do it for free," she said, when she finished training. And then she disappeared into the night. Rookies always get the dog watch, 10:00 p.m. to 6:00 a.m. A younger psychologist might be willing and able to ride along in the middle of the night just to stay in touch with the troops, but I need my sleep.

"I admire Chief Reagon's persistence and know her reputation for changing organizational culture." Pence turns and smiles in Reagon's direction. "I am happy to say that I have encountered no resistance bringing Officer Spelling on board at Kenilworth PD. The police association was very supportive, as they are for my candidacy." There is a smattering of applause from a group of officers in the audience.

"Bringing women into law enforcement is a priority for me. I wrote a paper on the topic for my class at the FBI National Academy. You can read it if you want; it's a good antidote for insomnia." He laughs again. "It is also the subject of my thesis for my masters in public administration, when and if things slow down enough for me to complete it."

Jacqueline Reagon bends to her microphone. "Pardon my interrupting, but if I may, I'd like to ask Acting Chief Pence why he thinks women make good police officers?" Her question, so simple and unexpected, seems to throw Pence off. His hand moves to his silky, perfectly combed, prematurely white hair, as if to ruffle it, and then drops to his side. I prefer shaggy men, like Frank—the way his gray hair curls at the base of his neck when he needs a haircut, the brushy feel of his beard on my face. I feel a rising flush, perimenopause or flashes of desire—it's hard to tell anymore.

"Women are good with children. They have good communication skills. They have a natural affinity for caretaking that is very helpful with domestic violence victims."

Chief Reagon rises from her seat. She is plain as a nun in her navy suit and white nylon shell. The only jewelry she wears is a silver watch. "I congratulate Chief Pence for trying to do the right thing, although, in my opinion, hiring one woman doesn't come close to what this department requires. And, in fact, it puts a great deal of pressure on that particular woman. It's critical to have a deep understanding of the contributions women can make to law enforcement. Without it, we risk exploiting a social trend for our own means." Jay Pence's cheeks are tinged with red. Despite her diplomatic use of the editorial "we," Chief Reagon is looking directly at him.

"As Chief Pence said, women have excellent communication skills. Police work involves physical aggression only ten percent of the time." She shifts her body toward the council. "Women are more likely to defuse an explosive situation by talking someone down and less likely to act aggressively when they are challenged. This is not to say women cannot or will not respond aggressively when needed. They will go to the mat to protect their safety, or the safety of others. Whereas male officers are more likely to respond aggressively because of their egos or their need to exercise control."

Pence is still standing, but all eyes are on Chief Reagon.

"Women are also at an advantage in undercover work, because they are unexpected. And research suggests they may be more stress resistant because they will seek help in a timely fashion and are less prone to alcoholism."

She sits down and then immediately stands back up.

"Law enforcement is and will remain a male-dominated profession for years to come. If women are to become a meaningful statistical presence in law enforcement, rather than tokens, special consideration must be paid to their recruitment and retention, including maternity policies, of which I can find none in the general orders. If Kenilworth is ready—and I think it is judging from the support on the council—then there is no better way to recruit women to the work force than to have a woman as top cop showing, in a highly visible manner, that women have a future in the Kenilworth Police Department and a leader who has walked in their shoes."

A week later, an announcement appears in the newspaper and on the bulletin board outside the briefing room. "Kenilworth Police welcomes its first ever female police chief. Her tenure to begin the first week of October." The following day, the chief's secretary removes a handmade sign pinned to the new chief's office door. Someone has blown up the announcement of her appointment. Written across it in large red letters is the message "Welcome C-U-N-T."

* * *

Within a week, Jay Pence is back in his old captain's office. I can smell fresh paint as soon as I turn the corner. Jay and his wife have apparently come in over the weekend and redecorated. I wonder if his new decorating theme is masking a grand sulk. On the other hand, he has suffered a huge disappointment and public humiliation. So what if he pours his feelings into a can of paint? He deserves to comfort himself however he can.

Pence looks up from his desk and sees me standing in the

doorway. "Looks good, doesn't it? The wife helped me. She's got the touch. What can I do for you?"

"How are you doing?"

"Great."

He doesn't ask me in. I put my briefcase on the floor. "Mind if I sit?"

"Help yourself."

"I know you had your sights set on being chief. You've worked really hard for the position."

"The council made its decision. I can live with it. If I can't, I can always apply to be chief somewhere else. I've worked for Kenilworth PD my whole career. Always planned to retire from here. But if the atmosphere changes, I'll reconsider my options."

"Have you had a chance to talk to Chief Reagon?"

"She's quite a lady. Very gracious. Wants us to work as a team. I need to give it a little time. In the meanwhile, I'll do my job like I always do." He stands up. "I appreciate your concern. People have been dropping by all day. My voice mail and in-box are filled. I didn't realize I had so much support." This isn't surprising to me. The police association publicly endorsed him and campaigned hard for his selection. Better the devil you know than the one you don't.

"Thanks for dropping by." He extends his hand and for the first time since I've been here, he smiles. "Don't worry about me, Doc. I'm good to go." And before bending his head to his paperwork, he winks at me—a big, theatrical wink that crinkles up his left cheek and pulls at the side of his mouth.

* * *

Frank turns over and nuzzles the back of my neck. Outside my window the afternoon light has turned dusky and dark. October in California is usually warm and bright. But this year—courtesy of climate change—we've had an early winter. Damp and unseasonably cold. I light the candle that I keep next to my bed.

"Nice appetizer; what's in store for dinner?" he asks, stretching over me, reaching for his glass of wine on the bed stand. "How come you're on my side of the bed?" he asks.

When did it get to be his side? We've grown close in the past year, but not close enough for him to lay claim to half my bed. At our age, Frank thinks we don't have time to waste. There's some truth to that. These days I look better dressed than naked and certainly more appealing from the front than the rear. There's a new bouquet of broken capillaries on my left calf and in the dim light, my upper arms are starting to look like driftwood. Frank challenges me wrinkle for wrinkle, shows me his liver spots and says he's going to get drunk and have them tattooed together with a Celtic chain. I don't find this funny.

On the other hand, Frank has filled the hole in my heart left by my ex-husband, Mark. I hardly think about him or his child bride Melinda and their baby Milo anymore. I feel only a hollow victory that he has surrendered his license as a psychologist after being charged with healthcare fraud. Never pays to have your unlicensed wife do your pre-employment evaluations, then sign and bill for them as though they were your own. I hear via the grapevine that Melinda is still beseeching the Psychology Examining Committee to let her sit for her license. Until her case is resolved, she's a stay-at-home mom.

Frank strokes my arms with a lascivious touch and yanks me back into the present.

"I'm hungry," he says. "Food, woman."

"I was hoping to tire you out so you wouldn't want to eat."

"I've worked up an appetite. I have to keep my strength up for the likes of you, you know."

"That's not all you need to keep up," I say.

He pushes me out from under the covers toward the shower and leans against the headboard. Candlelight blurs the lines on his face, and I can see the resemblance between the shaggy, bearded, silver-haired man in my bed and the young Navy lieutenant J.G.—tall, thin, black-haired, and clean-shaven—who hangs in a gold frame on the wall over the desk in his office. I turn on the water and wait for it to get hot. Frank has promised to install an instant hot something-or-other so I don't waste water. Hot showers are my vice, along with popcorn and red wine.

My phone rings before the water gets hot. Frank whacks me on the rear and steps past me into the shower stall, singing under his breath. It is Raylene, chief communications supervisor at KPD. She comes right to the point with no hello and no apology for calling me on a Saturday. "We have an officer down. It's a cluster. We're going to need you at University hospital, Code 3. Hold on." I can hear talking in the background. The dispatchers' normally calm voices sound high pitched and strained. Bad things aren't supposed to happen in upscale suburbs like Kenilworth where every other house is owned by a lawyer, a doctor, or a university professor. Bad things belong on the other side of the freeway in East Kenilworth, home to a working-class population of Hispanics and Pacific Islanders. People like that are known to get drunk and belligerent, while people like us—white and educated—commit our crimes behind closed doors or in our offices. Raylene comes back on the phone.

"Is anyone hurt?" I ask.

"Wish I could tell you. They're stepping all over each other on the radio. All I know is someone's on the way to the hospital. Let's hope it's the bad guy." She disconnects without another word.

I start pulling on clothes as Frank comes out of the shower, dripping and smiling. "I have to go." I mean it as an apology, but it comes out like an announcement.

The look on his face is part disappointment, part irritation.

"A cop's been hurt. I don't know any details or when I'll be back."

He shakes his head and bends to give me a quick kiss. "You wait. Someday one of my clients is going to have an emergency in the middle of the night, and I'll have to leave you naked, cold, and hungry."

"Will it be a burned-out light bulb or a busted pipe?"

"Something like that." He smiles. "You Ph.D. types aren't very handy, you know." He gives me a hug. "Should I wait for you? Not good to come home to a cold bed."

My chest tightens. I don't want him to stay here alone. Not that I don't trust him, I do. It just feels too soon—like we're living together in two different houses.

"Don't wait," I say. "I could be gone a long time."

CHAPTER TWO

There are two police cars on the edge of the hospital parking lot, parked driver's door to driver's door—the officers watching each other's back, wary of a nosy supervisor or worse, a bad guy looking to assassinate an inattentive cop. I drive past and wave. They look up, eyes wide, as though they are doing something wrong. This is the look I always get from the cops, even after a year. It's as though they think I keep a mini-cam in my bra sending a minute-by-minute feed to the chief's office.

A fire engine and a medic van are parked at odd angles in front of the entrance to the hospital emergency room. I park in the visitors' lot and walk down a long sidewalk to the door. Everything is quiet except for the fall leaves crunching underfoot. The big glass doors slide open as I approach. I step through onto a sound stage flooded with light and moving people. This is a teaching hospital; the medical personnel hardly look old enough to have graduated high school. They move quickly and quietly, dressed in pajama-like clothes and Day-Glo rubber clogs. If it weren't for the stethoscopes and name tags, I would be hard pressed to tell the patients from the personnel.

A harried-looking receptionist asks for my identification and then directs me to a private waiting room for cops only. Cops and ER staff are part of the same team and accord each other professional courtesies. Romantic liaisons between ER nurses and cops are common—after all, who else is up in the middle of the night? And who better to understand the pace and pressure of working a high-stress job. I walk down a short hall and through a door marked "private." The room is jammed with cops, most in uniform, some in street clothes. There is a low hum in the room that stops momentarily when I open the door. For a second, all eyes are on me and then they drop.

"We thought you were the ER doctor. We're waiting for him." Manny Ochoa steps out from behind the open door. He's wearing jeans and a police department t-shirt. I'm not supposed to have favorites, but I do, and Manny is it. He stood up for me, believed in me, almost lost his job because of me, after his fellow rookie, Ben Gomez, committed suicide, and everyone, myself included, blamed me for his death. Manny's matured into a confident, skillful officer, and I feel a special bond with him that I don't feel with the others. He owes me nothing. I owe him, but in his quiet way, I get the sense he's still keeping his eye on me.

"What's going on? Who's hurt?" I ask.

"Tom Rutgers. We don't how badly. We're waiting for the ER doc to tell us."

"What happened?"

"Rutgers and Randy Spelling were doing a welfare check on some homeless guys fighting down by the creek. There's an embankment. Rutgers went down first because some guy was laying on the ground, looked like he was unconscious. Spelling held the perimeter. All of a sudden this guy's up and on Rutgers with some kind of a sword, caught him in the neck and the arm. Rutgers yelled for help and—I don't exactly know what happened—but somebody said Rutgers said Spelling froze. He kept yelling for her. She finally got on the radio and called for help then ran down the hill. But by this time, the wacko's friends are jumping in, trying to grab Rutgers' gun. Spelling jumped on the pile, but somebody pulled her off and then she disappeared. Rutgers doesn't know what happened next."

The door to the waiting room opens, and the ER doc steps in. He's a tall, muscular man in green scrubs with a surgical mask pulled up over his forehead on top of dusty gray hair. All eyes are on him, appraising, measuring. He has the stature of a man cops can respect. Everyone falls quiet. The doctor gives a broad smile.

"Okay, guys. Sit down. Officer Rutgers is going to be fine. He's one lucky guy. The cut to his neck missed the vital arteries and caught muscle that I sewed up with an eye to his future. He's a good-looking dude and now he's going to be even more of a magnet for the ladies who are all going to want to know how he got such a beautiful scar."

"He's already fighting the women off, Doc," somebody says from the back.

"He's going to have to fight harder now." The doctor grins, supremely confident, enjoying the high-level locker room banter. "I'm going to keep him overnight, just to be sure. All the rest of his wounds are superficial and don't require suturing. There are no internal injuries. He's got a broken finger."

"The middle one, I bet," someone shouts.

"Which I splinted. Other than that, I think he's good to go. He's in good shape to start with, that always helps. A couple of you can see him; not all of you. He's in Room six. Don't stay long. He's tired, as you can imagine, and we gave him some pain meds, so he's going to get real sleepy in about twenty minutes. Any questions?"

"Yes," I say. "What about Officer Spelling?"

I can hear a low rumble behind me.

The doctor shakes his head. "If there was another officer who was injured, I haven't seen him."

"Her," I say.

He raises his eyebrows. "I don't know what to say. Check with the receptionist. The medic van only brought in one officer."

* * *

We file out of the waiting room, heading in different directions. Out in the cool night a small group of officers have stopped to talk at the edge of the parking lot under a bower of old oak trees, their voices rising in the quiet.

"Anyone seen the chief?"

"Where's Spelling?"

"Whoa. Don't go there." There is laughter and more comments I can't hear for the laughing. "The chief should pick on someone her own size."

"There is no one her own size. The broad is an Amazon." More laughter. In the weak yellow light from the streetlamps I can see Jay Pence's silky silver hair. The champion of women is laughing it up like one of the boys.

I turn back to the hospital. I don't want to walk by them to get to my car, hear them go silent until I pass, and then start in again, maybe talking about me, maybe not. It's eight-thirty. I feel a stab of regret that I didn't tell Frank to wait for me. I'm not looking forward to walking into a quiet, dark house. I think about calling him at his house, driving over, and spending the night. But I'd have to stop home first for a change of clothes and my pills. The last thing I want is a menopausal pregnancy. I walk back into the glare of the hospital. Truth is, the closer I get to Frank, the more I push him away. And the more I push him away, the more I want him closer.

* * *

Room 6 is near the emergency room, some kind of temporary holding for overnight patients. Two officers pass me on the way out, so engaged in conversation they don't notice me standing by the door. I push it open. The room is dark, except for the neon blinking of a gaggle of machines. A young blond woman is sitting next to the bed, stroking Rutgers' arm. He appears to be asleep. She turns when she hears the door move. Despite her tear-swollen eyes, she is pretty.

"You bitch, get out of here. You almost got him killed."

"Excuse me. I'm Dr. Dot Meyerhoff, the department psychologist."

She clasps her hands to her mouth. "I am so sorry. I thought you were Randy Spelling."

I could take this as a compliment. Randy Spelling is at least twenty-five years my junior, and while we're both about five feet tall, with short hair, hers is brown with blond streaks and mine is salt and pepper, with an emphasis on the salt.

"How's he doing?" I approach the bed. Rutgers is sleeping deeply.

"Okay, I guess."

"And you? How are you doing?"

The blinking lights turn her tears to alternating streaks of pink and green. "When they called me, I thought he was dead. I've never been so scared in my life. I can't stop shaking. He's alive, but I can't stop thinking that he could have been killed." Both hands cover her face, little ragged pieces of tissues cling to her fingers.

"That's why I'm here. I'll be talking to Tom and to you about what's happened, how it may affect you in the future and what you can do about it." I take a business card out of my pocket and put it on the bedside table. "I'll be in touch." This is something I learned from Ben—it's on me to pursue an injured officer, not wait for the officer to call me. "First things first, Mrs. Rutgers— Tom needs to rest and recover from his physical wounds."

She looks at me and dabs at her eyes. I see in the dim light that they are bright blue. "We're not married. I'm his girlfriend. My name is MaryAnne Forester." She extends her hand. "You're the lady who wrote the book about police families, right?" I nod. "I read it, but I skipped the scary parts. I didn't think we'd need them."

* * *

It's almost nine o'clock. I haven't gone to the bathroom since I got to the hospital, which must be a record for me. These days, I never pass a restroom that I don't need. I open the door. There is a pair of booted feet in the last stall. For a moment I think I've walked into the men's room by mistake until I hear someone crying.

"Randy, is that you?" I call through the door. The toilet flushes.

"It's Dr. Meyerhoff."

"I'm okay."

"Are you hurt? Do you need a doctor?"

"No."

She's still in the stall by the time I exit mine and wash my hands.

"Randy, please come out. I'll wait for you."

"I'm fine, really. I just want to be alone." She flushes a second time.

"You can't lock yourself in the bathroom forever. People are looking for you." She makes no response. "If you're worried about Tom, I just saw him. He's going to be fine. He's got a cut on the neck, a broken finger, and some bruises. They're keeping him overnight only as a precaution and they're going to release him tomorrow. He's okay. Really."

The door to her stall swings open. She's in full uniform, her tiny frame made more boyish by the chest-flattening effect of the bulletproof vest she's wearing under her shirt. She looks worse than Tom Rutgers' girlfriend. Her swollen eyes are red-rimmed and crusty.

"From what I heard, you've had a rough night."

"What else did you hear?" She has her back to me now, dabbing at her eyes with a wet paper towel, watching me in the mirror at the same time. "Did they tell you I froze, that I got bounced on my butt? Did they tell you Rutgers told me to pull my gun and I didn't?"

"You don't have to defend yourself to me. I'm not going to second guess any of your decisions."

"I should have used my Taser."

"With a pile of people rolling on the ground, wouldn't you have risked hitting Tom?" She pitches the wadded-up towel into the trash can with perfect aim. "I'm not trying to make you feel better. Your memory of what happened and Tom's memory of what happened won't be the same. Memory degrades under extreme stress. Give yourself forty-eight hours to settle down before you start judging yourself. Get some sleep."

"I let everyone down." She bends over the sink. The tap water runs over her hair and her neck, mixing with her tears. When she stands up, tears and water drip on the floor and streak down her uniform.

"I was so close."

"Close to Tom?"

"No, close to finishing probation." She mops at her hair with a towel and then separates the strands with her fingers, pulling spikes of hair into a cap. "Now they can fire me and they don't need a reason. Although being a coward is a pretty good reason."

"You are getting way ahead of yourself. Let's talk this over in my office. My private office on Catalan Court, not my office at the PD."

"Do I have to?" She wets a fresh towel, folds it carefully into a small square, and holds it over her eyes, one at a time.

"Sorry, department policy. You and Tom are both required to see me following a critical incident."

She turns around. "How do I look?"

"Fine. Where are you going?"

"Back to work. I have a report to write." She hoists her heavy leather belt around her tiny waist and throws her shoulders back. "After I hand in my report I'm going 10/8, back in service."

"Randy. That's crazy. You've just been through a very dangerous incident. You should go home." She opens the door to the hallway.

"Everyone's mad at me. They'll be even madder if they have to write all the paper and then stay overtime to backfill my beat."

The door closes behind her, and I listen to her footsteps as she walks down the hall.

CHAPTER THREE

Chief Reagon's office is lined with boxes, stacked three high, blocking most of the outside light from the one window behind her desk. The bookshelves are empty, and I can see nail holes where Jay Pence had hung plaques and photos during his tenure as acting chief. There is a large white gift box on her desk with a bright curly bow on top. It's the only color in the room. The chief is wearing the same dark blue suit she's worn three times this week. I wonder if she even notices. She stands to greet me.

"Good morning, Dr. Meyerhoff. I just came from visiting Officer Rutgers at the hospital; he's being released this afternoon. They kept him an extra day because of a minor infection. I understand you already talked to him. Is there anything I need to know?"

"I'll be debriefing Officer Rutgers and Officer Spelling later this week after they've rested, and he's had a chance to recover from his injuries."

"And Officer Spelling? How is she?"

"I talked with her briefly at the hospital." I stop here. What any officer says to me is confidential, even if the officers don't believe it.

"I see. And you have nothing to add?"

I start to say something and she interrupts. "Sorry, I know you can't tell me what she said. But I can tell you something if you don't know this already. Officer Rutgers is very upset. He believes Officer Spelling panicked at the scene, placing him in jeopardy. I won't, of course, know the specifics until all the reports are in. I've asked Jay Pence to conduct an investigation of the incident, nothing to the level of Internal Affairs, unless his investigation suggests it's warranted. I'm not jumping to conclusions until I see his report."

"Tough way to start your first week."

"As expected. Please, sit down." It is both a courtesy and a kindness. Standing up she is nearly a foot taller than I am.

"I understand you've been to all the briefings and met with every employee." No small task, some briefings start at six a.m. "How did it go?"

"As I expected it would."

Rumor has it she was stonewalled by the cops: long silences, no questions, no comments and then as she turned her back to the group to write something on a flip chart, there were small pantomimes about the size of her butt.

"I'm not a popular appointment. I think most employees favored the in-house candidate. I have a reputation as a—excuse the expression—ball-breaker." She enunciates the term like an elocution teacher. "Or should I say a hatchet man, or more properly, a hatchet woman?"

She says this without smiling. Her large, ringless hands rest on the edge of the desk. "I have been brought here to shake things up, I think that's obvious. This department is behind the times and its reputation still suffers from the actions of the previous chief. I firmly believe it takes an outsider with a fresh perspective to bring about change. That doesn't mean that I won't be fair or judicious about it. I know I will have to earn people's trust."

She asks me to explain the scope of my job. I do and she comments that creating my position might be the most proactive thing former Chief Baxter had done while in office. There is no animus in her voice, no sense of dishing the dirt—woman to woman—just a plain statement of fact.

"I have a great deal of respect for psychology. Too many officers' lives have been ruined because they refused to get psychological help when they needed it or because none was available." She pauses briefly as she whisks at something on her jacket, gathering her thoughts or brushing them away. "I might need some guidance from you regarding Jay Pence. He's a good man, earnest and hard-working. Being passed over for the chief's job has to be difficult. He needs to know that I bear him no rancor and I want us to work together as a team. Do you think he can do that or is he inclined to harbor bitter feelings?"

"I've been here just over a year myself and I don't really know him that well." I doubt anyone knows Jay Pence. He's always prepared, always pleasant, a bit too composed for my tastes. No spontaneity, no discomfort, nothing joyful or tense rubbing at him. Only the way he draws his lips together suggests a hint of moral superiority. He's the consummate politician—I saw this at the hospital—how easily he played to his constituents, laughing and joking like he was one of the boys.

"Well, at any rate, I hope I might call on you for some advice."

"Of course, I'm available to everyone in this organization from line staff all the way to the top." She smiles and nods her head once. "Someone gave you a present." I gesture toward the gift box, glad to have something to say.

"Indeed they did." She pushes the box towards me. "It was on my desk when I came in this morning. There is a card in it, unsigned. It says 'Police Chief's survival kit.'" She takes the top off and empties the contents one by one, placing them carefully on her desk as though they were valued objects: tampons, deodorant, douche powder, breath mints, and lipstick. I'm stunned. It's a puerile prank, more typical of junior high school boys than men who carry loaded guns. The chief sees the look on my face.

"I'm used to these kinds of practical jokes. They'll stop eventually. You must have experienced a few yourself."

"Nothing like this." I wonder how much she knows about my early-on struggles with Officer Eddie Rimbauer or what happened between me and Chief Baxter. It doesn't matter because it's not even relevant. None of that had anything to do with my being a woman, it had more to do with my persistent efforts to find out why Ben Gomez killed himself and who was at fault.

"Cops are not a monolithic block. In my experience, there's great peer pressure to join the resistance to an outside chief, especially someone with my reputation, but ultimately people sort themselves out. What concerns me is this: If I'm being harassed, I can only imagine what's happening to Officer Spelling. I've been where she's at, the only female. I would have rather cut off my hand than complain about the way I was being treated or ask for help. There was nobody like you around when I was a rookie. I'm going to talk to her myself today. If she's in some kind of trouble over last night's incident, she'll need a lot of support. I'm going to insist that she continue to see you after her debriefing." She pauses, picks up the tube of lipstick, pulls off the top, looks at the color—a garish pink—closes it and puts it down. "Is there anything in the general orders that authorizes me to mandate that she get therapy?"

"Don't do that," I say. "Please."

There is a slight lift to Chief Reagon's shoulders and one, tiny, breathy inhalation. I doubt many people tell her what to do or not do.

"Mandated therapy never works. She'll be angry at being ordered to do something she doesn't choose for herself. Therapy only works when the client wants help and trusts the therapist." Once again the memory of Ben Gomez swoops in on me reminding me how great my limitations and how small my talents are as a psychologist.

"Do whatever you think is right. The bottom line is, until I make a decision about this incident, I want you to keep an eye on Randy Spelling. There's no way she's not feeling some heat. After-action investigations take time, and if it turns into an Internal Affairs investigation, those can take forever."

* * *

There is a running controversy over post-incident debriefings in the world of psychology. Do they harm? Do they help? Do they do nothing at all to prevent PTSD? It's complicated and hard to study. There is little uniformity among debriefers or debriefing incidents and relatively little consistency of specific factors among the people being debriefed. Still, psychological debriefings have become so common that if you fell down in any major city in the United States, every other person who stepped on you would be trained to debrief you. All that aside, I am eager to check on Tom Rutgers and especially eager to speak with Randy Spelling. Neither of them are especially eager to speak with me.

I arrange to meet Tom Rutgers at his house. He's still on antibiotics and feeling queasy. He asked to postpone our meeting and only agreed to meet today when I said I would come to him. He lives in a suburb thirty minutes south of Kenilworth. It is a place where farmers once grew oranges, walnuts, and apples. Now leafy enclaves of high-tech businesses sprawl across college-like campuses surrounded by clusters of condominium developments built to look like small villages. Mounded shrubs edge sloping swaths of grass. Fountains arc in small ponds next to meandering walkways. I drive through an intersection, all four corners filled with shopping centers probably selling fruit flown in from New Zealand. Many of the smaller shops have window signs in English and Chinese or Vietnamese.

Tom's townhouse is at the end of a row of fifteen identical residences. It is quiet, the only sound is a lawnmower whining somewhere in the distance. I see no children, no playgrounds, no sandboxes, nothing to indicate that this is anything more than a bedroom community in disguise, a place for people to warm takeout food in their microwaves and sleep before going back to work. Not too different from where I live. And how I live.

MaryAnne Forester, Tom's girlfriend or fiancée—I haven't figured that out and perhaps neither have they—opens the front door dressed in a tank top, shorts, and flip flops. Her hair is pulled up in a gigantic plastic clip. She looks as though she hasn't slept for a week. Tom is sitting in a recliner. Tank tops, shorts, and flip flops seem to be both their preferred styles. He has a large bandage on his neck and his finger is in a metal splint. There's a glass of water and a bottle of pills on the table next to his chair. The rest of the furniture in the room is standard Rooms-R-Us fare: a functional, black Naugahyde sectional, a wood-and-glass coffee table, an entertainment center holding electronic things and the largest flat screen TV I've ever seen outside of a bar. No sign that MaryAnne has had any say or influence on the decor.

I take a place on the couch. MaryAnne sits on the other sectional at right angles to me. Tom is facing us. We sit in a mute triangle.

"How're you feeling?"

"Pretty good. A little nauseous from these." He picks up the bottle and rattles the pills. "I should be back to work in a week or two. Maybe do a little light duty until my finger heals. It's my shooting hand." He holds it up for my inspection.

"Sleeping all right?"

"Sure."

MaryAnne shifts in her seat. "Tom, that's not true." He gives her a searing look.

"What do you mean?" I ask.

"You have to tell her. She's here to help you." MaryAnne turns toward me, her eyes bright with tears. "He has nightmares. Rolls around, yells. I touched him to wake him up and he almost hit me. He didn't know who I was. It was scary. I don't know what to do."

"How about shutting the—" He pauses, looks at me, and says to MaryAnne, "Get me some water. I'll talk to the doc myself." She stands up, takes a step toward the back of the house, and turns. Her cheeks are wet and shiny.

She looks at me, avoiding Tom's eyes. "He's afraid to go back to work. He doesn't want to work with Randy Spelling. He's afraid she'll get him killed the next time something bad happens." And before Tom has a chance to react, she stomps out of the room, as much as anyone can stomp in flip flops. She's back in a minute with a bottle of water that she sets down on the table. "See you later." She nods in my direction and goes off somewhere. I hear a door slam. Tom takes a long swig from the bottle.

"She's upset. Always nervous. Scared I'm gonna get hurt."

"You did get hurt."

"Part of the job. And I'm not hurt bad. Tell you the truth, things aren't too good around here, even before this. She hates my hours, doesn't like my friends. I don't know where this is going."

"She's worried about you and she doesn't know how to help. There's no shame having nightmares. It's almost universal after an incident like yours."

"It was no big deal."

"Really? You mean that being outnumbered, thinking you might lose your gun, and getting hit in the neck by a crazed man with a sword is no big deal? I find that hard to believe, Tom."

He pulls the lever on his recliner and leans forward. The foot rest retracts with a groan.

"You want to know the big deal? I'll tell you. Randy Spelling. She froze. She panicked."

"She called for help."

"Big effing deal. She's supposed to call for help. And she's supposed to get in the fight."

"I thought she did."

"She couldn't fight her way out of a paper bag. She got thrown off the pile, and I never saw her again. If it wasn't for the other guys getting there so fast, I coulda been killed."

"Under the circumstances—you were in the dark, fighting for your life—how do you know who was where?"

He pulls back and looks at me. "Whose side are you on anyway?"

"I'm not on anyone's side."

"Doesn't sound like it."

"Captain Pence is doing an after-action report. Things will be clearer when he finishes interviewing everyone."

Tom leans forward again, pointing his splinted finger at me. "He hired her, she's his pet, he's not going to throw her under the bus. You watch."

"You don't trust him to write an unbiased report?"

"I don't give a rat's ass what he writes. Even if I have to go back to day shift, I'm not working with Randy Spelling again."

CHAPTER FOUR

Randy is sitting on the edge of the couch in my waiting room facing the stairs. She's dressed in jeans, a t-shirt, running shoes, and a small black fanny pack swiveled to the front where she keeps her gun. There's no need for a weapon in my office, but after what's she's been through, I doubt she feels safe enough to go anywhere without it. Her face is scrubbed to a shine. The only jewelry she wears is a large sports watch on her left wrist. She hears me before she sees me and is on her feet, her hand on the fanny pack, preparing for the unexpected.

"I see your startle response is working." She looks at me, her face taut. Her lips are chapped and red. "That was a joke," I say. She doesn't respond. I open the door to my office and motion her in. She looks around as though she's never been here before.

"Where do I sit?"

"On the couch, where you sat before, when I did your pre-employment psych." She sits down on the edge, ready to spring up again.

"Coffee, water, tea?"

"No, thanks." She reaches behind and pulls a phone from her back pocket and clicks it off.

"Do you need to answer your phone? It's okay, we've got plenty of time."

"How long?"

"Depends."

"On what?" This is definitely not the relaxed young woman I interviewed before.

I lean forward in my chair. "Here's the deal. Since I've been working here, the department has instituted a policy. When an officer has been involved in a serious incident, that means an incident where there's been violence and extreme danger, I automatically meet with that officer and his or her family."

"What for?"

"Well, we know that incidents, like the one you were just involved in, can affect you psychologically and emotionally. In the old days, cops would simply stuff their feelings or drown them at choir practice. Now we know it helps to talk about the incident so things don't pile up. This is not a brain drain. I'm going to talk too, tell you how people react to critical incidents so you don't think you're the only one or that you're going crazy."

Her left leg is jiggling and her hands are balled so tightly that her knuckles are bloodless. "So this is like a fit for duty?"

"Absolutely not. What we talk about is confidential. I won't take notes. I'm not going to make a report. This is for your benefit. The only thing the chief needs to know is that you showed up."

"What if I am crazy?"

"I doubt that's the case. The limits to confidentiality are the same ones you have as a police officer. I have to break confidentiality only if you tell me that you're going to kill yourself or someone else, that you're abusing a child or an elderly person, or that you can't take care of yourself. So, are you planning on doing any of those things?"

"No." A smile flickers and dies at the corners of her mouth. "What else do you want to know?"

"How are you sleeping?"

"Terrible."

"Nightmares?"

"You gotta sleep to have nightmares."

"So you're not sleeping at all because the incident is doing hot laps in your brain. You see it over and over and can't stop it." She looks at me, her eyebrows lifting slightly. For the first time since she's been here I feel like I've made a connection.

"That's me."

"Happens to almost everybody. Partly your brain is trying to figure things out, partly you've overdosed on your own adrenaline. As the adrenaline and some other body chemicals decrease, probably in a few more days, you can expect that hot-laps thing to slow down too."

"Is Tom Rutgers doing hot laps?"

"Randy, I can't tell you what he said. Any more than I can tell him what you said."

"So you saw him?"

"I told you, it is policy to see officers who are involved in critical incidents." I take a breath. It's getting dark outside. In a minute I'm going to have to get up and turn on the overhead light. "Let's get back to you. You said the incident keeps spinning in your head and you're going over it again and again. We can slow that down by reviewing it, frame by frame."

She wrinkles her nose. "Why would I want to do that?"

"It makes sense to avoid what's causing you discomfort. But here's the problem. Those same chemicals that have you so jacked up create a variety of perceptual distortions: time slows down or speeds up, you get tunnel vision, your hearing changes, your vision changes. Happens to almost everyone who's involved in a fight for survival. Which is why your recollection of the incident is probably not accurate."

"Tom have any of those distortion things?"

"I told you I can't repeat what someone else told me."

"So, if I had any of that, just saying, does it mean I'm crazy?"

"No, it means you're human."

She sinks back into the couch as though this announcement was so unexpected and so profound it has sucked all the fight out of her. Tears spill down her face. She wipes them away on her sleeve. "Busted," she says. "I hate being human." She pulls some tissues from the box on the coffee table and blows her nose. "So ask me."

"Ask you what?"

"Which of those things I have." She turns her hands over, palms up in an offering. "All of them. I have them all."

"So, tell me what happened. In as much detail as possible."

She takes a deep breath. "It's like they say. I got scared. I froze. I tried to help. There were so many of them, hands, legs, feet, everywhere, grabbing me, trying to get my gun. I couldn't see Tom. I couldn't see anything." Now she's breathing in shallow sips, her face drained of color. "It's dark. I can't see. Someone is lying on my face, I can't breathe, I can't scream. I am going to die. I have to run, get out of here." She scrambles to her feet, in panic mode caught in the terror of a past moment as if it is happening all over again.

"Randy." I'm on my feet. "Randy, look at me. Look at me." Her hands are on her chest.

"I can't breathe. I'm having a heart attack." Her eyes spin around the room looking for the door.

"You are not having a heart attack. You're having a panic attack. Take a deep breath, hold it, and let it out slowly." Her eyes are still flicking over the room looking for danger. I step directly in front of her so I'm the only thing she sees. "Keep looking at me, Randy. Take another breath, hold it, and let it out slowly." Her breathing eases just slightly. "Press your feet into the floor. Good. Keep breathing. Slowly. Tell me where you are."

"Your office."

"Good. Now look at me. What color is my shirt?"

"Gray."

"Good. Keep breathing, longer on the exhale. Can you sit down again?" She backs up a few steps until she's pressing against the couch. "Feel your legs against the sofa. Can you?" She nods. "Is it warm or cool? Hard or soft?"

"Soft."

"Warm or cool?"

"Hot." She sinks down, her head drops back, and she closes her eyes. Her face is flushed, dripping with sweat and tears, but at least she's stopped struggling for air.

"Good. Now I'm going to get you a glass of water from the cooler in the waiting room. I'll only be gone a minute and I'm right outside. I'll leave the door open. Do you hear me?" She nods her head. When I return, she's leaning forward, elbows on her knees, her head in her hands. She downs the water in a single gulp.

"What happened to me?"

"You had a panic attack. Have you had these before?"

She shakes her head no.

"We probably triggered it by talking about your incident. It happens sometimes."

"Still think I'm not crazy?"

"This has nothing to do with being crazy. The things that happened to you at the creek were beyond your conscious control, beyond anyone's conscious control. It's called an 'amygdala hijack,' meaning the alarm center in your brain is in charge, not the thinking part. When your life is threatened, or even if you just think your life is threatened, the amygdala goes into overdrive. It's been this way since the beginning of time. It's not a choice, it just happens."

"They weren't trying to kill me, they were trying to kill Tom."

"If someone was trying to cut Tom's head off with a sword, what do you think they were going to do to you, give you a haircut? Cut you a piece of cake? You didn't have time to analyze their behavior, all you had was a nanosecond to save your own life. That's why we have a survival instinct."

"I ran off and left him because I thought I was going to die. That makes me weak."

And there it is, the "W" word. Better to be crazy than weak if you're a cop.

"Look. We ask cops to do their best to protect each other. We don't ask them to commit suicide."

"I messed up. Jumped on the pile, couldn't handle the heat, and ran away."

"So, a good cop wins every fight? Tom Rutgers didn't win this one."

"That's my fault."

"Really? Let me offer another perspective. I've never been a cop and I don't want to second guess anyone's actions—"

"Go ahead. Everyone else is second guessing me."

"Maybe Tom Rutgers should have waited for backup before he ran down to the creek. Maybe he should have taken a minute to work out a plan with you. He was the senior officer." Randy scrapes at her eyes with a wad of damp tissue. "This never occurred to you?"

"No," she says softly. "I doubt it's occurred to anyone else either."

Her phone buzzes. She looks at the screen. "I gotta go. Rich's waiting for me."

"How's he doing?"

"Good." She looks at me quizzically.

"I mean, what does he think about what happened to you?"

"He doesn't know about it."

"You didn't tell your husband?"

"He's got enough to worry about at the jail. He needs to stay focused. He doesn't need to worry about me too."

"He might like to know what's going on with you. He might like to be included in something this important."

"I know. I read your book. We both did. I'll tell him what's going on, just not now."

"Well then, if you read my book, you both know that if there's one thing harder than being a cop, it's being married to one."

She smiles fully for the first time this session.

CHAPTER FIVE

It's Halloween. The cops are gearing up for pranks and praying for rain to keep everyone inside. They'll be disappointed: the weather prediction is crisp, clear, with unseasonably warm temperatures. Halloween isn't Halloween anymore, not like the Halloweens of my childhood. Parents are so afraid of kidnappings and candy spiked with pins or poison that most little kids go trick or treating at their schools. Even in a safe upscale suburb like Kenilworth. Captain Pence is being extra cautious. He's shuffled the shifts around so that there will be a lot of cops on the street in the late afternoon and evening. The briefing room is filled to capacity. The chairs are arranged classroom style. I make my way to the back, prepared to stand until Manny gives me his seat. "I'll be sitting in my patrol car all evening, I need to stand." It's a sweet lie. I spot Randy halfway to the front. If she's seen me, she doesn't give any sign. It's been nearly a month since the incident at the creek. So far as I know, Pence still hasn't completed his report. Thirty days is a long time to be dangling in the wind, waiting for someone to make a decision about your future.

Randy and I have met weekly since her incident and, unless she's lying to me, she hasn't had another panic attack. Sitting at home was not therapeutic. Too much time to think, plus she and Rich were getting on each other's nerves. We made a compromise. Randy could return to work, but only after she told Rich about the incident and how it affected her. Then she had to ask her internist to prescribe a fast-acting antianxiety drug, safe for short-term use if taken off duty. The downside? Addiction and a list of potential side effects long enough to cover the drug manufacturer's very large posterior. It was a hard sell. Cops will drink coffee and caffeine drinks until their hands shake, but they resist taking medication because the people they know who do are drug addicts and psychotic street people. Truth of the matter, I would have preferred Randy deal with her anxiety with deep breathing or meditation. Except meditation doesn't work with someone who is in such a state of hypervigilance she can't sit still.

The room quiets when Pence walks in. He is dressed in uniform instead of his usual business suit, a sign that he will be out in public tonight showing the citizens of Kenilworth that the department is on the job, even management. I have yet to see Chief Reagon in uniform. Pence looks sharp, broad shouldered and narrow at the waist. His silky silver hair, smooth as a pearl.

"Sorry some of you have to miss being home tonight with your kids. Hope Mom is taking a lot of photos with her iPhone. As you know, last year a couple of children nearly got hit by a car in a crosswalk, so we've got extra traffic patrols, and I've arranged for some crossing guards to be on duty." There's a murmur in the room and some raised eyebrows. "If that seems over the top, I'll tell you why in a minute. We'll also probably get some skateboarding on the sidewalk. That's a cite and release. Be polite, but firm. We don't want a repeat of last year where we had parents complaining we were too tough on their little darlings who were just out having some Halloween fun."

"They should complain to the neighbors. They're the ones who called us in the first place." Eddie Rimbauer is at the open door to the briefing room pushing a cart from Fran's Café piled with coffee and sandwiches. He's still on disability leave from the PD, filling his time volunteering at Fran's cafe, lurking around any place remotely related to police work. Three turns at Pinkerton's Rehabilitation Center, known as Pinky's to the cops, is finally getting results. He's lost about twenty pounds of the sixty he needs to lose and looks better than he has in a long time. Fran's husband BJ was killed in the line of duty years ago. Surrogate mother to every Kenilworth cop, including Eddie, she never misses an opportunity to send food to the PD when there's something special going on.

"Remember this," Eddie says, "there's assholes, dumbshits, and cops: it's the assholes who make the dumbshits call the cops."

"Thank you, Eddie," Pence says. He's smiling and scowling at the same time. "And thank Fran for the food. You can set up in the cafeteria." Pence and Eddie are opposites: one cool, trim and precise, the other loud, big-hearted, and not in control of his mouth or his appetite. Pence turns back to the room.

"Citizens are our most important link to solving crime. We want them to call us, to report skateboarders and anything else that's amiss. Seems to me you can do a lot of damage to yourself or someone else if you're high as a kite and moving at warp speed down a dark street. At any rate, if the little darlings want some fun, remind them that that's why we have a skateboard park. Okay? Got it?"

There's a murmur of affirmation from the troops.

"Now, here's why I'm suited up and why I'll be walking a beat downtown. Every year the community counts on us to keep the streets safe for legitimate trick-or-treaters. Word on the street is that some kids from East Kenilworth are going to be trick or treating on our side of the freeway. We had one or two last year, but this year there's going to be a gang of them. Big kids in masks. They're not interested in candy, they're interested in casing houses, cars, and who knows what else? I don't want any break-ins, any vandalism, or any broken windows. You know the drill."

"Want something good to eat or steal? Cross the freeway, come to Kenilworth," someone says and everybody laughs.

Pence's scowl is deep, pulling at his hairline and carving a "V" between his eyebrows. He raises his hand for quiet. "Settle down, guys. Bottom line is keep your eyes open, take your break when you can, drop by the cafeteria for free eats, and watch yourselves out there."

We file out of the briefing room. I try to catch Randy, but she scurries away and disappears into the police garage. I walk back down the hall. Jay Pence is still in the briefing room talking to a few officers.

"Hold up, Dot. I want to talk to you a minute." He finishes his conversation and motions me inside the now empty briefing room. "I've completed my report on the incident at the creek. I want to give you a heads up because I know you've talked to both Tom and Randy. I'm going to recommend that Tom get a letter of commendation from the chief and that Randy's probation is extended for a week. Plus she gets remediated in defensive tactics, for her own safety. Not a big deal."

I disagree. Remediation and extended probation is a big deal, no matter what Pence says. Official acknowledgement that you messed up and now everybody knows it.

"Why isn't Tom getting remediated or days off? Shouldn't he have waited for backup before he ran down the embankment in the dark?"

Pence looks at me. I can sense what's coming next. Just like former Chief Baxter, he's going to tell me to mind my own business and stick to what I know, which is not operational tactics. Only he won't be as direct or as crude as Baxter. He starts gathering up his things.

"Like I tell my wife, Doc, don't sweat the small stuff." I wonder if his wife wants to hit him like I do.

* * *

Eddie is in the empty cafeteria. Two large metal urns of coffee are sputtering and burbling on the counter. He is unpacking cartons filled with wrapped sandwiches and small plastic containers of potato salad. He gives me a big hug.

"Crazy lady. How's my favorite shrink?"

"Excellent. Totally buzzed to see my favorite non-client looking so hale and hearty. Looks like life is treating you well."

"I am F-I-N-E, meaning fucked up, insecure, neurotic, and emotional." He laughs and the remains of his once enormous gut shakes under his t-shirt. "I'd be a helluva lot better if I could come back to work, but I still got to pass a fit for duty and get interviewed by the new chief." He bends to my height. "What's the old broad like?"

"First of all, if you want to come back to work, don't call her an old broad."

"I hear she hates drunks."

"You're not a drunk anymore, are you?"

"Once a drunk, always a drunk. You know that. One day at a time. I've been sober now for seventy-two days." He fishes in his pocket for some coins and lays them on the counter. "Here's my thirty- and sixty-day coins."

"Congratulations."

"And it only took me three trips to the funny farm to do it. You can lead a horse to water, but you can't make it swim on its back." He dumps bags of chips into a huge metal bowl and puts the bowl on the counter next to the sandwiches. "Much as I hated it and hated you and Fran, and that backstabbing little prick Manny for dumping me in that joint, I gotta admit, once I got my head out of my ass and quit with the liquid therapy, I made a little progress. It was the best and the worst experience of my life. I was comfortable being numb and when they took away the booze, whoa." His eyes tear up and he turns away, rearranging things that don't need rearranging. "You told me I was a jackass. I told you to fuck yourself. Fran told me I was a jackass—fuck her too. But when the guys at Pinky's told me I was a jackass for the tenth time, I strapped on my saddle and went to work on all the shit I'd been burying under the booze and food."

Suddenly, there's shouting, doors slam, and people are running down the hall toward the garage. A minute later we hear tires screeching and a moment after that the wail of police sirens.

Eddie looks up from the food, puts one hand over his heart, and stands quietly until the sirens fade away. "I love it," he says, "when they play my song." His face settles. "I need to get back to work, Doc. Anything you can do to help me out?"

"Not my decision."

"Can you do my fit for duty?"

"Nope. It has to be someone who doesn't know you, who's never been in a position to counsel you."

"Does it help that I never listened to a thing you said?" He laughs, then his face sinks into seriousness.

"I've changed. I can talk about stuff now, tell you my whole life story, about my crappy parents, my dope-addict wife and how she killed our baby and herself. Nothing to hide. My life's an open book."

"It takes time, Eddie. Policing is stressful. You've said it yourself; you've only been sober for seventy-two days. Don't rush into things. Take your time. You've got a whole year to rest. That's what disability leave is for."

"I go to meetings all the time, drive all the way up to Pinky's and back."

"No AA groups locally?"

"Not unless I want sit next to some a-hole I arrested six times."

"Are you on medication?"

"I got something for sleeping, that's all."

"Having trouble sleeping?"

"Hell no, I sleep like a baby. First I cry, then I take a bottle, and then I piss myself."

Now I'm the one who wants to cry. Still using humor to cover up his feelings and deflect any real conversation. Nothing grows in alcohol, especially people. Eddie may not be drinking anymore, but he's one of those dry drunks, sober, but no wiser and, I fear, no better able to cope with the world. And now he's got the two worst things an alcoholic can have, money and time on his hands.

CHAPTER SIX

It's nearly nine p.m. The rainy season is in full display. Gusts of wind and rain are bending the fledgling trees in my tiny yard nearly in half, ripping the last remaining leaves off the branches and flattening them against the fence. Frank and I have finished dinner, downed an excellent bottle of pinot noir, and now he's giving me a foot massage. We both know where this is leading. Time has been easy on us despite our jokes about wrinkles and cellulite. We were both equally shy and apologetic about our bodies the first time we saw each other naked. It is an agreed-upon miracle that we have found each other at this point in life. We may not be as handsome as we once were, but we're a damn sight smarter about relationships. At least, I hope, I am.

"How 'bout we move upstairs to the bedroom? I have some other massage tricks in mind." Parts of me undulate at the suggestion. I grab my wine glass and let Frank lead me up the stairs. At the door to my bedroom, my cell phone buzzes in my jeans pocket. "Let it be," Frank says.

"I'm on twenty-four-hour call. Part of my job."

"You can call whoever it is back in twenty minutes, maybe thirty." He starts to undress, hooking his denim shirt over the back of a chair. I have another undulation and head for my closet when my cell phone goes off again. Frank scowls and gets into bed.

"Do what you have to do," he says.

I know what he's thinking. The closer we get, the more he expects that we will be first in each other's lives. I, on the other hand, am not so sure. I answer the phone, expecting to hear Raylene's voice. This time it's Chief Reagon.

"Sorry to bother you at home so late. I need you to come to headquarters right away. There's been an incident involving Randy Spelling. It's a bad one."

* * *

TV trucks from five stations are parked at odd angles in front of the police station as though someone had thrown them against the curb. Cop cars are pulling in and out of the parking lot. I edge, head down, through the crowded lobby to the elevator and push the button. Someone grabs my arm and asks me who I am. After the headlines around Ben Gomez' suicide, I can't believe there's a local reporter who doesn't know me.

"I'm Jack Shiller, new guy with the Kenilworth Daily. Someone said you're the department psychologist. Are you here to interview the officer who did the shooting?" My heart stops and then races.

"I don't know. I've been asked to come in because there's been an emergency."

"Have you treated this officer for psychological problems before this shooting?"

"I can't talk about my work here. And I've no idea what's just happened." I swear I'm going to pay for an upgrade to the ancient elevator myself if it doesn't get here in another minute. I could take the stairs, but it means pushing back through the crowd and being accosted by more reporters.

"So you don't know what happened?"

"No, I don't." I can see he's about to tell me when the elevator stops with a bounce. I slip in before the creaky doors grind fully open.

What's-his-name sticks his arm through the door and hands me his business card. "I can wait until you're done." I back against the rear of the elevator and will the doors to shut.

* * *

Randy is sitting on the floor of the conference room, wedged behind a rolling metal cabinet, her knees pulled up against her chest.

The minute she sees me she scrambles to her feet. She is in uniform. There are dark stains on the front of her shirt.

"Get me out of here. Please. Everybody's staring at me."

"Are you hurt?"

"I need a shower. But they won't let me. They're afraid I'm going to wash off the evidence. Said I needed a female escort in the locker room, and the only woman in the building is the chief. No way I'm going to undress in front of her."

I pick up the phone, dial the chief's extension, and offer to be Randy's escort. Five minutes later I'm in the women's locker room, stuffing Randy's blood-stained uniform into a plastic evidence bag and listening to the shower run. She exits, wrapped in a long white towel, her hair plastered to her head. She walks past me into the dressing room. I can hear the metal sound of her locker door opening. I stay in the bathroom, wanting to give her some privacy while she dresses. Whatever's happened is bad enough that her entire life is about to be lived in a fishbowl. I know what it's like to open the newspaper and see your name and photo on the first page and read about, not yourself, but a one-dimensional stranger created by some reporter who barely knows you.

The door to her locker slams closed. Then I hear her kicking the locker door with such ferocity that I'm afraid she's going to break her foot. I walk into the room as she sinks to a wooden bench, head in hands, her tears dripping on the tile floor. I sit next to her.

"What's happened, Randy? Talk to me."

"It was a girl. I told her to stop, but she just kept moving around, digging in her car for something. Her car was jammed with stuff, like she was living in it. I told her, put your hands where I can see them. I asked her over and over, and she just kept digging like she didn't hear me. And then when she got out of the car she had this metal thing in her hand. I thought it was a gun." She balls her fists against her forehead. "I shot her. I don't even know her name and I killed her." Her sobs bounce off the tiled walls. I put my hand on her back. "I want to go home," she says. "I want Rich."

"Not yet," I say. "The chief is waiting for you in her office."

* * *

DA Allen Herter and the chief are sitting among her still-unpacked boxes. I tell Randy to wait outside for a minute, I want to talk to the chief first. Herter is a small man with a rodent-like face and pale, thinning hair. His skin never sees the light of day. It strikes me as unusual that he is doing this interview himself, rather than sending one of his minions.

"Randy's exhausted. She needs to go home, see her husband, get some sleep. Is it possible to postpone this interview?"

"I appreciate that," Herter says, "but I need to speak with her now. It won't take long."

"You'll get more accurate information from her when she's rested. Sleep promotes memory consolidation. Better recall."

Herter squints at me. "This is not an inquisition, Doctor. The more information I have now, while the shooting is fresh in her mind, the better it is for the officer."

I wonder about this. The DA is an elected official. His office, and everyone who works in it, is vulnerable to the eddies and currents of county politics. There are segments of this county who are plenty mad at Herter for failing to file charges against an officer from another department who regularly brutalized members of the Vietnamese community. He'll need their votes in the next election. It's to his advantage to show he's tough on cops.

I take a short step in his direction. My hands are sweating and my heart is racing again. "Current research on memory suggests that it is a mistake to interview officers immediately after a shooting. They are the worst reporters of their own experiences because they're drunk on a cocktail of cortisol and adrenaline. They need forty-eight hours to rest, to feel safe, and as they do, bits and pieces of their experience come back to them, filling in the blanks and correcting any distortions in their recall. If you want, I can show you the research."

"Plus, she'll have time to concoct a better story. I don't need a lecture, Doctor. I've read the research on memory." Herter gets to his feet. I can see Randy through the open door, slumped in a chair, eyes closed, feet stretched out in front of her.

"What about the union attorney? Doesn't Randy need her attorney?"

Herter looks at Chief Reagon as if to ask why she isn't controlling this wacky psychologist. "I've asked if she wants representation," Reagon says. "She refused."

"Can she do that?"

"I advised against it, but yes, she can."

Herter picks up his briefcase without looking at me. "I'll talk to Randy in the interview room, Chief. And I'll need a blood sample before she goes home." He walks out to the hall and softly greets Randy by name. She opens her eyes and follows him like a beaten dog to the interview room.

* * *

After Herter leaves, the chief and I sit in silence, looking out the window behind her desk as fingers of pink push away the night sky. It's nearly seven a.m. There's a carafe of coffee on a small table. She pours us both a cup. Her hands are shaking. We sit for a moment sipping in unison. The coffee is lukewarm and vile.

"The victim's name was Lakeisha Gibbs. Her driver's license gives a residence in East Kenilworth, but it was apparent that she had been living in her vehicle. According to the information gathered thus far, Ms. Gibbs has been parked in front of someone's home here in Kenilworth for two days. He or she got fed up and called us. We ran the plate and found the car had been reported stolen. Officer Spelling was first on scene. She woke the young woman and asked her to step out of her car, but, according to what Randy told the next officer on scene, Ms. Gibbs kept rummaging around for something. When she finally exited her car, she did so quickly and had something in her hand. It was metallic and shiny. Officer Spelling thought it was a gun and shot her."

"Is she dead?"

"I'm afraid so."

"It wasn't a gun?"

"It was a cell phone." The chief sighs heavily. "Lakeisha Gibbs was seventeen years old. She's survived by her mother, grandmother, and two younger brothers. Chaplain Barnes, our volunteer police chaplain, has already notified the family. I'm going to follow up in person. I want you to come with me."

"Me?"

"The chaplain had another call out to attend. He indicated the family might need some psychological help. They almost always do."

* * *

No one recovers from the death of a child. They may go on with their lives and do wonderful things, but nothing sews up that hole in their heart. My job is to support the officers' mental and psychological well-being, not to provide crisis intervention to people in the community. There are other people who can do grief counseling. I'm going to have enough on my hands just helping Randy and her husband get through this. Chief Reagon stands up. There are deep purple shadows under her eyes. I can't imagine how hard this is for her, how alone she feels. Whatever her officers do, right or wrong, the buck stops with her.

"Ready?"

"I don't think so. I'm exhausted, and so are you."

"Being exhausted is a small inconvenience compared to losing a child," she says. And as she turns her back to me, her eyes swell with tears.

* * *

We drive in silence across town to East Kenilworth to where Althea Gibbs, Lakeisha's mother, lives. The commute traffic is beginning.

Long lines of cars pile up behind stop signs, drivers tilting their commute cups to get at the last drop of coffee. The sky is gunmetal gray.

There are three patrol cars in the parking area of Ms. Gibbs' condominium development, angled in a protective circle. Officers are leaning against their fenders, their darting eyes vigilant, watching as a growing knot of neighbors, some still in their bathrobes, gather in an empty carport. As we get out of the chief's car, the nearest officer straightens up and mumbles a greeting.

"Good luck, Chief. The mom's not a happy camper."

"I wouldn't expect her to be," the chief says and the officer's somber face reddens.

The woman who opens the door to the Gibbs' apartment is older than I was expecting, slender with long gray dreadlocks caught up in a metal clip. She's barefoot and wearing a floor-length caftan that is frayed at the hem.

The chief extends her hand. "I'm Chief Jacqueline Reagon. I've come here to tell you how sorry I am for your loss. I want you to know that I will personally oversee a thorough investigation, and if there's been any wrongdoing by my department, I will see to it that the offending parties are punished."

"Where's your uniform?" she asks. I'm pretty certain that if I had a daughter who had just been killed, clothes would not be the first thing on my mind.

"I'm new to the position. And I have to have all my uniforms custom made. I apologize for the informality. I mean no disrespect, Ms. Gibbs."

"Ms. Gibbs is my daughter. I'm the grandmother." She steps back and motions us inside. "My daughter is in her bedroom. I'll get her." She leaves us standing at the doorway and shuffles away unsteadily, touching the walls with her fingers as though she is blind as well as brokenhearted.

The apartment is decorated in black and white. There are plastic covers on all the upholstered furniture and lampshades, and boxes of coasters on every table. Somebody worked hard for this furniture and wants it to last. Framed photos of two identical teenage boys wearing suits and ties hang on a wall surrounded by a dozen smaller photos of them playing baseball and football. On an adjacent wall, there is a prom photo of a smiling young woman, presumably Lakeisha, leaning against a young man in a tuxedo. A corsage of dried flowers dangles from the gold frame by a satin ribbon. An eating area extends from the living room and opens out onto a small balcony filled with potted plants. The dining table is set with four place mats and matching napkins. In the center of the table an arrangement of black, white, and red silk flowers nestles in a glass bowl. There are five people living in this apartment. I wonder who eats in the kitchen and how comfortable a teenage girl would be inviting friends over to watch TV and eat pizza in this pristine room. If that's even what teenagers do these days. I have very little contact with adolescents and intend to keep it that way, although, lately, our new officers look hardly old enough to date, let alone carry weapons.

Grandmother shuffles back into the living room. She has re-pinned her hair and is wearing beaded sandals. She motions us to a love seat. "I told my daughter you're here." We sit while she leans against the back of a winged chair for support. She sways slightly. It is clearly an effort for her to hold herself upright, but she does, never taking her eyes off us, pinning us in her gaze, as if we might suddenly run off. The idea has a great deal of appeal.

A door opens and closes in the back of the apartment.

"My grandsons. Lakeisha's brothers. I told them to stay in their room." It is the first any of us have mentioned Lakeisha by name.

Another door opens and closes, followed by footfalls in the hall. Ms. Gibbs, dressed, accidentally or intentionally, in black and white to match her color scheme, comes into the room. She is a tall woman, though not as tall as the chief, well endowed with rounded hips. Her dark skin is smooth and polished. Lips and nails painted a deep, glossy red. It is obvious that she's been crying.

The chief stands and extends her hand. "I'm Chief Jacqueline Reagon. I've come here to tell you how sorry I am for your loss." Ms. Gibbs turns and walks toward the balcony door, leaving the chief with her outstretched hand in the air. "I want you to know that I will personally oversee a thorough investigation, and if there's been any wrongdoing by my department, I will see to it that the offending parties are punished."

The grandmother moves forward using the backs of chairs to support herself until she stands in front of her daughter. "You're dressed. Where are you going?"

"I don't work, I don't get paid."

"You can't go to work today. It's not right." The two women lock on each other's faces.

The chief steps closer. "I'm also here to offer you the services of our department psychologist, Dr. Dot Meyerhoff, and to give you some information about the county victims' services which are also available to you at no cost."

"It's not right that my daughter's dead, either. But that don't pay the rent."

"Is there someone I can call for you?" The chief is moving between them. I start to wonder if I should get one of the officers standing outside to come in and assist her.

"Ms. Gibbs," the chief's voice breaks into the tension. "Is there anything I can tell you about what we know so far?"

"My daughter's dead. What else I need to know?"

"Althea. Watch your mouth."

This is hardly the time for a fight or a lecture. I stand up and move next to the grandmother. "Is there somewhere you and I can talk while Ms. Gibbs and Chief Reagon finish their conversation?"

"Go on with the lady," Ms. Gibbs says. "Tell her what a bad mother I am. Tell her how Lakeisha been in trouble all her life because of how I raised her up."

Grandmother whirls around. The metal clip falls out of her hair and skitters across the bare wood floor. "You're the one who told her to get out. You're the one who said you had no time to be raising another child."

"Lakeisha's pregnant? Was pregnant?" My voice pitches an octave over normal.

"That's why she was out there living in a car," the grandmother says, looking at her daughter, not at me.

Ms. Gibbs takes two steps toward her mother at the same moment Chief Reagon moves sideways, placing herself between the two.

"Please," she says. "Remain calm. You're in shock, both of you. You're going to need each other for support."

Ms. Gibbs cocks her head. "I been supporting her ass for years. She got all those degrees and can't make a dime. Been mooching off me forever. And I got, had..." She looks at the chief, "three kids to support."

Grandmother sinks to the couch, one hand over her heart.

"Now what? You going to faint? My mother's a drama queen. She's gonna say different, but I'll tell you what happened. I didn't kick Lakeisha out—she stormed out of here, took my car and left me with no transportation." She puts her hands on her hips as if defying us to dispute that being shot to death isn't justified punishment for getting pregnant out of wedlock and taking your mother's car.

Chief Reagon continues unfazed. "When the reality of Lakeisha's death sets in, you may want or need some support."

"I need to go. I can't miss my ride." Ms. Gibbs picks up a large black patent leather bag, heads for the door, opens it, turns around, and walks back into the room. The two officers standing outside look at us, waiting for a signal from the chief to come in and help.

"I know what's she's going to do," Ms. Gibbs says. "She's going to tell you all kinda lies about me. Ask her what kind of mother she was. A good mother puts food on the table. Takes her kids to the doctor. Gets their teeth fixed. Puts a roof over their head." She's standing over her mother now, her big black bag swinging from her arm, her voice getting louder with every accusation. "You dragged me all over the place. Left me in libraries while you run with your friends. Reading about children ain't the same as raising them."

"All right, now. That's enough. Please stop." The chief moves in front, blocking Ms. Gibbs. "It's the shock and the loss. I understand how you feel. Let me call someone to be with you."

"You don't understand nothing about me." Ms. Gibbs shoves her face in front of the chief. "What are you going to do? Kill me too?" She is gripping the handles of her purse in both hands as though she's going to swing it, tears are streaking down her cheeks. "First I got no mother, now I got no daughter." The two officers rush inside, just in time to catch her as she collapses on the floor.

* * *

We are back in the living room, the chief, Lakeisha's grandmother and myself trying not to listen to Ms. Gibbs and her sons weeping in their bedrooms. One howl of pain generates another, then another.

"My name is Charla Gibbs Bernstein. Bernstein was my husband. We're divorced, but I kept his name." She fixes her eyes on me. "Meyerhoff, is that your maiden name or married name?"

"My maiden name. What a curious question."

"Names interest me. I meddle a bit in genealogy. Passes the time now that I'm retired." For a long moment we stare at each other like guests at a Mad Hatter's tea party. She faces the chief. "I hope I can believe you when you promise to find out why my granddaughter was murdered." She pauses to let the words sink in. "You can be sure my daughter and I will be holding you accountable—you and anyone else connected to my granddaughter's death." She looks at me, her eyes as green as tumbled sea glass. "I loved my granddaughter and my daughter loved her too, in her own way. I wasn't angry with her for being pregnant. Getting pregnant without marriage appears to be a family tradition, one that I apparently started when I gave birth to Althea."

"You don't owe us an explanation," the chief says.

Bernstein stiffens slightly. "But you owe me. And my daughter. You owe us the courtesy of trying to understand us as people, as a family. Because that's what we are, a family, however flawed. Don't put us in a category and don't judge my daughter too harshly. As she reminds me frequently, I was hardly a fit parent to her." She massages her long fingers as she talks. The joints are swollen and bent like broken twigs. "I believe I'm a better grandparent than I was a mother. Lakeisha and I were close. I moved in to help Althea with the children because I could see how difficult things were getting for everyone, Lakeisha especially. For some reason my daughter gets along better with her sons. Perhaps because she never knew her own father." She struggles to stand.

"You have my word that I will investigate the circumstances of your granddaughter's death thoroughly and fairly with absolute transparency." The chief extends her hand.

"I'm sure you're aware that people like us don't have much faith in the promises the police make."

Bernstein walks to the door, the hem of her caftan dragging along the floor, leaving the chief, once again, with her hand outstretched. She opens the door. A cuff of silver bracelets tinkles on her wrist. "Chief Reagon, your business card, please?" Chief Reagon pulls a card from her pocket. Her hands are trembling.

"Yours too, Dr. Meyerhoff." She smiles, her teeth are perfect.

* * *

"What did you think of Ms. Gibbs and her mother?" I ask as we get back into the car. The chief shrugs, looks over her shoulder and slowly pulls out of the parking area onto the street. The speedometer needle stays at the speed limit, not a mile faster or slower, as we drive back to headquarters.

"I can't imagine going to work hours after someone told me my daughter was killed. Can you?"

We pass first one, then two, then three intersections in silence before she responds, never taking her eyes off the road. "You never know how people will grapple with grief. I've done dozens of death notifications in my career, some with a chaplain, some without.

I've done so many I can almost tell the cries of children who have lost parents from the cries of mothers who have lost their children. It's one of the hardest parts of being a cop. People react in all sorts of ways. Some sink into silence. Others wail and shriek. Some turn on each other or assault the officer who has brought the bad news."

"And you remember them all?"

"I do."

"What about the people whose lives you saved? Do you remember them?"

"In this business, you don't remember the people you've saved. You remember the ones you killed."

CHAPTER SEVEN

I have time enough to go home, take a shower and change my clothes before going into the office. I want to get in early to prepare for the day's work. There is a note on the kitchen counter from Frank, stuck under the empty bottle of pinot noir. I read it on my way out the door. "If you aren't busy, let's pick up where we left off last night."

I have two appointments this morning starting at ten-thirty. The first is an officer who is six months away from retirement, panicking about what he'll do with the rest of his life. His identity is so melted into police work that he can only imagine himself as a security guard, asleep on his feet in a museum. Who will he be when he's no longer a cop? How he will get along with his wife without the long hours and overtime that has buffered him from the untended fissures in their relationship? How can he replace the fraternity of officers that filled his life? It's a serious consideration, one he should have begun planning for five years ago. My heart gives a little anxious thump. There's an uptick in the frequency of suicide among retired cops. I'm irritated with this client. Why is his failure to plan my problem? Except that it is my problem and my job to help him figure it out.

My second appointment is a pre-employment psych. Another nervous young applicant twittering with expectation, eager to suit up and save the community. They are like bookends, these two men, the young one, shiny and bright, the way Randy was not that long ago, the older man, bruised and dented. Police work changes people. It is my job to make sure that it doesn't damage them. That's what I want for Randy. I want to help her come through this wiser and stronger, however long it takes. I want her to find something positive to take away from this tragic experience so that she can retire at the end of thirty years with pride for the good things she's accomplished, the people she's helped, the problems she's solved. My father's voice rises in the quiet of my office: "Be careful what you wish for, Baby Girl. Hope for the best, but prepare for the worst."

I grab a cup of coffee in the staff room on the first floor of my office building and carry it up the stairs. It will have to hold me until lunch. I keep thinking about Lakeisha Gibbs. How lonely and frightened she must have been, pregnant and living in a car.

Randy Spelling and Rich are in my waiting room, sitting still as stones. A chair separates them. They are leaning forward, elbows propped on their knees, holding paper cups of coffee in their hands. They both have that thousand-mile stare. Rich is wearing jeans, a sweatshirt, and a backwards baseball cap with sunglasses resting on the bill. Like the Roman God Janus, looking into the future and the past. Randy, minus the baseball hat, is dressed the same. Rich and Randy, they sound like a sitcom.

"Randy, I wasn't expecting to see you so soon."

"Chief's orders," she says. So much for my little speech to the chief about mandatory counseling.

"Well, I would have suggested you wait a day or two, but since you're here we might as well...Just give me a minute to get settled."

"Take your time. I've got all day."

I wait for her to introduce her husband, and when she doesn't, I introduce myself.

He stands up and shakes my hand. He's quite tall and slender with the gangly body of a late-blooming adolescent. His light brown hair is brushy and spiky, his eyes are pale green. He is tan, a surprise for someone who works in the jail, and has ruddy cheeks. "Nice to meet you, ma'am."

"Nice to meet you, too, although we could have wished for better circumstances." He sits down without responding, picks up a magazine from the pile on the table in front of him and starts leafing through it.

"Give me a few minutes, please, to get organized."

My office is cold and damp. I turn on all the lights and sit down at my desk trying to recover from the surprise of finding Randy in my waiting room. I used to scuba dive. It was one of my ex's inspired solutions to our marital problems. We needed something to do together besides talking shop. Turns out we had as much trouble communicating underwater as we did above it. The night before a dive I would vibrate with anxiety at the prospect of submerging myself in the cold, gray Pacific Ocean off the San Francisco coastline where the visibility rarely exceeds ten feet and the water is home to large fish with sharp teeth. I feel that same night-before-a-dive churning in my gut now. It could be that my gut is reacting to drinking coffee on an empty stomach. Or it could be the enormity of facing a young woman who has just taken an innocent life. A mistake of this magnitude calls for a priest, not a psychologist.

*　*　*

Randy and Rich sit at opposite ends of my leather couch, putting their coffee cups on the table in tandem. Before I have a chance to start, Rich jumps in: "I want to put this out there right now. This is my fault. I tried to tell the DA that, but he didn't want to talk to me."

"It's not your fault. It's my fault. Mine. No one else's. I told you." Randy tilts her head in his direction without looking at him.

"After the creek thing, Rutgers bad mouthing her all over the place, I told her. Get tough. Show 'em what you can do. Beat the crap out of somebody so they'll leave you alone. I didn't mean for her to kill anyone." He shakes his head. I can see tears at the corners of his eyes.

This is how it is. Behind every cop who's been through something tragic is a loved one, suffering in silence, uncertain about how to help, a target for the misplaced rage that is fueled by a mix

of fury and fear. In a matter of seconds my client load has dou-
bled. Rich will need my help, maybe as much as Randy. But, for
the moment, Randy is my primary client, and I need to talk to her
first.

"Rich," I say. "You're in a lot of pain. That's understandable
and normal, given the circumstances. But, would you be willing to
give me a few minutes alone with Randy and then you and I can
talk?"

He's on his feet before I finish my sentence. "Whatever," he
says and walks out the door, leaving it partially ajar.

Randy gets up and pushes it shut. Then she walks to a side
chair next to the bookcase, pulls it out into the room and turns
it around. She straddles it, facing me, her arms crossed over the
back, creating a small barrier between us. Her legs are bouncing
and her jaw muscles clench and unclench rhythmically.

"It's not his problem. It's mine."

"He loves you. When you hurt, he hurts."

"He didn't kill someone, I did." She reaches into her back
pocket and pulls out a folded sheet of newspaper, unfolds it and
holds it in front of her face so I can read it. The headline says
"Cop Shoots Pregnant Teen."

"Why did I have to find out that she was pregnant from the
newspaper?" Her face puckers. "I killed a homeless, seventeen-
year-old pregnant girl who was only trying to call her mother.
Guess that makes me cop of the year. Jesus, I thought running
away from the creek was the worst thing that could happen to
me." Her head drops to her folded arms.

"You thought she had a gun. You did what you were trained
to do. What any reasonable cop would have done."

"Any reasonable cop would have handcuffed her and put her
in the back of a patrol car, not shoot her."

"Nobody can predict how they're going to react in a crisis.
It's not fair to second guess yourself based on what you know now
but didn't know at the time."

She lifts her head, her jaw juts forward. There are eggplant-colored shadows under her eyes. "Fair? What's fair about what I did? I can still taste her blood in my mouth."

I wince inwardly at the image. What other profession mandates that you attempt to resuscitate a person you've just tried to kill?

"Don't read the newspapers, Randy, and don't read the blogs. The minute Lindsey Lohan gets another DUI you'll be off the front page. What I mean is there's history here. The Kenilworth Daily hates the police department. Back in the sixties, there were campus demonstrations against the Vietnam War and the police broke into the Daily's office and confiscated photos of the demonstrators. The case went all the way to the Supreme Court. I doubt anyone from that era still works there, but they still carry a grudge against the police, particularly Kenilworth cops."

"Were you there?"

I wasn't, but demonstrating runs in my family. My father was a student agitator at UC Berkeley. I still have news clippings of him standing on a patrol car, giving the finger to the cops in riot gear, before they pulled him down and beat him senseless.

"Look at her." Randy opens the newspaper to an inside page and shows me a picture of Lakeisha Gibbs dressed for a prom. It is the same picture that is hanging in her mother's apartment. She was a pretty girl, slightly overweight, with a wide smile and deep dimples. She looks happy. Her braided hair is wound with flowers, and she's wearing a white satin strapless gown. The boy holding her hand is resplendent in his tuxedo. I wonder if he is the father of her child.

"Just a kid, a normal kid." At twenty-four, Randy is barely more than a kid herself.

"We don't know that. She seemed to be in a lot of trouble."

"She was scared. I can't imagine my parents kicking me out of the house for getting pregnant."

I start to tell her that Lakeisha may have run away from home, but I stop myself. It won't make any difference. Compassion is Randy's Achilles' heel. On the one hand, it will make her a better cop. On the other, it will obliterate the emotional distance she needs to do her job. My father's voice rises in my head. He would turn over in his grave if he heard me use the words compassion and cops in the same sentence. "Cops do what they do because they're sadistic bullies," he told me so many times that I could recite his rant by heart. "They liked beating me; they were laughing the whole time."

Randy stands up. "I want to talk to Lakeisha's mother. I need to tell her what happened. I didn't do this on purpose. I'm not a monster." Her eyes bulge with tears.

"I don't think that's a good idea. She's in mourning. She might not understand. It might even be dangerous. You can't presume anything about Lakeisha or her family. You just said that her mother kicked her out of the house. Maybe she had a good reason."

"You think she doesn't feel guilty? You think she isn't beating herself up over this, like I am? We could help each other."

"Do not do this, Randy, it's dangerous. Examine your own feelings first. I know you didn't intend to kill her. You were frightened, you thought your life was in danger. You went on automatic pilot, the way you were trained."

She folds the newspaper up into a flat square, sticks it back in her pocket, and sits down again.

"No," she says. "I didn't do what I was trained to do. I should have called for backup. That's how I was trained. But I didn't, because I was worried about what everyone would think if I couldn't handle a seventeen-year-old girl by myself? They already think I'm a wimp. I didn't want to hear it anymore, the snide comments, the snickering...and now they love me. Look at this." She leans to the left, lifts her backside off the chair, digs in her other pocket and pulls out a crumpled greeting card. "I found this on the front step this morning. It's a congratulations card. I'm one of the boys now because I killed somebody. The same creeps who called me names because of what happened at the creek. The same jerks who gave me extra whacks in defensive tactics, just for the fun of it. Now I'm their hero. Well, fuck them. If that's what it takes to join the good old boys' club, I don't want it." And before I can stop her, she's on her feet, out the door, through the waiting room, and down the stairs, Rich staring after her.

"My turn now, huh?" He stands, still holding the magazine he was reading.

"Don't you want to go after her?"

"She's probably better off alone. Let her cool off." He walks into my office, looks from the chair to the couch and chooses the couch.

"She needs time," I say. "It's not even twenty-four hours yet. Her bloodstream is still clogged with hormonal debris. She won't be easy to live with until she calms down and expels all that adrenaline. In the meantime, it's as though she thinks she's still fighting for her life."

"Last night I got out of bed to take a leak. When I got back into bed, she thought I was attacking her and started kicking and punching me. This morning I came up behind her to give her a hug, and she jumped two feet in the air. The phone's been ringing off the hook. Cops, calling to see how she is. She won't talk to anybody. Even the chief, who called three times already. I told her to call her family. They're all cops, they'll understand. She made me do it instead, just so they wouldn't hear it on the radio. I don't know what to do."

"These are early days, Rich. There are only a few things you can do. Let her talk if she wants, but don't force her. Keep her away from alcohol and caffeine, they potentiate the chemicals in her body, and try to get her to do some mild exercise. It's a good way to get the adrenaline out of her system. And keep her from watching TV news or reading the paper. It will only upset her. Sorry to say, but she's going to be irritable and have a short fuse for a week or two, maybe more."

He grimaces. "That long?"

"It's chemical, not voluntary. She doesn't get to vote on it and neither do you, so try not to take it personally. This is tough, but it's temporary. You're going to need a lot of patience." I say this knowing that patience is usually not a cop's best asset. "What about you, have you ever experienced anything like this in your career?"

He shakes his head. "I suppose I gave some extra love to a few folks in the jail who didn't love me back for it, but nothing like this. Never killed anyone although I felt like it sometimes. I can't even take my weapon into the jail. I knew she was having a hard time at work. The cops were ragging on her about wimping out in a fight. She's not a wimp. She's tough. I told her to man up, show them what she could do."

"Are you saying you think she shot Lakeisha Gibbs on purpose, to prove something?"

"No way. What I mean is she didn't call for backup because it would make her look like she couldn't handle the situation by herself. Stupid move. They may have been riding her, but when a cop puts out a Code 3 call for help, everybody comes. So what if they ragged on her some more? Big deal. It would have been better than this." He pulls his sunglasses off his hat and puts them on. "I'd better go look for her." He stands. Puts out his hand for me to shake. "Thanks, Doc. I hope you know what you're doing. She's stubborn. Always has been."

* * *

I check my office phone for messages. There's a message from Chief Reagon. She wants me to know that she has been trying to get Randy on the telephone, but that Randy isn't answering. She left a message strongly recommending that Randy meet me as soon as possible, hopefully today. She wants me to tell Randy to take all the time she needs. It is her inclination to have an outside agency investigate Randy's shooting to avoid any potential accusations of conflict of interest, but Captain Jay Pence has advised her that doing so would be an insult to the integrity of the department. Because he knows the department culture so much better than she does, she's accepting his advice and has, once again, put him in charge of the investigation. I am to keep him apprised of Randy's progress.

I call her back on her cell phone. When she picks up I can tell she's in her car. I can hear traffic noises in the background.

"You promised Lakeisha's mother and grandmother that you would personally oversee this investigation. And now you're handing the investigation to Jay Pence. Have I missed something? Is anything wrong?"

"Jay Pence reports directly to me. When I said I would personally oversee things I didn't mean that I would conduct all the interviews myself. I still have a department to run. I count on my staff to do the day-to-day work."

"But you're the public face of this department. Not Jay Pence."

There's a pause. Horns honk in the distance.

"I'm well aware of that."

"I don't think Ms. Gibbs or Ms. Bernstein will understand this. You gave them your word."

"They don't need to understand it. And frankly, Dr. Meyerhoff, neither do you. I'm sorry to be abrupt but I've arrived at my destination." She clicks off.

Heat rises in my cheeks, and I'm glad there's no one here to see me getting red in the face. How dare she talk to me like that? I'm a consultant, not a subordinate. Something is going on with her and I wish I knew what the hell it was.

CHAPTER EIGHT

Popcorn and red wine make up my fallback cuisine. I curl up on the couch in my bathrobe and turn on the evening news. Jay Pence stands like a cardboard cutout on the steps of police headquarters, stiff and emotionless, parsing his words so carefully that even I am inclined to think he's covering up something.

"There is an ongoing police investigation upon which I cannot comment. Rest assured, our investigation will be thorough, fair, and transparent." There's a barrage from the reporters, each one stepping on the other's question. Pence looks out over their heads and calls on none other than Jack Shiller, the young reporter who accosted me in the lobby.

"Where is the chief? Why isn't she in charge of this investigation?"

"I am keeping Chief Reagon in the loop, every step of the way. She is and continues to be fully informed. She has already made personal contact with the family of the young woman who was shot." I notice he avoids calling Lakeisha Gibbs a victim.

"When will we hear from the chief in person?" Shiller continues as though he hasn't heard a word of what Pence has just said.

"Thank you, ladies and gentlemen." Pence starts to close his briefing book.

"Who shot Lakeisha Gibbs?" Shiller has now edged closer to the steps.

Pence takes a long sigh as if he is condescending to tolerate an interrogation not his own. "I will not release the officer's name while there is an ongoing investigation."

"Randy Spelling. Isn't that the officer?" Two KPD officers

move in front of Pence, effectively blocking Shiller's physical access. He's a very skinny young man, hardly a match for the two broad-chested cops in front of him or for Pence, who's twice his age.

"I repeat; the law prevents me from releasing any names. As you know, when an officer is involved in a shooting, they are placed on administrative leave for a minimum of three days. Longer, if required."

"So, Spelling is suspended?"

"What is suspended, ladies and gentlemen, is our press briefing. Thank you for your attention." He turns his back to the TV cameras and starts up the steps while Shiller and the other reporters shout questions at him.

Now the TV screen fills with a close up of Althea Gibbs, dressed in black, clutching Lakeisha's prom photo in one hand. Tears roll down her face. "I want justice for my child and for the grandchild I'll never know." She leans against Chester Allen, Esquire, everyone's go-to guy in police brutality cases. He steadies her gently and bends toward the thicket of microphones. There is a whirring and clicking from the cameras.

"This is an outrage. A child, struck down in the prime of life, defenseless and unarmed, murdered in cold blood by the very people who are charged with protecting her. It is my duty and my honor to help Ms. Gibbs find justice and to provide my services pro bono." He has a booming bass voice and speaks in the rhythms and cadence of the black church. It is high drama of the first order. An address appears on the TV screen. Interested viewers may donate funds for Lakeisha Gibbs' funeral to an account in her name at the Monument Bank.

I turn off the TV. Had I been too quick to judge Ms. Gibbs this morning? Whatever the truth, the facts speak for themselves; a teenage girl is dead and a young officer's life is forever changed.

* * *

The telephone rings—never a good sign at night. It is my mother, taking time out from poker, line dancing, her investment club, and her Red Hat society hijinks to see if Frank and I have gotten married yet. She's only met him twice but considers him an ideal candidate for matrimony, the nicest man she's ever met.

"Having a good day, sweetie?"

"Hardly. Have you seen the news?"

"I don't watch the news anymore. Too depressing."

"We had a shooting. A young officer killed a pregnant teenager."

"Being pregnant isn't a crime."

"No mother, it's not a crime, it's a tragedy. The officer mistook a metal cell phone for a weapon and thought the young woman was going to shoot her."

"Shoot herself? I don't understand."

"There are two of them, mother. The officer and the teenager are both female."

"Oh, I see." I'm not sure that she does. My mother has always lived in a world of her own making, a perpetual optimist, picking and choosing her favorite realities and ignoring the rest. This despite of or because of my father's neverending diatribe against the world, most forms of humanity, and all forms of authority. "Why are you involved?"

"It's my job. I'm supposed to help the officer get through this. I'm sure it was a mistake on her part, not a deliberate act. I really can't tell you anymore, but listening to what she's going through made me think of Dad. How much he hated the police. How he could never imagine a cop feeling bad about anything."

"Well, you know how your father was."

"He never got over the beating he took. I feel sad that he let it poison the rest of his life."

"Oh my dear. Do you still believe that story?"

"Don't you? Didn't you?" I had no idea my mother doubted the truthfulness of my father's experience. The shock of it rumbles me. She heard him tell the story as often as I did and never contradicted him. "What are you saying, Mother? Do you think he lied about that? That he pulled his own arm out of the socket?"

"Of course not. But he was clumsy. I always suspected that he got hurt because he fell or got stepped on in one of those demonstrations. The police would never beat someone deliberately. It made him feel better to think that he was some kind of a hero of the student movement, like it wasn't for nothing that he got hurt. Why would I challenge him and make him feel even worse?"

CHAPTER NINE

Randy Spelling has no extra weight to lose. Yet, in less than a week she looks as though she's lost ten pounds—her jeans bag at the seat and her collarbones and shoulders protrude like sticks under her t-shirt. Her cheeks are sunken and her eyes are glossy from lack of sleep. She takes off her baseball cap. Her hair is matted and dull.

"How long does this last?"

"How long does what last?"

"This PTSD stuff."

"What's happening?"

"I can't sleep, I can't eat. I can't stop thinking about what I did. I don't dare go out. Rich told me not to watch TV, but what else am I going to do? Guess you know, somebody leaked my name so now my picture's in the paper. I don't know for sure, but I'll bet it's Tom Rutgers." She's walking around my office as she talks, pacing from the door to the window to the bookcase, tracing a wobbly triangle on the carpet.

"Did you hear the mother on TV talking about me like I'm a monster? I went out for groceries and got stopped twice by people asking me why I had to kill Lakeisha, why didn't I shoot her in the leg? I should've shot her in the leg, you know. I wish I had never seen her. I wish I had let someone else take the call." Now she sits, her leg jiggling like crazy, strangling her baseball cap between her hands. "Pence called this morning; told me I can't come back to work until the investigation is complete. Not even light duty. I'm going crazy at home. I feel like I'm in prison."

"Is there anyplace else you could go to wait this out?"

"Ms. Gibbs wants to sue me."

"That's standard procedure after this kind of incident." Her face goes red.

"That's just it. I'm a person, not an incident. Don't you get it?" Before I can apologize, the door opens and Rich comes in.

"I'm okay."

"No you're not. I want to talk to the doc."

"Have at it." She slaps her cap on her head.

"You got to stop her, Doc. She wants to talk to that girl's mother. She's been threatening to do it all weekend. She wants to apologize. Thinks that will make things better. She needs a lawyer. The POA will get her one, but no, she thinks lawyers make things worse. She wants to talk, woman to woman. I told her how crazy that is, but everything I do or say is wrong. How long is she going to be like this?"

"It hasn't even been a week. In my experience, life won't really return to normal until the investigation is over and the lawsuit—if there is one—is resolved."

"Hear that, Rich? That's what I told you. A year. Not a week. A year." She turns to me. "I must speak at a dog's pitch because only dogs and other women can hear me."

"This is my life too, Randy. Guys at work are slapping me on the back, congratulating me for hooking up with you 'cause you got balls. Asking if you strap on when you come to bed. They think you're hot. They don't know I'm living with a crazy person who can't sleep, won't eat, and yells at me every time I open my mouth. I didn't shoot that girl, but I wish I had. I'd have handled it better."

"You don't know how you would have handled it. Nobody does. Not until it happens." Randy springs up and heads for the door. "You have no idea how I feel."

He reaches for her arm. "I hate seeing you so miserable. If I could of switched places with you, I would have. You can't think or talk about anything else. It's like I'm invisible. You bark at everything I say, I snap back, and then I feel like shit for yelling at you. I want our lives back. I know this is happening to you, but it's happening to me too." He lets go of her arm and sits down on the couch, fighting tears.

Randy sits next to him, one hand on his leg. "I know how to fix this," she says. "Why won't anyone let me talk to the mother? Why does everyone know better than me?"

"Because if you apologize, it's going to sound like you did something wrong and you didn't," he says. "You did what you're trained to do. What I would have done. She was less than ten feet away. You had to shoot her. It's a legal shoot."

"It's a bad idea, Randy," I say. "Ms. Gibbs is very angry. Nothing you can say will help her—not now—maybe never. Like Rich says, it could be trouble for you."

Now I've done it. Lost my neutrality. Stepped over an invisible scrimmage line to Rich's side.

"How much more trouble could I be in than I'm in now? I'm not an executioner. I didn't get into this job to kill people." She puts her hands on her thighs and pushes herself into a standing position as though she is lifting a thousand pounds of dead weight. "I need a break." She opens the door and walks out. I look to Rich to follow her, but he is leaning back staring at the ceiling.

"No worries, Doc. She'll wait for me downstairs. She can't go anywhere alone. She thinks people are watching her. She even thinks she sees that girl's family on our street." He sits up. "What about meds? Can you give her anything?"

"Didn't her internist give her something to take after the incident at the creek?"

"She dumped them. Right after the shooting. Didn't want anybody to know she took drugs."

There's a brief pause in the conversation. I have to ask this question although I'm not sure I want to hear the answer. "On the night of the shooting, had she taken any medication?"

"I doubt it. She didn't like taking it. Made her feel weird. I'll bet the bottle was totally full when she dumped it. They took blood. Did they find any?"

"I don't know."

"She could use something now. She has these nightmares where dead people come up from under the ground chasing her."

"I'll look into it. There are a couple of drugs that help with nightmares." He stands up. "Looks like you need some support yourself. Who's backing you up?"

"I got friends. And my family. They know what's going on."

"No psychologist or peer support at work?"

"No way. We're in the dark ages. The crooks get counseling. Deputies get nothing."

"What about Randy's family?"

"They're not much help. I work with her brothers at the jail. Bunch of hard-asses. Telling her to 'man up,' and deal with it. Her mother said 'I told you to be a school teacher,' and her father scared the crap out of her by telling her about cops he worked with who shot someone and went to jail because of it. Took me two hours to get her to calm down after she talked to them. And then we got into another fight."

CHAPTER TEN

Randy and I are standing on the corner, two blocks away from the spot where Lakeisha was killed. It's a lovely neighborhood. The houses are old, each one a unique architectural gem, different from its neighbor. Totally unlike the cookie-cutter townhouses in my faux Italianate development. Bowers of magnolia trees create a canopy over the street, their huge leaves screening the early morning sun, dappling the sidewalk with splotches of light. I doubt the newly planted trees around my house, their spindly trunks encased in rubber sleeves and tethered to the ground, will ever grow to such magnificence.

I've persuaded Randy to do a walkthrough with me before she gives another statement to the DA or to the investigation team. She's wearing street clothes, her billed cap pulled down over her face just low enough that I can see her relentlessly chewing her bottom lip. She's shifting her weight from one foot to another as though she's preparing to sprint.

"Deep breaths, Randy," I say. "Take deep breaths."

"Suppose someone recognizes me?"

"No one is going to recognize you. You're not in uniform and we're using my car."

"Tell me again why you're making me do this."

"I'm not making you do anything. You agreed."

"Yeah, but why? I forgot."

"My point, exactly. When you're under extreme stress, your memory degrades. You thought you were going to be killed." She starts to protest. "It doesn't make any difference if that was true, that's what you thought at the time. It was dark, you couldn't see,

Lakeisha had a metal object in her hand and she wasn't cooperating. Remember?" I put my hand on her shoulder. It feels like a bird's wing, bony and cold. "When humans are forced to make quick decisions in response to sudden threats, all they can do is focus on the threat. It's called 'selective attention' or 'tunnel vision.' It makes sense, right? Focus on what's relevant to survival and ignore what isn't relevant." Randy continues to shift back and forth, her sneakers making soft, scratching sounds on the pavement.

"When people make decisions, they usually have enough time to use rational, logical, conscious thinking. Look at the houses around us. Think about the architects. All the planning that went into designing them so they are beautiful and structurally sound." Randy barely glances at them.

"You didn't have that kind of time to think. So you went on automatic pilot which is below the level of conscious awareness. And because it's below conscious awareness, it impairs your ability to recall parts of the incident or to articulate the reasons why you chose to do what you did. Things are going to look different to you in the daylight. It may jog your memory, help you fill in the blanks."

She takes a deep breath. "All right. Let's go." She starts to walk down the street.

It takes me a few seconds to catch up. "What were you thinking as you were driving to the call?" She closes her eyes for a second.

"Be there first. Don't cry."

"Anything else?"

"Can we please just get this over with?" she says and strides away from me. She is my height, but her legs are longer, and in no time at all she disappears around the corner. And that's where I find her frozen in front of a small memorial. Multicolored balloons are tied to a tree, a clutch of teddy bears and candles tucked among its enormous roots. Cards and placards are pinned to the trunk like dying leaves. Randy bends over them and reads. "RIP Lakeisha. We love U, baby. Not 2 B forgot. Revenge 4 Lakeisha. Spelling is a baby murderer."

A young woman jogs around the corner, pushing a sleek jog-ging stroller that looks more like a racing car than a baby carrier. She is tall and slender with a long blond ponytail tucked through the opening in the back of a billed cap. Her form-fitting spandex running suit looks as though it was sprayed on.

"Can I help you?" she asks, only slightly out of breath. Her sleeping baby murmurs discontentedly at the change in pace. "This is my house. I've asked the police to remove this, and they haven't responded. This is tragic, but I don't want it in front of my house. All this traffic, all those people. I told the police, we're having a party. Where is everyone going to park?"

Randy steps in front of the jogger. "Somebody died here, lady. Isn't that more important than your damn party?" She steps back again and turns to face me. "Great idea, Doc."

"Are you the cop who shot her? Oh, my God, you are."

"And are you the whining bitch who called the police because a black seventeen-year-old homeless girl was sleeping in front of your house. Bet you wouldn't have called if she was white."

Blondie straightens up. "I had every right. She didn't belong here. And not because she's black. I didn't know what color she was and I don't care. She's a vagrant. She should have gone to a homeless shelter if she needed a place to stay. Children play on this block. We did not move here to have homeless people living in our front yard."

"What did she ever do to you?" Randy's voice is a shrill whine.

"She played some boom-box thing, loud. And we could hear her talking on her cell phone when we were trying to sleep. You know, officer whatever-your-name-is, I just wanted the police to make her move. I didn't want you to kill her."

* * *

Back in the car, Randy's face is rain slicked and shiny with tears.

"I feel like I'm trapped in a box and the instructions to get out are written on the outside.'"

"We'll get through this, Randy. Not to worry. It's still early days." I reach to pat her shoulder and she jerks away.

I'm being prematurely reassuring and it's disingenuous. I think about an old friend who was driving down the freeway, minding her own business on the way to a shopping mall, when some man jumped off the overpass and landed on her car, his face smashed against her windshield, frozen in horror, eyes open and staring. She had nothing whatsoever to do with his death, yet years of therapy haven't erased the memory or released her to drive on a freeway. If she can't get past that, what hope is there for Randy?

"Don't give up," I say, this time mostly to reassure myself. "I'm not giving up on you. We'll get through this, whatever it takes."

CHAPTER ELEVEN

Sunday morning Frank wants to go to the farmer's market on the coast, and I want to stay home and watch Lakeisha Gibbs' funeral on local cable TV. I tell Frank to go ahead without me, but he opts to stay and make me breakfast instead. He is quiet and alternates between watching and playing games on his iPad. There is a large crowd in front of the church in East Kenilworth. Chester Allen has timed things so that the regular churchgoers stay around to swell the crowd of mourners, although the large, mostly black crowd needs little supplanting. Women in hats that look like birds in flight, teeter on delicate stiletto heels, oversized purses dangling from their arms as elderly men in a rainbow of suits with matching shoes and fedoras congregate, their faces drawn and serious.

Jack Shiller, still looking like a rookie reporter out of a grade B black-and-white movie, interviews Lakeisha's uncle, Samuel Gibbs, a handsome man with a trimmed silver goatee and a black beret.

"We want justice. My niece was taken from her family at the dawn of her life, pregnant with a child and pregnant with promise for her future. Instead, she was summarily executed for no reason at all. Officer Spelling was never in danger. My niece had a cell phone. Had Officer Spelling talked to Lakeisha instead of drawing her gun, we wouldn't be having a funeral. My niece was a bright girl, a good student, a loving daughter and sister."

"Why was she living in her car?" Shiller asks.

"She wasn't living in her car, and even if she was, that is not a capital crime in the United States." He turns directly to the television. "She and her mother had a temporary disagreement, not uncommon for a teenager. And certainly not grounds for execution. She and her mother were resolving their differences, and Lakeisha was intending to return home."

"Can you tell us the basis for their disagreement?" Shiller asks and then turns away from Samuel Gibbs before he has time to answer. "I believe the car that just pulled up to the church belongs to Chief Jacqueline Reagon." The camera moves left.

Jay Pence gets out first and holds the door for the chief. She is in uniform for the first time since I've known her. Her legs cased in neutral stockings and flat, black, walking shoes. Uniforms improve how men look, the sharp creases and expert tailoring making them look taller, straighter, and fitter than they might otherwise appear. Chief Reagon's uniform only emphasizes her height, her thick legs, and her lack of grace.

I have no idea what the chief is doing here. If she had asked me, I would have told her it was a bad idea, worse than Randy's impulse to apologize. Ms. Gibbs needs to hate someone other than herself for Lakeisha's death. Even if she didn't throw Lakeisha out of the house, what dreadful memories does she have of their last conversation? Who knows what horrible things they said to each other?

The camera follows the chief's ungainly exit from her car. She climbs the low steps in front of the church so close to Jay Pence that she appears to be leaning on him. There's movement on the right of the screen as Jack Shiller pushes through the crowd and mashes himself up against the chief.

"Did the family invite you to the funeral?" He is almost on tiptoes lifting the microphone to the chief's face.

"I'm here to pay my respects. This is a tragedy of immense magnitude. I hope my being here demonstrates the police department's deep concern for the Gibbs family and their loss."

This is insanity. Jay Pence should have stopped her. What is she trying to prove? Being here is provocative. She can't just show up and say 'sorry.' No matter how badly she feels, she isn't suffering as much as the Gibbs family, and it's offensive to suggest that whatever she or anyone else is experiencing comes close to the grief a mother feels for the death of her child. Unless, of course, it's Randy.

Chester Allen, elegant in a dove-gray suit and matching bowler, moves to the top of the stairs in between the chief and the TV cameras. He is joined by Lakeisha's uncle. Their heads bend in conversation. A minute later, Pence and the chief walk down the steps, get in their car and drive away.

Chester Allen turns to the reporters. "The family wishes to say Chief Reagon's attendance at Lakeisha's funeral is inappropriate, intrusive, and upsetting to the grieving family. What we need in this community is more than gestures of respect. We need genuine dialogue between the police and the community. There is no better evidence for the magnitude of this need than the tragedy that brings us here today, the death of Lakeisha Gibbs. It is not my place to speculate about the chief's reasons for coming here today, but if she hopes to avoid a lawsuit or intimidate me into calling off our planned demonstration demanding justice for Lakeisha, then she has underestimated my determination and only increased community outrage at this injustice." Two men emerge from the crowd holding picket signs saying "Justice for Lakeisha" and position themselves on the step below Chester Allen, careful not to obscure his face.

This is spin of the first order. I don't know why the chief came here and I intend to find out, but I seriously doubt it was to forestall a lawsuit or prevent a demonstration.

The camera pans the crowd as solemn monitors usher people into a line that slowly files into the church, their feet shuffling in time with the solemn music of a hidden organ. I've had enough. I'm about to turn off the TV when I see a quick movement at the corner of the screen. Someone dodges into a grove of trees planted between the church and a small grave-yard surrounded by a low, wrought iron fence. It's hardly more than a blur, but I don't have to see her face to know it is Randy Spelling.

CHAPTER TWELVE

My office at police headquarters is on the flight path between the locker room and the briefing room. Mostly a place to hang my coat and leave my laptop. It's a controversial location, given the reluctance most cops have to being seen talking to a psychologist. On the other hand, some of my best conversations have taken place in the hallway. Evidently, the police have a belief akin to my belief that food eaten while standing has no calories. If they're moving or talking to me while leaning on the doorjamb with their feet in the hall, it isn't therapy. But if they come into my office, sit down and close the door, that is therapy. When things get serious, cops prefer to see me in my private office on Catalan Court in a nondescript two-story building hidden behind a bank and a real estate firm.

My private office is on the second floor. It has two doors, one exiting down an external staircase, so that my clients, who are almost all cops and fire fighters, can avoid each other. Emergency response is a small world, everyone seems to know everyone else, and small departments, like Kenilworth's, train and share mutual aid with the other small departments that line the peninsula from San Francisco to San Jose. I share the building with my old friend Gary Morse, his wife, Janice, and three other therapists.

Monday morning, I decide to swing by the station before heading to Catalan Court. It's still early, the sky is gray, streaked with long flat fingers of cloud. There is a brisk, chilly wind in the air and a small traffic jam on my cul-de-sac as my neighbors back out of their driveways, and we line up at the corner stop sign waiting to turn onto the El Camino and head to the freeway. Back in the day, traffic on the El Camino Real would have been horses, cows, and vaqueros. Now it is one long strip mall lined with fast food chains, auto parts stores, and shopping centers. The curving streetlamps that are supposed to be quaint reminders of our Spanish past do little to mitigate the haphazard commercial mess.

There is a palpable buzz at HQ. I can feel it as I walk down the hall, open the door to my office, put down my briefcase, and hang up my jacket.

"You're here early, Doc."

"Hey, Manny. How you doing?"

"You got your hands full today. Plenty of pissed-off cops." He smiles.

"What's going on?"

"You don't know? I thought that's why you were here so early. The whole department's jacked up because the chief went to the Gibbs funeral. She's supposed to defend the troops, not line up with the bad guys."

This doesn't sound like Manny, who has never been a badge-heavy kind of cop. I want to remind him that Lakeisha was seventeen and pregnant, not my definition of a bad guy. But that's stupid; anyone with a weapon is a threat, even a child. Two officers, one tall and thin, the other short and round, are walking down the hall. They stop when they hear what we're talking about.

"Spelling let her get way too close. Never should have happened." They are looking at Manny, not me.

He answers quickly. "The only one who knows what happened is Spelling. Second guess this all you want, she was there, you weren't." That sounds more like the Manny I know—being his own person, staying out of the locker room gossip.

"Bet your fucking ass," the tall one says. "Excuse my French, Doc." He grimaces. Am I offended? Disgusted? Going to report him to the chief? Truth is I am more offended by the apology than the language. It's an unconscious stab at making sure I don't forget who I am and that who I am doesn't fit in.

"No fucking problem," I say. They look at each other, eyes wide, not sure if I'm kidding or serious.

The skinny officer continues. "All I'm saying is if it was me, it wouldn't have gone down that way. First off, I'd have waited for backup. Spelling's a hothead." The shorter officer winces—clearly this is dangerous territory to be discussing in front of me. He cranks his head toward the end of the hall. "We got to go. Later."

Cops love to Monday morning quarterback. They want to believe that they're invincible. Blame someone for making a mistake, convince yourself that you'd have done something different and presto, you banish random violence and your own human limitations.

Manny shakes his head as he watches the two officers walk away. "Half the department thinks Spelling acted right, and half thinks she blew it. It's tearing the place apart. People aren't speaking to each other. Morale is heading down the tubes. Been this way since the shooting and it isn't getting any better. There's only one thing everybody agrees on."

"What's that?"

"Everybody's freaking mad at the chief."

* * *

The door to the chief's office is open. She's bent over her desk, dressed in a gray suit, a pale beige shell and flat shoes. It's the same outfit she wears every day, but in different colors. I picture her closet, four suits, four blouses, four pairs of shoes, neatly lined up, all ready to mix and match. Frank buys his t-shirts online, six at a time. I wonder if the chief does the same with her suits.

"Knock, knock," I say. She looks up.

"Come in." She stands up. Her predecessor, Chief Bob Baxter, was a fireplug of a man, short and broad. She is so tall that she blocks most of the light coming through the window behind her desk. The sun is still fighting to break through the clouds. "Have a seat." She gestures to the small grouping of three chairs and a round table. "Coffee?" I nod. She fills my cup, but not her own.

"How is Randy doing?"

"As expected, under the circumstances. I really came by to see how you're doing." The light reflects off her glasses, making it hard for me to see her eyes. She sits straight, retreating into stillness as though she has suddenly gone into deep meditation. A minute passes.

"I was surprised you and Captain Pence went to Lakeisha's funeral. Apparently this has upset the troops."

"They're upset with me, not him. I give the orders."

"So, if I may ask, why did you go? Especially because you seem to be backing away from the investigation."

Her eyebrows knit together and she pushes her chair toward the window as though trying to put distance between us. "Is there a reason you continue to question my decisions?"

"Yes. I'm concerned about you."

"Really? Why?"

"I'm a psychologist. I have pretty good intuition based on twenty-plus years of experience. Call it a hunch, whatever. Something seems off with you."

"Your concern belongs with my officers."

"My concern is with the entire organization, from you on down."

She takes off her glasses, removes a cleaning cloth from a case on her desk and cleans them as though they haven't been touched in years. Her eyes are deeply sunk and ringed by purplish-gray circles. She replaces her glasses and straightens the earpieces, leaving a sprig of hair sticking out at an angle. If she were my friend, I would tell her to fix it, but I cannot even bring myself to call her by her first name.

"In my experience, police chiefs are the most isolated people in a police department. The cops have each other to talk to, but no one talks to the chief."

"I appreciate your concern, but I'm not here to make friends." She says this with no emotion in her voice, just a rendering of fact.

"Neither am I," I lie. "But it does help to have someone to talk to. You're under a microscope here. Everyone is watching you. The cops and the community."

"What makes you think I have no one but you to consult with?"

"I don't know. It's hard to read you."

She smiles, a small twitch to her mouth, enigmatic, bemused, nothing more. "So I've been told. Rest assured, Doctor, I take care of myself and wouldn't hesitate to ask for help when I need it. This is not the first time I've dealt with an officer-involved fatality, nor, I imagine, will it be my last."

"Are you aware that the organization is divided into two camps? One supporting Randy Spelling, the other against her."

"There's a third camp you haven't mentioned. A rather unified movement for a vote of no confidence in me. Some officers seem to think I should not have attempted to go to Lakeisha Gibbs' funeral. They are interpreting it as consorting with the enemy rather than a spectacularly failed attempt to stave off community outrage."

Now I want to get in her face. If she recognizes that going to the funeral was a fiasco, does she have any idea why she went?

"Was this your idea or Jay Pence's? You seem to be relying on his opinion a lot."

"I take responsibility for all my decisions."

"You didn't answer my question. Did Jay Pence tell you go to the funeral?"

I wouldn't put it past him to act out in a passive-aggressive way. Losing his bid for chief was a blow to his ego.

"There is nothing I can do to stop the association from a vote of no confidence. In fact, it means very little, and I don't have time to concern myself with it. I have a police department to run."

"You could talk to the troops, explain your reasoning."

"It would be a waste of time. They're too angry and they need someone to blame."

"You're the chief, not a sacrificial lamb."

Her face whitens slightly. I've pushed her as far as I dare. "Dr. Meyerhoff. I don't want to be misunderstood. I do appreciate your concern. But, rest assured, I know when I need help and I won't hesitate to get it. Now I must excuse myself. I have work to do. Please close the door as you leave."

She picks up a stack of files. I still don't know what's going on with her, but I do know that burying herself in paperwork won't fix it.

CHAPTER THIRTEEN

I have another appointment with Randy this afternoon at my office on Catalan Court. It's been ten days since the shooting. We were to have met last Friday, but Rich called at the last minute and canceled, saying Randy was afraid to leave home. When I asked to talk with her, he said she was asleep and he didn't want to wake her because she had been up all night again. I called later that evening and got a recorded message in Rich's voice. "Hey, thanks for calling, we appreciate the support, hope you understand we can't return all the calls we get. We'll catch up with you later. Bye."

It's lunchtime and I'm starving. There's a small break room in headquarters with vending machines. Former Chief Baxter's dream for a new public safety building included a cafeteria with homemade food and a salad bar. Until we're fully staffed and have enough patrol cars, KPD cops will need to choose between bringing their lunches and going out to eat. Kenilworth has a high-end restaurant serving every kind of cuisine known to man and dozens of coffee bars with gleaming espresso machines, outrageously priced pastries, and patrons with less-than-cop-friendly attitudes.

Which is why most officers feel a whole lot more comfortable going to Fran's coffee shop for super-sized dinners served by the super-sized woman whom they all consider the patron saint of KPD. It's been a while since I've had lunch at Fran's, only because she insists on feeding me enough food for an army. I usually leave with the makings of two dinners at home. Still, it's way better than soft drinks, sour coffee, fatty snacks, and plastic-wrapped cold sandwiches with mystery filling. When I get to Fran's, the place is crowded with lunch patrons. Eddie Rimbauer is shuttling between the counter and the few tables in the back.

"Hey, crazy lady. Joint's jumping, eh? There's a seat at the end of the counter." I squeeze in next to a man wearing jeans, a smudged t-shirt, and laced-up Red Wing boots like Frank wears. He doesn't give me a second look. Eddie stops in front of me holding a ladle in one hand and a bowl in the other. His face is red and sweaty. He leans forward. "Give that little lady cop an atta boy from me when you see her, because I know you're on her ass. Tell her not to listen to all the crap in the station. Opinions are like assholes, everybody's got one."

The man next to me lifts his head and just as quickly bends back to his newspaper. Eddie gives me a conspiratorial wink. "I seen that extravaganza on the TV; Chester Allen is angling for a payday. I don't believe that pro bono bullshit. Tell the little copper she did the right thing. No matter what happens, it's better to be tried by twelve than carried by six."

"Hey, Eddie," a voice calls from the back. "I want my soup before it clots."

Eddie starts sloshing soup into a bowl. "Fucking cops, always in a hurry. While you're at it, Doc, take another message for me. Tell Chief Ray-Gun, or whatever her name is, I want my fucking job back. I can't stay sober forever, waiting for it."

* * *

By the time I get to my office on Catalan Court, I'm so full and so sleepy I think I'll keel over unless I can grab a nap on my couch before my appointment with Randy. Forty winks as my father would say. I sneak past the open door to Gary's office, hoping he won't see me and usurp the few minutes I have to spare.

"Avoiding me, are you?"

"Hey." I stick my head in the door. He's seated at his desk, looking at his computer screen.

"What are you and Frank doing for Thanksgiving?" Frank

remodeled Gary and Janice's house. That's how we met. Gary introduced us and now he takes an avuncular interest in how our romance is progressing.

"Frank's going to Iowa to be with his family, and I'm having turkey with my mother and her so-called girls' club."

"Still afraid to meet Frank's family? One of these days you are going to have to admit you're a couple and couples spend holidays together."

Frank has been wanting me to meet his family for nearly a year, and they have been equally eager to meet me, too. But the thought of traveling during the heaviest travel season of the year to a snowbound state where people think green Jell-O is a vegetable has little appeal to me. So far, all our contacts have been via telephone or Skype. His sisters are warm and friendly and love to "visit." From what I can tell, visiting is a Midwestern form of conversation entirely devoid of abstract ideas. I'm not good at visiting. I don't cook much, have no hobbies other than work, no children, no livestock, and someone else repairs my car. The truth of the matter is I'm not ready. Meeting Frank's family is a de facto declaration that we are a serious couple. I don't know what is holding me back. My girlfriends think I'm nuts. Anyone of them would love to meet someone like Frank.

"So, Gary. When did you switch from psych assessment to premarital counseling?"

"Premarital is it?" he says. "That's progress."

* * *

I unlock the door to my office. I have four voice mail messages, one from an officer's wife wanting to make an appointment. It's the wife who usually makes that first call for help, rarely the husband. I can hear the stifled tears, even as she tries to disguise her distress with a brittle cheerfulness, laughing nervously at the end of every sentence. When I hang up, Randy is standing in the door dressed as always in jeans and a t-shirt. She flops on the couch and looks at me.

"You look like you haven't slept in a week."

"I'll do the diagnosing, thank you. I do need a cup of coffee. Want one?"

She shakes her head. "Help yourself. I got nowhere to go."

The coffee in the staff room needs warming and there is no milk, only little packets of powdered creamer that I absolutely detest. But I need the caffeine. I turn around, coffee in hand. Randy is standing in the doorway.

"Not a lot better than the break room at HQ. I thought psychologists made a ton of money."

"We do. Only we spend it on leather couches, not coffee rooms." We walk back to my office and sit. "So, how was the weekend? I missed seeing you on Friday."

"Yeah, sorry about that. I fell asleep. Rich didn't want to wake me up."

"And the weekend?"

"Terrible, like every other day. I can't go out. I can't stay home. I'm uncomfortable in my own skin."

"Tell me."

"I just did." She splays her legs, puts her elbows on her knees and cups her hands across the back of her neck, her face turned to the floor. "I feel like I'm going crazy. I have these dreams where people are coming out of the ground. Dead people. Buried people. I can't read. I can't concentrate. I can't do anything. I finally got Rich to go back to work because I thought it would be better than having him sit around the house staring at me, jumping up every time I move. But I can't stand it. I check the windows and the doors. Every time there's a noise I want to jump out of my skin. Talking about it only makes it worse."

"Are you doing perimeter checks? Making sure all the doors are locked?"

"About a million times a day."

"This is PTSD. Your brain is on overdrive, churning out chemicals from your alarm system. I have a model of the brain. Let me show you how it works."

"I don't care how my brain works, Doc, just make this stop. Please." She grips her head in her hands, her bony little shoulders poking through the seams of her shirt.

"Most cops never have to shoot their guns in the line of duty unless they're on the range. You took a life because you thought you were going to die. Your brain has to absorb what has happened, give it some meaning, learn from it, and then get rid of all the toxic stuff it doesn't need."

"What stuff?"

"The if-onlys and what-ifs. The idea that things could have turned out differently if only. You fill in the blanks."

She leans forward. "That's it. I keep thinking if only I had let someone else take the call. If only I had waited another second, just one more second, and made sure she had a gun."

"If you had waited, and she did have a gun, you'd be dead. It takes three-quarters of a second to move your gun from the holster to a cocked position." I can't remember where on earth I learned this or why I can remember it when I can't remember what I just had for lunch.

"Maybe that would have been better." A sudden torrent of tears washes down her cheeks. "I'm a cop because I want to help people, not kill them."

"Randy, I'm concerned that you're not sleeping. No one can function or get better without sleep. There's medication that can help people with PTSD."

"Uh-uh. No medication. That Ativan stuff the doctor gave me? Made me nuts. I felt like I'd been run over by an eighteen-wheeler."

"The medication I'm talking about is for sleep and to stop the nightmares."

"No. They won't let me back to work if I'm on meds."

"It's only temporary, until you start sleeping again."

"What don't you understand about no?" She stands up. "I'm out of here."

I stand up, ready to stop her. "Okay, I got it. No medication. Let's talk about some other alternatives."

"Such as?"

"Cognitive behavioral therapy, eye movement desensitization and reprocessing..."

"Give me something I can pronounce, something that works for cops. You know, plain talk, no psychobabble."

"Okay. How about talking to another cop? Someone with a lot of experience?"

"One of those peer-counselor types?"

"KPD doesn't have a peer support program yet. I'm supposed to be setting one up this year."

"So who left a flyer under my door? Some stuff about we know what you're going through—we can help, we've been through it ourselves." She pulls a crumpled piece of florescent pink paper from her pocket and hands it to me. "Keep it, it's yours."

"The person I'm thinking about is Eddie Rimbauer."

"Him? He's more of a joke than I am."

"Eddie's been through some hard times in his life, on the job and off, and he hasn't always made the best choices. I know he's a diamond in the rough, but only today he was asking about you, wanting me to tell you to keep your head up."

"I'm not supposed to talk to anyone in the department about the shooting until the chief or the DA says I can."

I hate this policy. When a cop's in trouble they're forbidden to talk to the very people who could support them. Although, given the turmoil in the department, only half the people are standing behind Randy and, from her point of view, for all the wrong reasons.

"Eddie's like you, on leave and facing an uncertain future, meaning he doesn't know if he's going to be reinstated. You two actually have some things in common, hard as that may be to imagine."

"Whatever. If you think it will help me."

"I do think it would help, and it might just help Eddie, too."
Now all I have to do is get him to agree.

* * *

After Randy leaves I unfold the flyer she gave me and smooth
it out on my desk. It announces the formation of a county-wide
multidisciplinary peer support and crisis intervention team
composed of volunteer cops, fire fighters, EMTs, dispatchers,
chaplains, and therapists. Given the fact that someone found
out where Randy lived and had the temerity to put a flyer under her door suggests that there are some ambulance chasers on
the team as well. There are testimonials about how much the
team's free services have already helped various consumers, identified only by their initials. At the bottom of the page is a studio
portrait of a smiling young blond, blue-eyed woman, Dr. Marvel Johnson. She has a string of letters after her name indicating
that she is a psychologist, a certified trauma specialist, an alcohol counselor, and the totally-thrilled-to-be-helping-the-brave-
men-and-women-of-public-safety founder of the team. I aim the
flyer toward my wastebasket and miss.

CHAPTER FOURTEEN

Meeting at Fran's was Eddie's idea. "She can't talk in a shrink's office," he told me on the phone. "Probably thinks the place is wired with a microphone that goes right to the chief's office. My place is out of the question—it'd take me a month to clean it up and haul off the old beer cans." There is a break in the conversation. "Old beer cans, Doc. Not new ones. I'm still on the wagon. And we can't go to your place 'cause I know how you feel about clients coming to your house. You try to bean 'em in the head with a ten-pound weight."

Poor Eddie. He was only trying to help me after Ben's suicide. He came to my house, saw an open window, thought I was being burglarized and snuck in, trying to catch the thief. I heard him on the steps and freaked out. When he came into my bedroom, I jumped out of a closet and attacked him with a ten-pound hand weight. I missed, but just thinking about it today makes my cheeks burn.

"I thought you were a burglar, remember?"

"Yeah, well, whatever. Let's meet at Fran's. Out in back, in the garden. Fran never lets anyone but the worker bees use it. Tell Randy to come through the back gate, not the restaurant, that way she won't run into any coppers."

* * *

The garden behind Fran's is no bigger than two parking spaces mashed together. We're sitting on bent metal lawn chairs surrounded by old coffee cans filled with scraggly succulents reaching for the late afternoon sun. Eddie is dressed for the occasion, wearing a clean apron over his stained t-shirt.

"Beats me why the Doc here thinks I can help. Maybe because I made more mistakes in my life than you could ever dream of. I don't believe in shrinks. I don't believe in all that psychobabble kumbaya-you-tell-me-yours-I'll-tell-you-mine bullshit." Randy smiles the tiniest of smiles, hardly more than a twitch at the ends of her mouth. "Unfortunately, what I did believe in"—he makes a gesture with his hand, thumb to his mouth, miming downing a drink—"almost killed me. What you can learn from me is how not to do things."

"I don't drink. Never have. Hate the taste." Randy is curled up in her chair with her legs tucked under her, only the tips of her sneakers sticking out from under her knees.

"So, how can I help?"

Randy scoots forward in her chair, stretches her legs out, and puts her hands over her cap, pulling the bill down over her face. I can see the tomboy in her, imagine her as a little girl, rough housing with her brothers, willing herself not to cry.

"You know what I did, right? I killed a pregnant seventeen-year-old girl because I thought she had a gun. It was a cell phone. I want to apologize to her mother, to her whole family. Nobody thinks this is a good idea. What do you think?"

"Bad idea. Never piss in your own canteen."

Randy's eyebrows shoot up. "What?"

"An apology is the same as admitting you screwed up."

"I did screw up, big time."

"Let me tell you something," Eddie leans in. "You're a cop. It's inevitable. You're going to hurt somebody and somebody's going to hurt you. Part of the job. You tell someone what to do and sometimes they don't like it. And when they don't like it, they fight back." He leans back, hands folded over his belly. "Which would you rather have, a gold watch or a gold casket? You did the right thing. It was a good shoot."

"You don't know that."

"What's done is done. These people are coming after you. For Christ's sake, don't give them any help. You did the right thing. Don't apologize."

Randy's face reddens. "I hate what I did. I'll hate it all my life. That's what I want to tell the mother. How is that admitting fault?"

"Because it is. I can't explain it. It just is." Eddie shifts around in his chair.

"That's all anybody tells me. I heard it in the academy. I heard it from my brothers and my father and my husband. 'Keep your mouth shut. Don't admit anything. Don't ever say you're sorry.' My union rep? Same thing. Even my shrink agrees." She pushes her chair back. The metal legs scrape over the concrete pad. "I made a mistake. Everyone tells me to man up and keep my mouth shut. I want to own up and admit it." She crosses her arms over her chest, daring us to disagree.

Eddie looks at me. "I don't know what else to say. Been there, done that. Beat myself up over shit I did and was a miserable son-of-a-bitch to everyone around me. It's your choice."

"I killed a pregnant girl who was trying to call her mother. What did you do?"

"Treated a sick addict like she was a piece of shit. My own wife, I'm talking about. Let me tell you something. In ten years nobody's going to remember who you shot, why you shot her, or if you followed tactics. They'll remember that you were the one who lived."

Randy points to the back fence. "There are people out there walking around with my picture on a poster, demanding I go to jail. And why shouldn't I? People who kill people should go to jail. I had a gun, she had a phone. It wasn't fair."

"The only unfair fight is the one you lose. If you're in a fair fight, your tactics suck. I was an FTO. Know what I told my recruits? Anything worth shooting is worth shooting twice. The only thing worse than a miss is a slow miss." Now his face is scarlet. He swipes at his forehead and wipes his sweaty hands on his apron.

"Know your mistake? You think that kid was a victim. Let me tell you, there are no victims, only volunteers. She walked right into trouble. A cop tells you 'get out of the car, put your hands where I can see 'em,' that's what you're supposed to do. Then you get to tell your bullshit story and whine for your mommy."

Randy looks at me and back at Eddie. Her hands are in the air as though she's about to clap them over her ears.

"Let me tell you something. You're making your own trouble. Misery is optional. Try being happy for six months. If you don't like it, I'll refund your misery." Eddie gets up, knocking his chair over. "Fucking A," he says. "I need a drink," and storms back into the restaurant.

Randy stands, wiping her hands on her pants, and looks at me. "This was a total waste. Why did you think this jerk could help me? He's a complete idiot. Thanks a lot for nothing." And before I can respond, she darts through the patio and out the back gate.

CHAPTER FIFTEEN

There isn't a worse day in the entire year to travel than the day before Thanksgiving. I'm late leaving the office and Frank is clearly irritated. He is standing in front of his house, ready to go, cell phone in hand, as I drive up. I pull away from the curb and do a U-turn, tires screeching to emphasize how sorry I am. We scarcely speak for the first fifteen minutes. He keeps looking at his watch as the commute traffic melts into the airport traffic and we creep along at fifteen miles an hour. I have convinced Frank to go to Iowa without me by telling him my mother would be heartbroken if I left her alone for the holiday. The truth is my mother detests most holidays, considering them to be artificial events created to get people to spend time and money on things they don't need and shouldn't eat. In this way she shares my father's endless conspiracy theories about capitalism. It is her habit to go out for dinner and to a movie with her friends on Thanksgiving and Christmas. She is thrilled that I'm going to join in the fun. Frank, on the other hand, has been sulky ever since I told him.

"I'm sorry. I had a very upset client. Her husband just asked her for a divorce. It was a big shock. She fell apart, and I couldn't stop the session on time. You know—time's up, quit crying please."

"Well, I'm gonna cry if I miss my plane."

"You won't miss your plane. You have an hour."

"I still have to go through security. The airport's going to be mobbed. There's only one connection to Des Moines. If I miss it, I'm stuck in Chicago overnight."

"Sorry. I couldn't help it."

"Yeah. Well, maybe next time I'll take a taxi."

The airport is a mess, cars, people, luggage, and red-faced traffic officers clogging the departure lane. Frank gets out of the car and walks the last few yards to the terminal, we barely have time for a good-bye peck on the cheek. "Happy Turkey Day. Hi to the family," I say, but he doesn't hear me.

* * *

My mother lives in a seniors-only community near Morro Bay. It's the kind of over-controlled, over-manicured development my father would have hated, but it suits her fine. She's made friends, mostly women—men are a scarce commodity at her age—and her schedule is so full that if I want to see her, I have to go her house because she can't bear to miss her exercise classes or line dancing. It's a pleasure to see her happy, although in her own goofy way, she's never been anything but. I wish I had inherited her perennially sunny, flower-child disposition and not my father's skeptical, sour view of humanity.

I take Highway 101 south past San Jose into the flat, fallow farmlands and small dusty towns. The air smells of peat and fertilizer. People on the streets of these communities are brown skinned. Old men sit in a corner park wearing cowboy hats and boots. A gray drizzle reflects my mood. There is little traffic. Most travelers have taken the quicker route down Highway 5. I stop for coffee in a fast food restaurant right off the highway. Fast food joints are not happy places to eat or work in on a national holiday. I get my coffee to go. By the time I get to the central valley a weak sun is warming the now barren grapevines that carpet the low hills to the east and west. The sheer volume of plantings reeks of agribusiness, not boutique wineries like the ones Frank and I like to visit in Napa or the Santa Cruz mountains.

By now, Frank and his family are into the traditional hors d'oeuvres, seven-layer bean dip and cheese whiz on Ritz crackers. He'll be helping his brother-in-law put the extension in the table and bring in extra chairs from the Morton building. I don't exactly know what a Morton building is, except that's where all the farm equipment is stored during the winter. The TV in the living room will be tuned to the hunting channel with the sound turned down. His nephews and nieces will be sprawled in front of it, playing with their iPhones and iPads. I remind myself that I didn't want to go. I was invited and I turned him down. If I feel like crap, it's my own fault.

**

My mother's manufactured home sits on a low berm surrounded by other manufactured homes. The artificial turf is perpetually shamrock green and never needs mowing. She has a small patio with chairs, a table, a dozen potted plants, and four bird feeders, all different. Off to the left is a community garden, looking forlorn, the way California gardens get in the late fall. Some whirligig things stuck in the ground spin around in a wet breeze. The sun has given up trying.

A small wreath of artificial fall leaves hangs on the front door, the latest enterprise of my mother's crafts class. Two homemade bushy gray squirrels nestle serenely next to a cluster of acorns. My mother opens the door before I have a chance to ring the bell. She is dressed in jeans and a long-sleeved t-shirt completely covered with Marc Chagall's painting of the "Blue Circus." She twirls around.

"Like it? I got it last month when we all went to The Contemporary Jewish Museum in San Francisco."

"You passed right through Kenilworth and didn't stop to see me?"

"We were a busload. I couldn't stop."

"She waved at you through the window. She really did." I can't remember all my mother's friend's names, but Sophie I never forget. She's my height with Day-Glo red hair and wide as the two of us laying end to end. She probably needed two bus seats to herself.

"Come in, sweetie. You know everyone, don't you, and

everyone, this is my gorgeous, talented, so-smart daughter—
the doctor." My mother twirls me around so they get a good
look, front and back.

"I forget, what kind of doctor is she?" someone asks.

"A head doctor, for the politsey," Sophie beams, proud to be
in the inner circle of my mother's friends.

"So, let me ask you a question."

A silver-haired woman holding a glass of white wine steps towards me. My mother pulls me closer and whispers. "That's Iris.
She's from Berkeley." This is not news to me. Everyone here is from
someplace else, starting over after being widowed, downsized, or
underwater on the mortgage. Rents are cheap, you don't own the
land under your home, and the monthly fees are far less than the
luxury high-rise senior developments in the Bay Area. Plus, there is
open space, groves of eucalyptus, and the smell of the ocean.

"Can I put my suitcase away first? And pee? It's been a long
ride." I know what's coming. I have asked my mother just to tell
her friends that I'm a psychologist and leave out the part that I
work with cops, but she can't. She gets a social bonus because I do
something out of the ordinary and that compensates for the fact
that I'm divorced and never gave her any grandchildren.

Iris narrows her eyes. She's a beautiful woman, stylish, slender, and not to be deterred. "Why didn't that officer shoot that
young women in the leg instead of killing her? She couldn't have
posed much of a threat, being pregnant and armed with a cell
phone." She narrows her gray eyes and stands with one hand on
her hip, making sure I don't mistake her for a harmless old woman who can be brushed off with a facile comment. For all I know
she's a retired attorney or past president of the ACLU.

"That officer works for the same department Dot works for.
Isn't that wonderful?"

Iris dips her head. She's got me now. No escape. I think about
peeing on the floor as a distraction, but that would be gross and
wouldn't stop Iris the Determined from interrogating me after I
cleaned up the mess.

"For one thing, cops are trained to shoot to stop a threat. They aim for central body mass, because, if you shoot someone in the leg, they can still kill you." A low murmur ruffles through the group.

"But she had a cell phone," Iris says.

"In the dark it's hard to tell a shiny metal object like a phone from a gun. If you take the time to examine it, you could be dead." Iris isn't buying any of this.

"That's a convenient defense, but it doesn't wash. If the officer had stepped away from the car or waited a few minutes in some safe position, she would have seen that this young girl wasn't armed. I used to live in Kenilworth. I have some direct experience with the police and I can tell you the officers are far too aggressive for the community."

"I thought you were from Berkeley," my mother says.

"Same thing," somebody else remarks.

"I don't know how long it's been since you lived there, but we have a new police chief, a woman, Jacqueline Reagon, and I think she's going to turn things around."

"Well, I hope so," Iris says.

"Now, girls," my mother intervenes. She never could tolerate the slightest discord. "Today is a holiday, and we're going bowling and for Mexican food. We'll have the restaurant to ourselves. So let's have another glass of wine and let Dot go to the bathroom and unpack." She picks up my overnight bag and heads to the guest bedroom.

"And when you come back," says Sophie, ahead of the others in terms of wine consumption, "tell us about Chester Allen. He's a very attractive man for a..." She uses the Yiddish word for African American. Everyone laughs but Iris, who doesn't look Jewish, and me. "He certainly knows how to talk. He had the whole crowd eating from his hand."

"What crowd?"

"The crowd in front of city hall. You didn't see? This morning. A Thanksgiving celebration of what's-her-name's young life.

The whole plaza was filled. They had tables set for Thanksgiving, served food and everything. Where the family sat was an empty chair with a stuffed bear instead of the girl. The mother cried the whole time."

"Her name is, was, Lakeisha," I say.

"What kind of name is that?" one of my mother's friends asks.

"They make them up, you know," someone answers.

"You could see it on TV. They keep showing it." Sophie turns to the flat screen TV on the rear wall. It is one of my mother's few extravagances. "Where's the remote?"

"Not now, Sophie. We have to go. Later, we'll see it later," my mother says. I could kiss her.

CHAPTER SIXTEEN

Randy's Thanksgiving was worse than mine, at least that's how it sounds Monday morning in my office.

"What do I have to be thankful for?"

"That you're alive?"

"That's what Rich said. I wasn't in a celebratory mood. I'd bring everybody down. So I stayed home. Anyhow, all they want to do is talk about it, get me to tell the story over and over. I can't get away from it no matter where I go. What's happening now? When are you going back to work? Is the family going to sue?"

"What is happening now, Randy? Any news?"

"Pence gave me his report for an early Thanksgiving present. Lawful shooting. I got five days off with no pay and a letter in my file that goes away in a year if I don't shoot any more pregnant girls. All I have to do is see some shrink for a fitness for duty. If she passes me, I go back to work. A slap on the wrist. Day shift, so they can keep an eye on me. I heard Tom Rutgers was doing high fives because he won't have to work with me again."

I'm happy for Randy that this part, at least, is over. And I'm worried. She wants to be punished, and since the department isn't going to punish her, I'm going to have to work hard to keep her from punishing herself, because—if and when she does—it won't be a slap on the wrist.

"You missed the demonstration, I guess. They want me fired. I watched the whole thing on cable TV. Ms. Gibbs rocking that stuffed bear and sobbing. I did that." She stops for a minute, jaw clenched, hands balled in fists, trying to push back her tears. "So, Doc, can you understand why I didn't feel much like celebrating?

Not to mention Captain Pence had to call in a whole bunch of cops for mandatory overtime to cover the demonstration. If they can't eat turkey with their families, why should I?"

"Rich watch with you?"

"He wasn't home. I told him to go without me. Like I said, I'm no fun to be around. No reason he shouldn't have a good time."

"Did you at least talk when he got home?"

She pauses for a second. "He spent the weekend at his mom's. Went straight to work from her place. I haven't seen him since Thursday morning."

She laughs, a small gurgle from the back of her throat.

"What's funny?"

"I'm a nobody and hundreds of people hate me. You should have seen their faces. Black, white; didn't make a difference."

And then it hits me. She didn't watch the demonstration on television, she was there. That's why she didn't go to her family's house or to Rich's.

"You went to the demonstration."

"I refuse to answer on the grounds I might incriminate myself." She spins her baseball cap to the side, crosses her arms, and stretches her legs out, daring me to push.

"That's pretty provocative. And dangerous. And self-destructive." I have to play this carefully. If Randy is pushing Rich away, I'm next. I know where this is going—she wants to destroy herself without involving the rest of us. It's the flawed logic of post-traumatic stress, endless self-blame and relentless reckless behavior.

"I'm not on house arrest. I can go anywhere I want. Unless you commit me to some mental hospital."

She's baiting me. Trying to start a fight.

"Randy, you're being harder on yourself than anyone else. You're the only one holding yourself responsible."

"Me and the hundreds of people at that demonstration."

"You did the best you could at the time. Would a more experienced officer have handled things differently? Maybe. If you hadn't still been reeling from the incident at the creek, feeling that you had to prove something to everyone, would things have gone differently? That's another maybe. But there's no way anyone—not even you—can convince me that you got up that morning intending to kill anyone, let alone a teenage girl with no weapon."

* * *

Frank and I stop at a little dumpling joint in downtown Kenilworth on our way home from the airport. We're back to our give-and-take banter, all traces of his tense departure banished by stories about a hilarious trip to pick out the Thanksgiving turkey at his cousin's farm. He stops himself, a dumpling midflight between the plate and his mouth. "So how are you doing? I saw the demonstration. Made the evening news all the way to Pick City." I'm surprised and secretly relieved. Now I have extra cover for explaining why I didn't go to Iowa. Not only do I have an aging mother to care for in California, I have a seriously traumatized officer on my hands.

CHAPTER SEVENTEEN

Attitude is everything and after a warm homecoming reunion with Frank, I'm in a fine mood. A little sleep deprived but nothing that the cappuccino the tattooed barista is making for me won't fix. Amazing how two middle-aged people—middle aged providing we live to be nearly one hundred—can still stir up some pretty powerful sex. Whoever thinks people over fifty don't enjoy sex obviously isn't over fifty.

"Penny for your thoughts, Doc?" Jack Shiller, cub reporter, is smiling more than I am, delighted to catch me off guard. "You look pleased about something. Care to share?"

"Not on your life." I smile as broadly as my lips can stretch. "Come here often or have you been following me?"

"Not following you, never, but you have been on my mind lately. I was wondering how things are going for Officer Spelling?" He's on a not-so-subtle fishing expedition.

"I heard the in-house investigation is over and she can come back to work as soon as you clear her as fit for duty."

He's got this all wrong. As Randy's therapist, I can't do her fitness-for-duty assessment. Industry standard. You can't expect to create a therapeutic alliance with someone who knows that you could get them fired for being unfit. All you'd hear would be how well they were sleeping and that they have no symptoms to report.

"What about the vote of no confidence?"

This guy has really good sources. I wonder who's on his payroll. The barista calls my name and shoves my half-caf, half-decaf, wet with nonfat milk cappuccino across the marble counter. I wave good-bye to Jack Shiller and hit the door running. I can see him in my rearview mirror as I pull out of the parking lot heading to my office. He's standing on the sidewalk, coffee in hand, looking for me.

* * *

I keep notes, like all psychologists, but I'm cautious about writing too much, just in case my records get subpoenaed by the court. This is highly unlikely, unless of course, my client just killed an innocent person and the community is in an uproar. In which case, the less written, the better.

December 2: Preparation for upcoming Fitness-for-Duty evaluation on 12/5. Review of self-soothing grounding exercises and deep-breathing techniques. Client agrees to call with an update on her progress with the examining psychologist.

December 5: First fitness-for-duty session was okay. Client scheduled to see FFD psychologist again on 12/10 and 12/12 requiring her to cancel appointments with me. Returned call, client not home. Husband doesn't know where she is. He reports that client likes the examining doctor. Client is still hard to live with. Not the same since the shooting. All wrapped up in herself and her problems.

December 13: Appointments canceled per v.m. Examiner requests to meet twice this week with client and her husband.

Dec. 20: Appointment canceled per v.m. Examiner meeting again with client and her husband.

Dec. 24: Appointments canceled per v.m. Client scheduled to receive results of her FFD in the week between Christmas and New Year's. Her outlook is optimistic and she believes she will pass.

I've done several FFD evaluations so I know how long and complex they can be. But this one is a record breaker. I like the fact that the doctor did collateral interviews with Rich to get his perspective on things. And I like that she is going to explain her findings to Randy before she delivers her report to the department. That shows respect for Randy and an appreciation of how stressful these evaluations are. What I don't like is that she hasn't called me. I'm an important source of collateral information, too. I wouldn't think of doing an FFD without talking to an officer's treating therapist. She should have called me, unless Randy refused to sign a release of information allowing me to share information about her treatment. I can't imagine why Randy would refuse. On the other hand, I know the doctor can't force her to sign the release. The only option she has is to report Randy's refusal to Chief Reagon, who could consider it an act of insubordination.

I call Randy. I'm just not buying her cheerful message, not with everything she's still facing at work along with Christmas and its own nasty brand of stress. There's no answer. It's Christmas Eve. I can only hope she's doing something celebratory.

* * *

Jewish people are at loose ends during Christmas. Mostly we go to the movies because there isn't any line for tickets or we eat Chinese food. Not the same for Frank who loves Christmas and insists on cooking a gargantuan meal for our friends. Our friends, some of whom used to be my friends or his friends. It's an Iowa Christmas redux: ham, turkey, mashed potatoes, sweet potatoes, gravy and Jell-O mold salad. Not a fresh green vegetable in sight.

I check my messages before rolling into bed at midnight. Frank warns me not to.

"It's a holiday, for Pete's sake. Leave it alone."

There's only one message and it's from Randy.

"Hey, Doc. Thanks for calling. Sorry I didn't call you right back. Good news. Dr. Johnson is going to recommend I return to work. Didn't want to ruin my Christmas by making me wait for the results." There's a pause. "Dr. Johnson has been real helpful to me and Rich too, so...we're going to continue seeing her for a while. Separately and together. Thanks for everything. Merry Christmas."

Dr. Johnson? The smarmy, smiling blond with the over-the-top sales brochure? I had no idea she was doing the evaluation and I have no idea why I have no idea. Why the hell didn't I ask? What was I thinking? Something's not right. Fitness examiners don't continue as treating therapists. And the protocol when a client switches therapists is for the new therapist to consult the old therapist first. There are a lot of reasons clients quit therapy prematurely. Randy was far from ready to stop one month ago. She was still symptomatic. If Randy wants to switch therapists, I can't stop her. It is her choice, but there is a process for termination. You just don't up and quit. Johnson should have called me and she should have sent Randy back to me for a final session to handle any unfinished business. Apparently every therapist knows this except the eager-to-help Dr. Marvel Johnson.

When Frank sees that I'm still awake at four a.m., he asks me what's wrong. I tell him dinner was delicious and I'm too full to sleep.

* * *

Frank waves a cup of coffee under my nose.

"Merry Christmas, Dr. Meyerhoff." He's sitting on the bed, fully dressed, smiling like the proverbial Cheshire cat. "Wake up, time's a-wasting."

I slide into a sitting position. A dim light filters in through the window. The sky is half black, half gray.

"What time is it?"

"Six-thirty. A.M."

"Why are you waking me up this early?"

"I'm a contractor. We're on the job at the crack of dawn."

"I'm a psychologist. I sleep 'til nine and take August and the week between Christmas and New Year's OFF." I try sliding back under the covers without spilling my coffee. It doesn't work.

"Merry Christmas," Frank leans over to kiss me and plops a small, wrapped, ring-sized box on my stomach. He's smiling so hard his lips are stretched thin and I can see his teeth. This can't be. Not a ring. I'm not ready for this. I just want to enjoy things. This is too much pressure. He wants too much from me.

"Open it." He sees the expression on my face. "It's not a ring, Dot, for Christ's sake." He looks disappointed, like I've taken all the joy out of whatever kind of surprise this is. Inside the box is a folded piece of paper. A copy of a reservation for two at the Big Sur B&B. I hide my relief behind my exuberance.

"How lovely. I've always wanted to go there. When?"

He's smiling again. "Right now. Get a move on. You can stop by your place, get whatever you need; it's gonna be cold, maybe rainy. Maybe we'll have to spend the whole time inside." He gives me a playful leer. "We'll grab breakfast on the road." He kisses my cheek. "Christmas in Big Sur: no crowds, no stupid music, no TV, and no cell phones."

"But—"

"No buts. We're out of here. Before your damn phone rings. Contractor's orders. Now, get your sweet ass out of bed and get going."

I have to talk myself down in the shower. Today is another big demonstration in front of city hall. 'Christmas for Lakeisha.' I'd planned to watch it on TV. What if Randy shows up like she did at the funeral? What if she falls apart and needs help? I turn the water off, grab a towel, and think to myself, "so what?" I'm not her therapist anymore. I'm going to Big Sur with Frank, maybe the best man I've ever known. Kind, generous, funny, and still sexy. If Randy needs someone, she can call Marvel Johnson.

CHAPTER EIGHTEEN

It's the first Monday after the holidays. I'm in the chief's office before the staff meeting.

"How was your holiday?" I ask.

"Quiet. And yours?"

"Go anywhere special?"

"No." Talking with her is like bottom fishing. She gives nothing away: no emotion, no give and take.

"I was out of town on Christmas myself. How did the demonstration go?"

"Captain Pence said it was peaceful—emotional, but peaceful. There was a crowd of approximately 175. Several speeches, including one by Ms. Gibbs." She might as well be describing a trip to the supermarket, all the while sorting through papers and putting them in the folder she carries into the staff meeting.

"You didn't go?"

"I thought it best to stay away. Particularly after the reception I got at the funeral. Captain Pence is perfectly capable of dealing with any problems. I appreciate his willingness to come in on Christmas Day. He has children."

I presume from this that Chief Reagon does not. If so, it makes me wonder why she wasn't here for the demonstration. It's traditional for officers who don't have kids to work the holidays and let officers with families stay home to celebrate. This was a high-profile event, potentially explosive. I can see why Jay Pence would be eager to stand in the spotlight. But it's a missed opportunity for the chief. Just showing up at HQ for a few hours would have gotten her some Brownie points with the troops.

I don't understand how this woman rose so high in the profession. Most chiefs I've known had egos as big as their mobile command centers. And they needed them. Everyone takes pot shots at the chief: the community, the city council, the troops, and the media. An image of former Chief Baxter, a little fireplug of a man with a huge secret ego, flashes in my mind.

She stops sorting papers for a minute. "How is Randy doing? You know, of course, that the fitness-for-duty evaluator found her fit to return to work."

"You haven't spoken with her yourself?"

"I left messages on her voice mail. She never calls back."

"Did you keep trying? It means a great deal to the troops when the chief takes a personal interest in them."

She dips her head and looks at me over the top of her reading glasses warning me not to push her.

"There are times, Doctor, when it is best to leave people alone."

I don't know if she's talking about Randy or about herself.

"I haven't seen Randy in almost a month," I say. The chief's eyebrows lift, just slightly. "She's been preoccupied with the fitness evaluation. Then last week she informed me by telephone that she's going to continue her therapy with the evaluator, not me."

"Good."

"No. It's not good. In fact it's very irregular."

"What do you mean, irregular?"

"Where did you find this evaluator?" Now she cocks her head to one side.

"Dr. Johnson approached me. Asked to speak with me about a county-wide crisis intervention team she was forming for first responders. One of the additional services she offers is fitness for duty."

"Did you ask for credentials, references?"

"Of course."

"Does she have police-specific experience?"

"Apparently so, though from another state. Why are you asking?"

"I wish you had asked me to recommend an evaluator, or at the very least, asked if I'd ever heard of Dr. Johnson."

"Counseling and evaluating are two entirely separate functions. I believe you said so yourself. What has Dr. Johnson done to upset you?"

"First of all, she's stolen my client. It's unethical for fitness evaluators to provide therapy to someone they've just evaluated. Check the guidelines issued by the International Association of Chiefs of Police. Secondly, if a client chooses to engage another therapist, industry standards dictate that the second therapist should consult with the first and encourage the client to have at least one final visit to discuss her reasons for termination."

Chief Reagon closes her folder of papers and stands. "With all due respect, Randy Spelling is not your client. Kenilworth PD is your client. You see our officers as a service to the department. You're on retainer to meet your basic expenses and to assure that you're available. Do not exploit this arrangement to build your private practice."

I can't believe what I'm hearing. Amortize all the hours I've spent worrying about Randy, not sleeping because of Randy, and I would have made more money flipping burgers at McDonald's.

"As I said a moment ago, I thought we both agreed that it was best to keep the fitness and counseling functions separate. For your information, I did call a few other psychologists, but very few of them are doing fitness evaluations these days, apparently because they have become so litigious. Those who do have long waiting lists. I felt Dr. Johnson was a good fit. She's closer to Randy's age than you are, and I hoped that might make it easier for Randy to talk to her. She's from out of town and has no preconceived notions about our department. And no waiting list." She looks at her watch. "I have to go. It's past time." She opens the door of her office and walks down the hall towards the conference room.

It takes me a minute to catch my breath. I feel like I'm in a fun house of mirrors. First she shoots me down. Then she picks me up and dusts me off. Who is this woman? And will I ever understand her?

CHAPTER NINETEEN

Dr. Marvel—accent on the "vel"—Johnson, brimming with Midwestern enthusiasm, is sitting in my office, on my leather couch, absolutely elated to meet me because she's read all my books, and I don't know this, but I'm her hero and her mentor. She's a farm-fresh blond, tall and lanky with big hands and feet, wearing tailored slacks and one of those 1950s style sweater sets that are all the rage, pale blue to match her eyes. Probably exercises regularly and eats only organic food. Her voice twangs cheerfully, with trilled Rs and As flat as the plains where she grew up.

"I admire you so much. You were so helpful to Randy. She said so herself."

"Well then," I say, trying to keep the anger out of my voice, "Why didn't you send her back to me so we could finish our work?"

She smiles. Her too-white teeth remind me of evenly spaced kernels on an ear of corn. "I tried. I told her she needed to see you at least one more time for a proper termination, but she just wouldn't. She kept saying she felt more comfortable talking to me. For a variety of reasons."

I wonder if Dr. Johnson has ever heard about idealized transference. A therapist is rarely as good or, for that matter, as bad as her client thinks. "And I'm working with Rich, too. With all the attention on Randy, he's been feeling abandoned."

"Where was it that you went to school?"

She shrugs and smiles. "You probably have never heard of it. Christian Connect Institute of Psychology. In

Nebraska, where I'm from. I had great teachers. It was one of my professors there who recommended your books." She rolls the word "great" out like a ribbon. She looks at me and when I say nothing in response, she continues in the grand Midwestern tradition to chat me up. "I put myself through college as an EMT, driving an ambulance. I could see the stress we were all under. My father was a fire fighter. He died of a heart attack when he was forty-seven. I'm not saying it was job stress that caused his heart attack, but maybe. All the smoke, the chemicals, the heavy lifting, being around people in pain. He loved his job, but he always used to say that his best day at work fighting fires was someone else's worst day ever. Anyhow, since I was a kid I knew, in my heart—" she points to her heart for emphasis, "—that working with first responders was my calling."

"So you have a Psy.D. in psychology. Not a Ph.D.?"

"That's right. I wanted the Psy.D. because it's a practitioner's degree. Ph.Ds. are interested in research. I want to help people." I can feel my face getting flushed. She scrambles to recover her status as a sycophant. "Not that your research hasn't helped a lot of people."

And then it hits me. I'm not just feeling old. I am old. Fifty on my next birthday. Marvel's winding up at the same time I'm winding down. Her eager, optimistic attitude is a sharp contrast to my own sense of limitation. I'm being slowly replaced by younger people. A woman half my age stole my husband. Marvel has only stolen my favorite client.

"I don't want there to be any misunderstanding," Marvel is saying, shaking me out of my morose reflections. "I am a bona fide psychologist with a license to practice in two states. I can show you." She reaches for her purse and I stop her. My urge to humiliate this woman has its limits. "Christian psychologists do not reject science; we use all the same modalities as secular therapists. It's just that we recognize the place that God has in our lives and the suffering that comes with a spiritual disconnect. As you know, losing God can be one of the most painful consequences of post-traumatic stress."

I know this only intellectually. I'm an atheist. I never had anything to lose in the first place.

Marvel takes a long breath. "One of the reasons that Randy, Rich too, wanted to continue seeing me, despite your skill and caring, is that she felt that you couldn't understand how important her faith is to her and the pain that taking a human life—which is against her religious beliefs—has caused her."

She folds her hands in her lap and waits. She's said what she needed to say and now she smiles benevolently, her mouth making a tiny crescent. She searches my face with her eyes, looking earnest and concerned. I don't buy a word of this. Everything about her has an air of theatricality, as though she's practiced this little charade in front of a mirror, arranging and rearranging her face to match the desired emotion. The insides of my stomach are roiling and so is my brain. I want to throttle her, call her a fake, and throw her out of my office. It's only because I don't want to give her the satisfaction of seeing how upset I am that I hold my tongue. The smart thing for me to do would be to thank her for stopping by and the second she leaves call Gary for a consultation. Only I don't want Gary to ask me why I'm feeling so threatened and competitive.

"Well. This is a surprise," I say. "Neither Randy nor Rich ever mentioned any of this. I had no idea either one was a devout Christian."

"This is exactly why Christian-based psychology is becoming so popular. Most secular therapists never raise this issue. Nor do they think to ask about their client's spiritual or religious beliefs. This sends a message that they are uncomfortable talking about God, so it never comes up. What has given Randy great relief is to give her suffering over to God. To recognize that what happened was God's plan. Do you practice your faith?"

My father's religion was a combination of socialism and paranoia. He was a cultural Jew, not a religious one. My mother's religion is optimism with side trips to Buddhism, Sufism, yoga, feminism, and macrobiotic cooking. I'm not about to explain any of this.

"Police officers relate well to Romans 13, verses 1 and 2," she says. "I use them so often I can almost say them from memory." She closes her eyes. A wintry blast slaps against my office window. "There is no authority except that which God has established. Consequently, whoever rebels against the authority is rebelling against what God has instituted, and those who do so will bring judgment on themselves." She opens her eyes. "Do you see? That unfortunate young woman caused her own death. She defied God when she defied Randy's orders to get out of the car and put her hands in plain sight."

"So you think that the appropriate punishment for defying God's orders is death, regardless of the circumstances? Remember, there was no crime involved. Lakeisha was just a scared kid living in her mother's car."

"That's not for me to say. The point is that police officers are ministers of God's authority on this earth, as it says in Romans, and as such are in a spiritual war against the forces of evil. I'm not saying the young woman was herself evil, but she clearly was in the grasp of evil forces. Once Randy realized this, she felt a great deal better."

Now I know this woman is full of crap. Randy has her own ideas about policing and wasn't afraid to question authority. Religion aside, I cannot picture her joining up with a squad of self-inflated members of anyone's chosen army to keep the rest of us safe from the forces of evil.

"One more thing, Dr. Meyerhoff, and I do appreciate your giving me so much of your valuable time. I want to leave you with this." She takes a laminated index card from her purse. "This program is an outgrowth of my dissertation research on Post-Traumatic Stress Disorder. It's a twelve-step plan to heal from PTSD, similar to the twelve-step Alcoholics Anonymous program. In the short time that we've been working together, Randy has moved very quickly. As of this week, she's already on step nine. I'll just leave this for you. You might find it helpful."

The only thing that will help me now is to kick this nutcase out of my office and my life.

She stands, we shake hands. She thanks me again for my time and reassures me that Randy will be just fine. At the door she turns, flashes a smile, and wishes me a "blessed day."

As soon as she leaves I dig out Randy's files. Now I wish I had taken more notes. There is nothing to indicate that we ever spoke about her religious beliefs. My pre-employment psych evaluations are locked in a file cabinet in my closet. I find Randy's and pull it out. It's over a year old. While I'm not legally permitted to ask applicants about their religious beliefs there is a section on my questionnaire that asks "Is there anything else about you that is important for me to know?" Applicants who have deep religious beliefs usually write something about their faith. That block on Randy's questionnaire is blank.

It's raining now. Pellets of water are hitting the roof and the window, making a clatter. The commute home is going to be a mess. I start to tidy up, put all my files back where they belong, and lock the cabinets. There's an accumulation of coffee cups and water glasses from previous clients to be washed and dried. I sweep Marvel's parting gift into the trash without looking at it and go into the waiting room. As always, the stacks of magazines need tidying. Lying on top of every flat surface is one of Marvel's laminated cards with her contact information prominently displayed next to a smiling photo of her oh-so-helpful self. That little ambulance-chasing bitch. I flip the card over. On the other side are her twelve steps. Step number nine is making amends. My heart races and my brain follows. It hits me like a ton of bricks. Randy's defection has nothing to do with religion. She still believes that the only way to heal herself is to make amends to Ms. Gibbs, face to face, woman to woman. She's back where she started. Where we started. She's been conning Dr. Johnson. Randy's not looking for spiritual guidance—what she wants is validation and encouragement to confront Ms. Gibbs. She can't forgive herself, so she needs Ms. Gibbs to do that. Well, she's found the perfect foil to support her delusion. Not only does she have Marvel's approval, Marvel is cheering her on.

CHAPTER TWENTY

Four police cars, lights on and sirens blaring, pass me as I turn the corner on my way to police headquarters. This is a rare sight in Kenilworth. Most of the crime here happens behind closed doors. Lakeisha Gibbs' death was an anomaly, the first officer-involved shooting in several years. A fifth and a sixth car speed past. I pull into the parking lot. Chief Reagon and Captain Pence are running down the stairs. There's an unmarked patrol car with a driver waiting for them at the bottom.

"What's happened?"

"Get in," the chief motions me toward the car. "Tell you when we're on the way." Pence jumps into the front passenger seat, and the chief and I get in the back. Pence's jaw muscles are twitching. The chief's face is in lockdown. She doesn't look at me but stares at the back of the driver's head. "They've found a body. We think it's Randy Spelling."

Tiny black dots push at the edges of my eyes. I grasp the back of Pence's seat to keep from falling forward.

"How?" I ask.

"Don't know yet."

"Where?"

"At a park in East Kenilworth," Pence answers without turning around. "Some guy walking a dog found her under a bench."

"Under a bench. What was she doing?"

"Beats me. You're her psychologist."

"Was," I say. Pence looks at me but doesn't say anything. "How?" I ask again.

"How what?"

"How did she kill herself?"

The chief turns to me for the first time. Her face is drained of color. There is a small quiver at the corner of her mouth. "She didn't kill herself, someone shot her to death with her own gun."

* * *

They won't let me near her body. Too many people spoil a crime scene. I watch from inside the car. Just as well, I doubt that my legs could hold me if I tried to walk. Cops and crime technicians are everywhere, ringed in by yellow caution tape like circus performers under a tent of gray sky. A crowd of onlookers has begun to assemble. A blue tarp lays over Randy's small body. Either the bench has been moved back or her body has been moved forward, I can't tell. Someone is interviewing the dog walker, a tall African American male dressed in jeans and a black-and-orange San Francisco Giants windbreaker. Three small mop-like dogs and two Chihuahuas are winding around his legs. The officer is leaning on the hood of his patrol car, writing furiously on his clipboard. The dog walker is shaking his head and pointing toward a newly constructed apartment complex painted in the colors of Tuscany.

There is a low rumble in the sky and a few drops of rain splatter against the pavement. I can hear Pence telling the troops to move fast before the rain washes away any usable evidence. More people drift toward the scene, some holding umbrellas and small folding stools as though they are planning to watch for awhile. Why not? This is the morning news and it's happening right in front of them. A uniformed officer pushes them back and puts up a second line of caution tape to expand the circle around Randy's body.

"I seen her," an older man shouts to no one in particular. "It's that cop what shot that little girl. Got what she deserve, you ask me."

Suddenly, I recognize where I am. This park with its crayon-colored slides and swings belongs to Althea Gibbs' apartment complex.

A car pulls up next to me. Jack Shiller gets out and lopes to the edge of the caution tape. I don't have to hear what passes between him and the officer who's trying to hold the growing crowd back to know what's going on. The only thing I can't tell is which of them is yelling louder. Shiller turns to the crowd and starts asking questions. There are a lot of eager takers, what better than to be on the TV news, only Shiller is a print journalist. Still, the TV crews can't be far behind. Too late, I slink down in my seat hoping I haven't been seen. He turns away from the crowd toward me, the older man in pursuit, daring him to tell the truth about terroristic cops who murder black youth for target practice.

The driver's side window is open. "One of your kind, Doc. A bona fide nut job," he says. "Can you help cure him?" He laughs. I don't. "So, who do the cops think is good for this? Lakeisha's family? The father of her kid?"

"They just found her body. I don't think they have a suspect."

"It's gotta be revenge."

I suddenly feel exhausted, all I can think about is my bed, my comforter, and my pillow. I want to sleep for a week. I see the chief, Pence, and the driver walking back to the car. Shiller follows my eyes, turns around and sprints toward them. They keep walking. I can't hear what they're saying. Shiller points to the car and then turns back to the crowd.

The driver gets in first, followed by the chief and Pence who does not look happy. "What did he want with you?"

"He wanted to know if you had a suspect. I told him it's too early for that."

"You don't know that." He motions for the driver to start the car. "Next time a reporter asks you a question, just say 'no comment.'"

"Do you have a suspect?" I can hear him curse under his breath. "Is this a revenge killing?"

Pence turns around. He is beet red and scowling. "We're police officers, not psychologists. We collect evidence, not theories." He turns to the front again as surprised as I am at this rupture in his airtight demeanor.

"It's all right, Jay." The chief leans forward and puts her hand on the front seat almost touching his shoulder, but not quite. "No harm done. We're all on edge and we need to be considerate of each other's feelings." She turns to me. "And we all need to be careful about talking to the press and making unverifiable inferences about anything."

There's a sudden undulation in the gathered crowd. Those working the scene stop doing whatever they're doing and turn toward the commotion. The cops all have their hands on their weapons.

"They didn't do it, they didn't do it." It's Ms. Gibbs. "Don't let them do my boys like they did Lakeisha." She falls to her knees, sobbing and heaving, tears cascading down her face. "Oh God," she screams. "Save my boys." Two young men rush to scoop her off the ground. She strikes at them. "Get away, don't let them see you. Get away." They lift her to her feet and turn her back toward the apartment building. I can hear her yelling, over and over, "Don't let them take my boys," until the crowd closes ranks behind them. The older man is still pacing back and forth, warning no one in particular about a lynching that's going to happen. We pull out of the parking lot as the crowd disperses, past the playground where Lakeisha's grandmother, Charla Gibbs Bernstein, is gripping the bars on a child's jungle gym with both hands. Her eyes are closed, her head is tilted upward, and tears are sliding down her face.

* * *

We ride in silence for several minutes. I can see the driver's stony face in the rearview mirror. He'd rather be out in the field trying to find a cop killer than cooped up with three of the most useless people on the planet: his chief, his captain, and the department shrink.

"That was an Academy Award performance, wasn't it?" Pence says. "What do you think?" He nudges the driver who wouldn't speak unless spoken to.

"Yes, sir."

"Really, what do you think? Am I wrong?" It's a safe bet he won't get any disagreement from a low-ranking street cop.

"Don't know about the mother, Captain. We've arrested the Gibbs boys several times. Petty stuff." Pence takes this in, working his mouth around as though chewing on the possibilities.

"Chief?" He looks over his shoulder. "Your thoughts? Was this a performance or not?"

"I think not. Grief is horrible." I wonder if she knows this firsthand. "This woman has lost one child. The idea that we might come after her other children must be terrifying. She's obviously lost trust in us, if she ever had it to begin with."

"What about you, Doc? Was she faking it?"

"I'm with the chief. Hard to imagine someone who wasn't a professional actress faking being overwrought. She was in agony."

"I thought she did a pretty good job of turning on the tears at those demonstrations."

"Enough, please," the chief says. "Let's not pre-judge anyone or anything. We need open minds. And we need to remember that different cultures express their emotions differently—some do it loudly, others hold things in." She is looking out the side window as she says this, turning her face away from us all.

CHAPTER TWENTY-ONE

There is an odd stillness in the police department when we get back despite the fact that almost every officer in the department has shown up, even those who were on vacation or weren't scheduled to work. The murder of a police officer is unthinkable. The ache of it settles on everyone like a fine dust. I pass Manny in the hall and when I reach out to him, he raises his hands defensively and backs away saying, "Not now, Doc. Not now," as if the mere touch of my hand would shatter him into a thousand pieces.

The chief calls a hastily assembled department meeting in the council chambers. The mayor and several council people are present. The last Kenilworth officer to be killed on the job was Fran's husband BJ. I make a mental note to check on her. It doesn't make any difference that BJ died fifteen years ago. Randy's death will trigger her most painful memories.

The first order of business is for the chief and Jay Pence to give the troops who aren't working the crime scene as much information as they can and to start laying out a strategy to find witnesses and develop a suspect profile. The department conference room has already been turned into a situation room, wallpapered with sheets of flip chart paper to track information. It's an effective, though ironically low-tech method, considering that Kenilworth sits in the middle of Silicon Valley.

Jay Pence was wrong about police officers not jumping to conclusions. The troops are unanimous in their certainty that someone in Lakeisha Gibbs' family is responsible for Randy's death.

"Let's be careful not to judge events or people prematurely," the chief says. There's a murmur in the crowd. She steps to the front of the room, raises her hand, and waits until the noise settles. "It is our responsibility to the community to investigate Officer Spelling's death as thoroughly and impartially as we are capable of doing." The murmur rises and then falls. "The loss of an officer is a tragedy. I know we're all feeling grief and anger. But, we cannot let anger get the best of us and distort our judgment. We have policies and procedures in place and we will follow them to the letter. Any questions?"

The questions come in a rush.

"What about the guy who got the Gibbs girl pregnant? Somebody interviewing him?"

"Did Randy have a gun on her? Were there any finger-prints?"

"What was she doing in East Kenilworth?"

"Was she in uniform?"

The chief raises her hands. "I need to ask for your patience. As of right now, we don't know what Officer Spelling was doing in East Kenilworth. We're still searching the area for evidence and witnesses. Captain Pence and I will keep you informed as details come in from the field. For now, you're all in service."

The chief motions for me to stay. She looks exhausted. "Rich Spelling is in my office. Will you talk to him, please? I tried to talk to him, but he was not receptive. He wants to be part of the investigation. This is understandable—he's a law enforcement of-ficer—but I can't permit such a thing. He's quite angry about it. I understand Randy's entire family is in law enforcement. They're going to want to be involved, and I can't let them. They don't seem to understand how much harm they could do to the investi-gation and to themselves."

I slowly walk to the chief's office, trying to find the right words to say to Rich. My mind is blank. Randy's murder is be-yond words. I pause at the door, wishing I were Catholic so I could cross myself.

Rich looks like hell. His face is drawn and the area beneath his eyes is red and flaky. He stands when I come in. "Got what she wanted, didn't she? Face to face with that lunatic woman and her gangbanger sons. Mea culpa, Ms. Gibbs, mea culpa. I didn't mean it. Please forgive me." He whines and bobbles his head as he puts his hands over his heart in a poor imitation of Randy being obsequious in a way that doesn't fit the Randy I knew.

He sits down again with a thud, head in hands. "Stupid, stupid, stupid." He looks up at me. "She had me, you know. I'm one stupid son of a bitch. Promised me she wouldn't do this. Told me she and Marvel had talked it through and she was over it. Not going to talk to Gibbs. She was going to leave it alone, get back to work, get on with her life. Her life, not our life—her life." He stands again, so agitated he doesn't seem to know where his body belongs.

"I didn't count, did I? It was all about her. Her tragedy, her cross to bear, her life ruined. You know what? I ought to thank Ms. Gibbs and her sons. They did me a favor." Air whooshes out of him and he slumps on the edge of the chief's desk, all his anger momentarily spent. "Tough guys, huh? No balls, two guys ambushing a 105-pound woman."

I doubt either of the Gibbs boys weigh more than that themselves.

Rich winces back tears. "She did this on purpose, didn't she? Got herself killed."

* * *

By the time I get home it's almost ten o'clock at night. There's a message from Frank offering his support. I'm too tired to call him back. He wants to know how I am, and I don't know how to answer his question. Blunted and muddy come to mind. I pour myself a glass of wine and sit on the couch with the lights out. Randy was tough, hard to reach, sometimes even hard to like. But I admired her spunk. And I was touched by her compassion for Lakeisha Gibbs. I can't imagine the burden of guilt she was carrying and would carry for the rest of her life. I take another sip of wine. Who am I kidding? I know exactly what it feels like to carry that kind of burden although I never said that to Randy. It's not like I killed Ben Gomez—he did that to himself—but to this day I still feel responsible. So, if I haven't cured myself of relentless guilt, how much help was I to Randy? Not as much as the youthful Dr. Marvel with her step-by-step game plan to certain disaster. I wonder how and what she's feeling right now. The wine sours in my mouth.

I know what to tell Frank if he calls back; so what if he's disgusted and never wants to see me again? Honesty is important in relationships. Relieved, that's what I'm feeling. Relieved everyone believes Randy was murdered and didn't kill herself. Relieved that if there's anyone to blame beside whoever killed her, it's Dr. Marvel Johnson, not me.

CHAPTER TWENTY-TWO

The halls are crowded with cops. I pass several officers I don't recognize. Mutual aid from a neighboring town is filling in so Kenilworth cops can work Randy's murder. No one, myself included, looks like they've slept more than a few hours. I spot Manny in the briefing room, bent over his computer.

"How's it going?"

He shakes his head.

"No leads?"

He looks at me. His smooth skin showing tiny break lines. He's unshaven.

"Did you go home last night?" He shakes his head.

"What about the Gibbs brothers?"

"In the wind. So is Darnell Taylor."

"Who's that?"

"The father of Lakeisha Gibbs' baby."

"Who told you that?"

"The grandmother." He looks at his notes. "Bernstein. Dr. Bernstein."

"Doctor?"

"That's what she says."

* * *

I walk up to the chief's office. The door is closed. I can hear voices, loud voices. The chief's secretary shrugs her shoulders and shakes her head at the commotion. "She's been waiting for you. Go right in, if you dare."

Chief Reagon and Captain Pence are on their feet. They

both look rumpled and sleep deprived. Pence's pristine hair needs another coat of gel, there are sweat stains under his arms, and his tie hangs loosely around his unbuttoned shirt collar. The minute he sees me, he turns to the chief.

"What is she doing here?"

"I asked her to join us," the chief says. "I want her input."

"Whatever. You're the chief," he says and drops into a chair. Petulant, sulky. I don't know how or when I got on his bad side. Talking to the reporter yesterday wasn't exactly a felony.

The chief swipes at her forehead and then wipes her hands on her skirt. Her face is slick with sweat. I take a chair across from Pence. The sky outside the window is the color of concrete. "Captain Pence and I have been discussing the protocol for Randy's funeral. The family insists on a funeral with full honors. Captain Pence and some members of the POA are opposed. It is their belief that a funeral with full honors is accorded only to officers who have died in the line of duty. Since we don't know what Randy was doing at the Gibbs' apartment complex, it is difficult to ascertain whether this falls into a category one or two funeral. I thought perhaps you might help us understand what Randy was doing when she died."

"Dr. Johnson knows more about Randy's current behavior than I do. Remember, she's no longer my client."

"Randy's family and her husband are convinced that Randy was investigating Lakeisha Gibbs. Trying to assemble evidence to mitigate her decision to shoot." The chief walks to her desk and sits down hard, as though her legs have suddenly given way. The chair squeaks in protest.

"And Dr. Johnson?"

"She hasn't returned my calls."

"I don't agree with the family's theory," I say. "And I'm surprised that Rich agrees. I think Randy went there to talk to Ms. Gibbs, face to face, to apologize for killing her daughter." A red scrawl inches up the chief's neck and across her cheeks.

Pence groans and leans back, his hands to his head.

"Stupid little bitch." And just as quickly he sits bolt upright, shocked at this sudden display of his normally hidden inner thoughts. "Sorry, ladies," he says. "I'm really tired." He turns to the chief. "What I mean is that if she went there to apologize, that has nothing to do with police work. She doesn't deserve a full-honors funeral. It would cheapen everything we do to honor the men—and the women—who make the ultimate sacrifice."

He stands up, apparently energized by his own thoughts. "I'm not a psychologist, but I'll tell you what I think. I think Randy brought this on herself. If she was nuts enough to want to apologize to the mother, then she was nuts enough to want to be punished for her so-called crimes."

I can't believe it. My exact thoughts coming out of Jay Pence's mouth.

"Suicide by crook. She let them kill her. Offered herself up like a sacrificial lamb. Maybe even handed them the gun and told them to wipe the fingerprints after they did her."

"Who is them?" I ask.

"Anyone of them. The brothers, the mother, the grandmother, the guy that got Lakeisha pregnant."

"No one is to know about the missing fingerprints," the chief says. "No one. Understood?"

Pence walks toward the chief and stands in front of her desk. "We don't give full honors to cops who kill themselves, that's all I'm saying."

Without warning the chief stands. Her hands balled into fists. "That was Chief Baxter's decision, not mine. Don't forget that. Randy Spelling took a life, not as a result of malice or negligence. She was a victim, too, and she deserves our respect."

"She was doing her job," Pence says. "She didn't need forgiveness."

"How do you know what she needed? Have you ever killed someone?" Her eyes are flaring. Whatever she's kept hidden behind that even-keeled façade is bursting its seams, splintering her emotional armor into fragments. Pence backs up. He looks at me. I'm the psychologist. I'm supposed to do something.

I move toward the chief, but before I have a chance to say a word, she makes a beeline towards her private bathroom and slams the door. A moment later we hear water running. Pence looks at me and shrugs. Neither one of us dares move an inch.

The door to the bathroom opens after several minutes, and the chief walks back into the room mopping her face and neck with a wadded-up wet paper towel.

"My apologies. I, too, am tired. And under a lot of strain, as you have no doubt noticed."

Pence and I mutter some trivialities in response.

"Randy's incident is personal to me. By way of explanation, I would like to share something with you and I ask each of you to keep this information confidential. I'm not ashamed of what I've done, but I don't want anyone, the media or the POA, to use it for their own ends." She looks at us. "Can I trust you?" We nod our heads. "When I was a young officer, I was involved in a high-speed pursuit and I killed a fourteen-year-old girl who was crossing the street on her bicycle. The pursuit was deemed legal after a protracted investigation. Still, I couldn't forgive myself. I wanted to apologize to her parents, but my chief wouldn't let me for fear that the girl's parents would understand my apology to mean that I was guilty of negligence and bring an even larger lawsuit than the one they were planning. Shortly thereafter, the department suspended the use of high-speed pursuits. That did not make me popular with the troops who blamed me for limiting their ability to catch criminals."

It takes me a minute to absorb the magnitude of what she's saying. I remember her comment the morning we went to see Ms. Gibbs—about not remembering the people you save, only the ones you kill. A person is only as sick as their secrets, and she's been dragging this secret around for years. Whoever did her background failed to investigate her experiences as a street cop because they didn't find them relevant to her ability to manage budgets and city politics.

"I can't imagine how difficult this has been for you," I say. "Thank you for telling us." I can see Pence out of the corner of my eye. He is standing stock still. Without a command to bark or a smart remark, he has no idea what to say. Empathy, sympathy, kind remarks are not in his lexicon.

"Did Randy know?" I ask. The chief holds the damp towel to her forehead and closes her eyes.

"No. Nothing anyone said to me at the time of my incident eased my pain. I didn't think I could ease hers. I thought, in time, she would find a way to live with herself, just as I have. Isn't this a police officer's fate? To be stuck with remorse for what we've done and regret for what we failed to do?"

I want to launch myself at her, guns blazing. Knowing her chief had survived a similarly tragic incident and built a career in spite of it, might have been just the thing Randy needed to hear. A glimmer of hope to hang onto.

"Why didn't you tell me? I could have helped you and then you could have helped me help her. Randy's dead. She might not be if you had reached out."

The color in the chief's face drains to a pallid gray. She takes a sharp breath. There's a quiver at the corners of her mouth. Pence backs up a step.

"I'm sorry," I say, "that was over the top."

"Indeed it was," she says. She's staring at her desk, struggling to regain her composure. It takes a minute before she looks up. "I don't hold myself responsible for Randy's murder and neither should you."

"I don't hold you responsible," Pence says. "Never have. Randy did this to herself." It's the first thing he has said in several minutes, and he looks pleased with himself for finally figuring out what to say.

"If there was anything I learned from what happened to me it's that while our actions have consequences, our intentions matter too. I never intended to kill that girl, and Randy never intended to kill Lakeisha Gibbs. She didn't have to tell me that for me to know it."

"But it would have helped her to know that you understood that." There is another silence. We are all on shaky ground. "I am sorry. I should never have spoken to you like that," I say.

The chief's face shifts again and softens slightly. Her eyes are indescribably sad. "You might work on your delivery," she says, "but I appreciate your candor. I will think about what you said. Now we need to move on." She pulls her chair closer to her desk. Gavel down. Case closed.

"Regarding the funeral." She looks directly at Pence. "This is my decision alone, and I am going to accord Randy a full-honors funeral."

Pence moves forward again. "Are you sure? We still don't know precisely who killed her or why." He's backpedaling, throwing his suicide-by-crook theory under the bus. "Let me remind you that if you insist on a full-honors funeral, you're going to lose that vote of confidence. The POA is split 60/40 against this."

The chief drops her shoulders and straightens her spine. "Captain Pence. Let me remind you of something. I don't make decisions, big or small, for political gain. And I don't have much regard for people who do."

CHAPTER TWENTY-THREE

It is Frank's first police funeral. He insisted on coming to keep me company. The convention center is filled to capacity. Enormous flower arrangements, taller than Randy herself, stand like sentinels along the front of the elevated platform. Rich walks past Randy's flag-draped casket, a uniformed officer at each elbow guiding him forward. He stops for a moment, brushes his hand over the gleaming lid and mounts the stage to join the other speakers. Randy's family is seated in the front row of the audience, her father and her brothers in dress uniforms from their respective agencies. Police Chaplain Barnes gives an ecumenical benediction. He stands tall, his dark skin burnished under the bright stage lights, speaking in measured terms about the grief that hangs in the air like secondhand smoke. He is followed by a heartfelt statement of compassion from the mayor of Kenilworth before Chief Reagon, in uniform, comes to the microphone. Her voice drones with condolence and everyone shifts restlessly in their seats. If the audience is looking for inspiration, some way to wrap their minds around this senseless loss and move forward, it doesn't come from her. My ill-timed attack in her office seems to have driven her back into her emotional armor.

Next up is Manny in his role as POA president. He walks to the front of the stage. Time on the street has strengthened his bearing, made him look taller, stronger, and more confident. He leans in to the microphone. His voice sails out, clear and strong, over the convention floor and up to the balconies.

"On behalf of the Peace Officers' Association of Kenilworth, our hearts go out to Randy's family, to her parents, her brothers, and to her husband, Rich. Randy was one of us. I ask her family to please, look around you. You are surrounded by hundreds of Randy's brothers and sisters in uniform, who are also your brothers and sisters. You may never meet us personally or know our names, but we stand with you, now and always." He lifts his head and looks over the crowd to the back of room where the TV cameras are positioned. "To the cowards who did this, be warned, kill one of us, and all of us will join the fight to bring you to justice."

Too bad, I think to myself, that this display of solidarity didn't include Randy when she was alive.

Rich is the last speaker. Bowed with grief, a handkerchief clutched in his hand, he stands mute. Seconds feel like hours before he finally bends toward the microphone, his hands gripping the edge of the podium for balance. "I loved her. She didn't deserve this. Find the bastards," he says before his knees give way and he crumples forward into the lectern. Someone in the audience begins sobbing loudly. I look first at Randy's family who are sitting ramrod straight with stony faces. Then I see her, a speck of pale pink in a sea of dark blue. Dr. Marvel Johnson, slumped forward in her seat, her back heaving.

CHAPTER TWENTY-FOUR

Nobody except Pence looks rested at the Monday staff meeting. I can't remember seeing him at the funeral. Pulling together a funeral of that size takes work, not to mention money and the aid of several surrounding agencies. There's still a psychological debriefing to do, but Pence has requested that any unnecessary meetings be postponed because all hands are needed for the continuing investigation. "And the bad guys aren't giving us a break. We still have police work to do. Okay with you, Chief?" She nods her head in agreement and turns to me. Her eyes are dulled from lack of sleep.

"What about you, Dr. Meyerhoff? Do you agree?"

I nod affirmatively. Psychological debriefings don't seem to work well when a cop has been murdered and the killers are still at large.

She continues. "I've asked the liaison officer to give us a report on how Randy's husband is doing. He should be here in a minute."

There's a hard knock on the door and it swings open banging against the wall. Manny is standing in the doorway, cheeks bright, bristling with excitement. "Sorry for interrupting, Chief. But we have three in custody." He clenches his fists triumphantly.

* * *

The three men in the detention center are in separate holding cells. Small, concrete block rooms furnished with hard metal benches and barred windows in the doors. There are several officers milling around in the hall in front of the evidence room giving each other high fives. Manny and Tom Rutgers are among them. I haven't seen Rutgers very often since the incident at the creek. Pence is grinning, shaking hands, and slapping backs. Congratulating everyone on their good police work. "This is what it's all about," he says. "Getting the bad guys off the street." It's not what it's all about, of course. Cops do hundreds of other things. Comfort victims, aid the frightened, participate in the community, and help the disadvantaged. But this is what gets everyone's adrenaline going: the thrill of the chase and the triumphant capture. If adrenaline smelled bad, this hallway would reek.

Chief Reagon is conspicuously not joining the back slapping. She walks over to Tom Rutgers.

"You were the officer in charge?"

"Yes, ma'am." He salutes, smiling so hard his mouth is in danger of ripping at the corners.

"How did these suspects sustain their injuries?"

There is a sudden silence.

"I repeat. How did these suspects sustain their injuries?"

Rutgers shrugs. "Don't know, ma'am. It was a pretty long chase. We went over a bunch of fences, through bushes, backyards, you know, could have happened anywhere. We didn't just yell stop and they stopped."

Another officer steps forward. "And when they did stop, it's not like they stuck their hands out and let us put the cuffs on without a fight."

"None of you appears to be injured," she says.

"Yeah, well. Good for us."

The chief turns around until she sees Pence. "Captain Pence, I want these suspects transported to the hospital immediately and then I want a report from you on how this happened."

The minute she leaves the hall, they start rumbling.

"Jesus fucking Christ. They run from us. What does she expect us to do? They just killed a cop."

Somebody kicks an evidence locker. The sound of it—the violence of it—echoes through the hall.

"Give 'em some love. That's what we do."

"Shoulda shot the fuckers," someone else mutters, "Save the public a bundle."

"Shhhh!" Somebody sees me standing there.

"Okay, everybody," Pence says. "You heard the chief, let's get these men to the hospital."

I watch them as they walk out, one by one, shackled at their hands and feet. First come the Gibbs boys, skinny as rails, their terror-stricken faces bruised and bloated. Blood spatters down the front of their white t-shirts. They look more like their grandmother than their mother, with the same delicate frame and the same light-colored skin. The third boy, Darnell Taylor, is a shirtless, husky kid with cornrowed hair and tattooed arms. He is dark skinned, but I can clearly see the bruises on his face and the name Lakeisha written in bold script across his chest.

I watch as the officers walk them into the police garage. I wait as each boy is placed in the hard back seat of a patrol car, with the guiding hand of a grim cop bending his charge through the passenger door. Tom Rutgers is standing behind Darnell Taylor. He shoves Darnell forward, cracking his skull against the roof of the patrol car. "Oopsy," he says loud enough for me to hear. "My bad."

* * *

Manny and I walk upstairs together. He's still jazzed.

"Good day," he says. "Damn fine day."

"Do you know how those boys got hurt?"

He stops on a step and looks at me. "No," he says, drawing out the O. "I wasn't there."

"And if you did know? Cops talk. You must have heard something."

"Where are you going with this, Doc?"

"You were the guy who was willing to turn in anyone who contributed to Ben Gomez' suicide."

"That was different. Somebody drove him over the edge. I wanted to find out who. So did you."

"And I admired you for it. You risked a lot to help me. Are you going to do the same for Chief Reagon?"

"Look, Doc. there are people out there who would kill a cop for no reason. I don't know who they are and I don't know when one of them is going after me. But I do know who has my back. And I'm not about to throw any of them under the bus."

The air in the stairwell is stale. Manny is standing on the step ahead of me, half-turned in my direction. Even in the dim light I can see his face begin to redden.

"How can you be sure it's one of those three boys who killed Randy?"

"You have any other suggestions?"

"Lakeisha's mother or her grandmother. Maybe Darnell Taylor has a jealous girlfriend. Maybe that crazy guy I saw in the parking lot."

Manny laughs, a short bark that bounces off the walls. "Maybe her father came back from Mars on a spaceship."

"Nobody knows her father's whereabouts."

"My point exactly. Look, Doc. I'm sorry to disappoint you, but you're the one who told me that police work changes people. It doesn't take much. Get lied to once or twice, you start believing everyone's a liar. Get bounced on your butt, you start believing everyone wants to hurt you."

"There are many ways to get hurt, Manny. One of them is to shut down emotionally and lose touch with the person you used to be."

He steps down to my level and puts his hands on both my shoulders. His cheeks have returned to their normal color and the tightness around his mouth has softened. "You worry too much, Doc. I'm still the same guy. I still know right from wrong. My skin's a little thicker and I'm more wary of people, but I'm pretty much the same. Losing a cop is the worst thing that can happen in any department. If we're heavy handed with suspects, you need to cut us a little slack. So does the chief." And with that he takes the stairs, two at a time, and doesn't wait at the top to hold the door open for me.

* * *

I get it—and I don't. I get that it's nearly impossible to turn off your adrenaline after a hard chase. Or when someone has killed a fellow cop. A gust of wind slaps at the windows in my kitchen and pushes the rain across the patio. I can see my reflection in the glass doors. My face is rain streaked as though I'm crying and then, suddenly, I am crying. Safe here in my own home, no need to be brave or competent or helpful. Am I crying for Randy? Or am I crying for my father? Are the Kenilworth police any different from the cops who beat my father, rendering his arm useless for life, breaking his spirit, and leaving him with a fearful disdain for authority. My father was provocative, dared the cops to attack him, served himself up as a youthful martyr for a cause that didn't outlast his injuries. But is that what the Gibbs boys did, or Darnell Taylor? Were they running because they were guilty or because they were scared and knew they would be beaten? And what am I doing? Am I working for an upscale, community-minded police organization or a bunch of thugs?

CHAPTER TWENTY-FIVE

There are ten messages on my voice mail, mostly from frightened parents and spouses. The risks of loving a dangerous job fall to the officer's family. The phalanx of cops who came to Randy's funeral will fade away. With few exceptions, their promises to be there for Randy's family and for Rich will be reabsorbed into the grind of their own everyday lives. The family's grief will be prolonged and deepened by the public spectacle that surrounds the murder of a police officer—the national memorials, the annual graveside ceremonies, the highway signs, the scholarships in her name, and a statue that won't look like her and is covered in bird shit. Rich has a hard road ahead of him. I make a note to call him in a few days to see how he's doing.

The next-to-last message is from Jack Shiller, cub reporter. He talks fast, trying to beat the bleep that will cut him off. His voice wavers between registers, suggesting he really is as young as he looks. "So, I was nosing around, I'm a curious kind of guy. Just wanted to let you know that the Gibbs brothers and Darnell Taylor have been discharged from the hospital. Guess their injuries weren't all that bad. Chester Allen is asking that they be released on their own recognizance, but in case the judge doesn't go for that, he has offered to put up the bail himself. Ms. Gibbs is so distraught, she can't work and doesn't have any money. If you have anything to say about this, give me a call on my cell." I delete his message.

The last call is from Charla Gibbs Bernstein, requesting an appointment with me. My first reaction is to refer her to the county's victim services. Counseling citizens is not in my job description although the chief seems to think it is. I'm not eager to get involved in the machinations of a family suffering from decades of dysfunction. Grandmother may be the most articulate and emotionally contained member of the household, but there was something about her that didn't feel right, some malice underneath her cool composure. I remember how she spoke to her daughter the day Lakeisha was killed. She was cold and cruel. But more than what she did say was what she didn't. She offered no words of support or comfort, only a cool analysis edged with contempt. As much as I don't want to, I reach for the phone. I know the chief wants me to be involved and I want to do something to make up for the way I talked to her in her office.

* * *

Charla Gibbs Bernstein arrives at my office dressed like she's going to the opening of an art gallery. Flowing silky pants and a kimono-like jacket adorned with an eye-popping handcrafted necklace that must weigh two pounds. She composes herself on my couch before she starts to speak.

"I am deeply aggrieved by Officer Spelling's murder, not just for her family but for my own family and my community," she says. "I have lost my beloved granddaughter to careless police behavior. If you care to know, I don't believe Lakeisha's death was malevolent on Officer Spelling's part, despite what others might say. What concerns me is what is happening now. Because it is malevolent."

"What do you mean?"

"The police are on a campaign to blame my grandsons. They're on a witch hunt, racing toward a conclusion for which they haven't a shred of evidence. My grandsons were at church when Officer Spelling was murdered. But, of course, my word is worthless because I'm their grandmother. They've already been convicted in the press, ruining any chances they might have to get a decent job or join the military. As I told you before, I all but abandoned Althea because I was so caught up in the headiness of the sixties. I'm not going to turn away from my grand-sons like I turned away from my daughter. I have a chance to redeem myself and I'm going to use everything in my power to make this right."

I can't tell if this is a declaration or a threat. "How can I help?" I ask.

"I come to you because, as a psychologist, I am hopeful that you will understand how tilted the odds are for my grandsons. That you will be a force for balance, slow things down, keep the police from jumping to conclusions."

"That's the police chief's job, not mine."

"I understand. But I don't know the police chief, beyond her one visit to our home and what I see on television or read in the paper. She appears to be a thoughtful person, but she has limited control over her department and, from what I read, is struggling to retain the confidence of her employees." She digs in a large black leather satchel, pulls out a business card, rises from the sofa with some difficulty, and hands it to me. It says Charla Gibbs Bernstein, Ph.D. Professor of Sociology Emeritus. "I believe we have something in common, you and I. Perhaps several things. Our training and our ability to look at the larger picture, for one. It is for this reason that I want to give you some information that I believe validates my fear that my grandsons will not get a fair shake."

She pulls a large envelope stuffed with papers from her bag and lays it on the coffee table. "I have some information for you, including a study by the Pew Research center about racism in law enforcement."

She looks to me for a reaction. I'm feeling warm and sweaty, about to have a hot flash that I hope won't turn my face scarlet.

"You'll find one statistic that speaks directly to my concern for my grandsons. And that is the disproportionate number of black students who are arrested, referred to criminal court, and sent to adult prisons." She pauses, waits for me to speak, and when I remain silent, she asks me for a glass of water.

I go out to the empty waiting room and draw two glasses of water from the bottle of water that sits inverted on a wooden stand. Not exactly a Zen fountain, still, the sound and cool feel of the water glasses is an antidote to the oppressive heat spreading through my body.

Dr. Bernstein thanks me, straightens her back, wincing slightly, and takes a long drink. "Do you see why I'm frightened? And not just for myself. The community is like a tinderbox, ready to explode with very little provocation." She takes another long drink and sets her glass on the table. "So, Dr. Meyerhoff, what is your reaction to what I'm saying?"

"I'm afraid you've gone to a lot of effort for nothing. I don't know what I can do to help. This is out of my hands."

"I see." She pauses without taking her eyes off my face. "Is it that you can't do anything or that you won't do anything?"

"Number one, I don't know what to do. Number two, I have no authority over the police, even if I knew what to do. I am a consultant here. My job is to counsel police officers. I do not make policy nor give advice about tactical operations."

"I'm not talking tactical operations. I'm talking attitudes, perceptions, just the kind of things about which psychologists are the supposed experts."

"I'm sorry. But it won't make any difference. I am not in a position to help you."

Her once soft green eyes glint like shards of broken glass. She scoots forward to the edge of the couch.

"I wasn't going to bring this up, but you haven't left me any choice."

"Bring what up?"

"My grandsons are in danger of being blamed for something they didn't do. They will not be treated fairly. You know that and I know that."

"I don't know that."

"Knowing about the injustices that are about to occur, your

father would have figured something out. He wouldn't have slept until he did."

"My father? What do you know about my father?" Suddenly my heart is pumping. I feel lightheaded and grip the arms of my chair.

"We were students together at Berkeley in the sixties. And very good friends." She pauses to let this sink in. "I thought I recognized you when you and the chief came to my apartment. You have your father's facial structure and your hair is graying just like his. Your name confirmed it. As I recall, he began graying shortly after he was beaten by the police."

My father never had a secret life. We shared everything. If he had had a good friend, I would have met her or heard about her. My mother would have known her.

Bernstein's voice grows soft. "It's possible, though not probable, that my daughter could be your half-sister, my dead granddaughter your half-niece, my grandsons, your half-nephews."

"You need to leave right now." She doesn't move.

"Your father would have wanted you to help me. He would have expected you to do so and would have been exceptionally disappointed at your refusal. And, it goes without saying, that he wouldn't have wanted your mother to know about his and my special friendship."

"Are you threatening to tell my mother that you had an affair with my father if I don't help you?"

"Of course not. I want you on my side." She picks up her satchel and stands. "Haven't I given you enough reasons to help me slow this rush to judgment? Don't hide in your office. Get involved. If for no other reason than to honor your father's memory. Come to my apartment, meet my grandsons, face to face. Judge for yourself."

She loops the handles of her bag over her shoulder, walks to the door with a newfound alacrity, and places her hand on the doorknob. "I remember your mother. A cheerful sort of woman. Struck me as living in some kind of rosy unreality. A world of her own making. I don't imagine she would take kindly to learning that the world she thought she inhabited might be a fiction."

* * *

The door closes behind her. My shirt is damp with sweat, and I don't trust myself to stand. If my father had another child beside me, he would never have abandoned either one of us. Is that why we were so poor? Was he splitting his meager salary between two families? Is that why he was always so tired, scuttling back and forth between two worlds, supporting a subterfuge of lies and promises?

I have exactly fifteen minutes to pull myself together before meeting my next client for her first session. I need to clear my head. I duck under the bathroom faucet and hope she won't notice my shiny naked face and my wet hair. My mirrored self begins a cross-examination. Have I just been blackmailed? Is Charla Bernstein telling the truth? Should I ignore her or talk to my mother before Bernstein gets to her? The bathroom door opens. Judging from the look on her face, this is my new client, and she has just discovered her new therapist standing in the bathroom talking to herself.

CHAPTER TWENTY-SIX

I turn on the evening news to fill the silence. I'm exhausted after my encounter with Charla Bernstein. Frank is off meeting a potential client. Chester Allen's face fills the screen.

"An outrage is what this is. Look at this boy." He shoves Darnell Taylor in front of the cameras. The left side of his face is distorted, and his eye is swollen shut. "Look at this." Allen sticks his fingers in the boy's face and parts his lips. He is missing several teeth, and there is a visible cut on his upper lip. "And this." He raises Darnell's hand which is wrapped in bandages. "Three fingers broken." He starts to pull at the boy's pant leg, but Darnell pushes him off. "Who did this to you, Darnell—tell the people." He shoves a microphone in Darnell's face.

"The guard." His voice is a mumble.

"What guard?"

"Dunno. Too many. Couldn't see."

Allen takes back the microphone. "It was Rich Spelling, was it not? Husband of slain officer Randy Spelling. Imagine, putting this young man in Spelling's charge, when he is a suspect in the death of Spelling's wife."

He's right, I can't imagine it any more than I can imagine that Rich is back to work barely a week after Randy's death, a mere four days after her funeral.

"Who is he, no matter how grievous his loss, to be both judge and jury, to administer street justice to a man who has not been convicted, has not had his day in court?"

"What about the Gibbs boys?" Jack Shiller shouts. "Were they beaten, too?"

"All three sustained injuries during their arrest. The Gibbs brothers went to juvenile hall. As of last night, they were released to the custody of their grandmother. I'll be interviewing them later today. I hope they were treated better than Darnell was at the county jail."

* * *

Dr. Bernstein never mentioned that her grandsons had been released. Nor had she mentioned Darnell Taylor. Her concern for the plight of black men and boys everywhere, apparently doesn't extend to him.

I call Rich at home, planning to leave a message. He answers the phone. "I have two questions," I say. "Is it true about the beating and are you all right?"

"What did they expect? I'm supposed to watch this creep? Make sure he eats his din-din and wipes his ass? He was mocking me. Going 'boo-hoo, who gonna be your bitch now?' I shoved him once when he wouldn't shut up. Didn't even break skin. They pulled me off, sent me home. I guess my buddies finished what I started." There's noise in the background. "Hold on a minute. Someone's at the door." He lays the phone down with a clunk. I can hear faint voices. One of them sounds like a woman. "I got to go. Some friends just dropped by."

"I was surprised to learn that you went back to work so soon."

"I was going nuts at home. It's like a mausoleum. Couldn't stand it. Her stuff is everywhere. Never occurred to me I'd be assigned to the same floor as that asshole. Maybe somebody thought they were doing me a favor, giving me a crack at the guy." There's more noise behind him. "Some favor, huh? Now I'll probably lose my job. Maybe even go to jail. She took it all, didn't she? Got what she wanted." He muffles the phone with his hand and says something to the people in his house.

"Randy never wanted to hurt you," I say.
"Think so? Anyhow, Doc, do me a favor, will you?"
I perk up.
"Sure, Rich. Anything."
"Don't call me again."

CHAPTER TWENTY-SEVEN

The Gibbs boys are sitting ramrod straight at the dining table, dressed in starched-white dress shirts and black pants. They fit right in with the decor. So does Althea Gibbs, who is seated on her plastic-covered couch wearing black pants and a white sweater. Bernstein is wearing a zebra print caftan and silver slippers. I feel like I'm in a fun house of black and white, everyone but me, camouflaged, able to disappear into the background, leaving me, the blotch in a green suit, standing alone. An easy target.

The boys stand as Bernstein introduces me first to Omari and then to Rashan, their handshakes are limp and tentative. I suppress an urge to try the homie, hand bumping, jive shaking, finger wrapping greeting I see among young people, only I don't know how to do it and I'd look pretty stupid trying. I'm here against my better judgment, ignoring all the warnings I gave Randy, about how dangerous it would have been for her to visit Ms. Gibbs. The only difference is that I have, euphemistically speaking, been invited. I'm getting more like my mother every day, able to spin dross into gold.

I join Bernstein and the boys at the table. Althea Gibbs swings her body to the right, staring past us out the window.

"Ms. Gibbs, would you join us?" I ask.

"This her brainy idea." She acknowledges her mother with a bounce of her head. "I don't want nothing to do with it."

These two women are so different that if I didn't know they were mother and daughter, someone would have to tell me. They don't look alike, they don't talk alike, and they don't think alike. The only things they have in common are the way they flaunt their differences in each other's faces, their fondness for dressing in black and white, and their determination to protect Omari and Rashan. A determination so fierce, I imagine the boys will have to run away from home if they ever want lives of their own. And then what? Without Omari and Rashan to hold them together, they'll be at each other's throats.

Bernstein hisses a lengthy sigh. "Tell the doctor about yourselves, boys, please."

It's like a job interview. Omari, who is sixteen, is a high school junior, member of the marching band, a C+ student, and an avid churchgoer. After high school, he wants to join the army and learn computers. Rashan has an almost identical bio, except that he wants to go into the air force and be an airplane mechanic. Their presentations are stiff and halting, their eyes darting back and forth between me, their grandmother, who has clearly orchestrated this event, and their mother. I drift between listening to their words and studying their faces, charting every feature, looking for a bump in the nose, a narrow chin, steep cheekbones, a high forehead—anything that would resemble my father. Somewhere there is a white ancestor in all their lives, but short of DNA testing, I doubt we are even distantly related. Their closing remarks are short eulogies to Lakeisha, how much they looked up to her and how much they miss her. Small drops of sweat drip off their newly barbered heads. It is a weak performance, and we all know it. They haven't proven anything. Still, neither one seems capable of an aggressive act like murder. In this family, it is the women who are powerful and full of rage.

"I expected to meet Darnell here today, as well," I say.

"Darnell don't come in this house. He's not welcome here," Ms. Gibbs is suddenly engaged. "He beat her. She pregnant and he beat her."

I turn in my chair to face her. The sun is blazing through the sliding glass door to the balcony, striping the room with bars of white. "If you are so concerned, were so concerned for her safety, why did you throw her out?"

Ms. Gibbs stands up. "I told you once. I did not throw her out. We had a fight and she left. Took my car. She could have stayed. But she stubborn, she wouldn't do what I told her."

"And what was that?"

"Get rid of Darnell."

"I don't think this is relevant to Dr. Meyerhoff's interests." Bernstein is now standing.

Althea Gibbs cocks her head, glaring at her mother. "I told you her interests ain't my interests. My interests are my boys. Lakeisha's gone. I can't get her back. But I'm not going to lose my boys."

"And I'm not going to lose my grandsons. That's why I asked Dr. Meyerhoff here to meet them. I've explained that to you once. She can help us."

"Yeah, you explained it. It still wrong. Those boys should have been on a plane to Atlanta, to stay with their aunt." She looks at me directly for the first time since I've been here. "You think she's gonna help us? You crazy."

The boys are sitting stock still in their chairs. There are tears running down Rashan's face. He is too frozen to wipe them away. Omari is lost in the swirling pattern of his placemat.

"I agree. This interview isn't very helpful." I turn to the boys. "Do you know anything that could help me find out who killed Officer Spelling?"

They shake their heads no in unison.

"They already told the cops that, about a million times," Ms. Gibbs says.

"What about Darnell?" I ask them.

"They don't know nothing about him. They don't run with him. He older. I won't let them. Bad enough their sister did."

"But they were arrested together." I remember Manny, his face bright with excitement, bursting into the staff meeting to announce "three in custody."

"No way. They all picked up the same night. I don't know

where they got Darnell, but my boys were at church for game night. The police already checked."

***

Dr. Bernstein calls me the first thing the next morning. I recognize her phone number and debate letting her call go to voice mail, but at the last minute I pick up the phone. Stupid move.

"I apologize for my daughter's behavior yesterday. She is genuinely fearful for her children, as am I, only she doesn't handle her emotions with much equanimity." I wonder if Bernstein ever talks like an ordinary person instead of a dictionary. "Nor were my grandsons entirely truthful. After you left I spoke to them. Darnell has dropped out of sight again. I don't know how my grandsons know this, but they told me you could find him at 1704 Travis Avenue in East Kenilworth where he is staying with friends. "

"Why are you telling me this?"

"Omari and Rashan looked up to Darnell when he was dating Lakeisha. They had no other male role models. Their sister loved him, so they loved him too. That's why they didn't tell you where he lives. Darnell has influence over my grandsons. As you saw, they're rather passive. Comes from being raised by a domineering mother who controls every aspect of their lives. The police are going to believe that Omari and Rashan, in some way, helped Darnell murder Officer Spelling. In which case, he is the only one who can exonerate them."

"If you are so sure Darnell is guilty and you know where he is, call the police."

"Unlike my grandsons, who are good boys and would do whatever the police asked them to do, Darnell would fight the police or run away. In either case, I can almost guarantee that he will be killed. I don't like him but I don't want his blood on my hands. He will talk to you because he doesn't know you."

"I was in the police station the night he was arrested."

"I'll take the chance that he was too preoccupied watching the officers who beat him than he was looking at you."

"So you want me to convince Darnell to confess to something he may or may not have done in order to save your grandsons from suspicion? And you won't call the police yourself because you're afraid Darnell will be killed in the confrontation?"

"Exactly."

"No. Absolutely not. It's too dangerous. Darnell is dangerous, you said so yourself. If you want to talk to him, you do it."

"I would if I were a younger woman, but I'm not. In fact, I'm at the age where I'm seriously contemplating moving to a retirement community. I understand your mother lives in such a community near Morro Bay. Perhaps I'll pay her a visit to see if she likes it."

CHAPTER TWENTY-EIGHT

1704 Travis Avenue is an apartment building, not a house. It's built like a motel, three stories high, ten apartments to a floor. Darnell Taylor is bunking behind one of those thirty doors, and I have no clue which one nor what I would do if he opened the door and saw me standing here. A sharp wind blows across the parking lot from the bay. On the street behind me, a long line of cars, caught in the evening commute, their headlights reflecting a light rain, inch slowly toward the East Bay Bridge. This end of East Kenilworth—wide, flat and open to the water—is the last affordable real estate in the Bay Area. Small, tidy, working-class bungalows are slowly being replaced by gargantuan homes, built from lot line to lot line, closed off to the neighbors by ornate, electrified, wrought iron fences. I imagine the residents, instant millionaires from Silicon Valley, barely old enough to be living on their own, roaming through the empty rooms of their faux palaces, trying to fill homes big enough for ten, their enormous mortgages precariously balanced on the undulating waves of an uncertain economy.

A door opens on the first floor and a large, older woman steps out holding a leaking bag of garbage. She stops when she sees me, her eyes alert. I don't fit in and people who don't fit in are mostly here to cause trouble: bill collectors, social workers from Child Protective Services, and the police.

"Excuse me," I say. "I didn't mean to frighten you. I'm looking for a young man—"

She steps back into her apartment. "Lo siento, no hablo inglés," she says as she closes the door. Better to spend the evening with a smelly bag of garbage than risk running into a stranger.

This is crazy. I should leave. Frank's at his house, cooking posole, a savory stew of hominy and chicken with chili peppers that he roasts by hand and grinds into a sauce. His favorite cooking show is on the TV, one he's seen so often he could recite it by heart, a glass of wine is in his hand. He is totally in his element while I am totally out of mine, freezing my butt off in a dark parking lot in a drizzling rain in the "wrong" part of town. I should call to tell him I'll be late, but then he'll ask where I am and I don't want to tell him because he'll tell me what I already know, that I should get the hell out of here while I can.

Why do I think Charla Bernstein would actually follow through on her threat to tell my mother that she and my father had an affair? What if they did? Is it worth my getting killed over? An image rises, my father and Charla Gibbs Bernstein, both of them young and beautiful, wound together by their passions for each other and for the fight to overcome oppression. True? Not true? I don't know and at this moment it doesn't much matter. What matters is my mother. There is no way I am going to let Charla Bernstein break my mother's aging heart. I'll do this for her and her grandsons and then I'll tell her to go to hell.

A car whips into the space next to where I'm standing. All four doors open at once and four young African American males get out, bang their doors shut, and head wordlessly toward the steps. Much to my surprise, they are ignoring me.

"Pardon me," I say. They turn around in unison and stare. "I'm looking for Darnell Taylor. Do you know him? Or where he's staying? I am an associate of his attorney and I have some important information for him." It is so dark now that Darnell could be standing right in front of me and I wouldn't recognize him.

One of the boys steps forward, the first non-synchronized move anyone has made. "You police?"

I laugh, a phony fearful tinkle. "No. As I said, I'm working with his attorney."

"What his attorney's name?" a voice asks from the back of group. I can't see his face but I know I'm being tested.

"Chester Allen."

The boy, man, whatever he is, closest to me steps back to the group for a confab. All I can hear is a low buzz. He steps forward again. "Why we gonna help you? You going to pay us?"

"You're not helping me, you're helping Darnell. If he doesn't get this information right away he'll be in trouble. Big trouble. And so will you for interfering with a legal process."

"You a process server?"

"Yes, I am." I'm not even sure what a process server serves.

"Leave it with me. I'll give it to him," the tallest boy says.

"He has to sign it himself, and I have to witness his signature. Or he could come to the police station and do it. Something I doubt he will want to do since he appears to be avoiding the police."

There's another short confab, and the tall boy takes a step in my direction. He looks around and lowers his voice.

"You didn't hear this from me. He in 3C. But he ain't home now." I look up, almost all the front-facing windows on the third level are dark.

"Do you know when he'll be back?" There's yet another buzz from the group.

"He be at home during the day, sleeping. He work at night."

"Thanks," I say and turn toward my car which is parked at the sidewalk.

"Watch yourself now." The voice follows me. "This neighborhood ain't safe at night."

I don't know whether that's a concerned warning for which I should be grateful or a not-too-well-disguised threat.

CHAPTER TWENTY-NINE

Frank is irritated with me. He's trying to hide it, but I can tell. He's sitting in a chair watching a young Julia Child make duck confit. The half-empty wine bottle on the counter means he's several glasses of wine ahead of me.

"Sorry, I couldn't help it...something at work. Couldn't be delayed. Did I ruin dinner?"

"Not a problem. Posole holds, so does salad. Take your time." His voice is clipped and flat. His eyes never move from the TV.

I can't stand it when we have these silent fights.

"So, how was your day?" I ask.

"Okay. Nothing special."

"Get that job you bid on the other day?"

"Look, Dot. You don't have to try so hard. You're late. I'm pissed. That's all. Let's eat." He switches off the TV, walks into the kitchen, picks up a long-handled wooden spoon and takes the lid off the posole, releasing a cloud of fragrant steam. "You could have called."

"I'm sorry. You're right. I should have called to say I would be late."

"So why didn't you?" My stomach tightens, getting ready for a fight, not a bowl of posole.

"I couldn't."

"Why not?"

"I was busy."

He whacks the spoon on the counter splattering drops of red on the wall. His face is a scowl. "I can take waiting for you. I don't like it, but by now I know you well enough to know that your work comes first. I love cooking and I love cooking for you. What I can't take is being shut out. So, are you going to tell me what's going on? I'm not stupid, you know." He rinses a sponge in the sink and wipes down the wall behind the stove, his lips pressed into invisibility.

We are like half a dozen couples I've seen this week. The wives begging to be included, wanting to know what's going on at the police department, why their husbands come home from work with that "look" on their faces. The more they pursue, the harder their husbands pull away. Cops have a long list of reasons not to talk. They think only other cops understand what they go through at work. They want their homes to be sanctuaries, uncontaminated by the tragedy and cruelty they see every day. And they have secrets—some official, some personal. Psychologists have only one reason. Client confidentiality. Charla Bernstein, Althea Gibbs and her sons, and Darnell Taylor, are not my clients. I pour myself a glass of wine. The only reason I'm keeping things to myself is to avoid getting grief.

"I tried to find Darnell Taylor."

"Who?"

"One of the boys suspected of killing Randy Spelling."

Frank slams the lid down on the posole. "Alone? You went alone to see a suspected murderer?"

"Yeah."

"Why didn't you take an officer with you?"

"The department doesn't know I'm involved."

He sits down on a metal stool at the end of the counter. "Just how involved are you and why?"

I sit on the end of his couch, facing him and take a sip of wine. "It's a long story," I say.

"I have all the time in the world," he says, wiping his hands on his denim apron. "The posole will hold."

CHAPTER THIRTY

I have two cancellations in a row. Ordinarily I'd be upset at losing therapeutic momentum with my clients, not to mention the loss of fees. But today I'm relieved to have time in the afternoon to catch Darnell before he goes to work. 1704 Travis looks different in the daylight. There's a small playground to the side with slides and a sandbox. Six or seven young children are chasing each other under and over a multicolored jungle gym. Two women, probably day-care workers, watch from a bench, calling out warnings in Spanish. A fight erupts between two boys and one of the workers rises reluctantly to separate the two tearful combatants. It is the woman I met the day before, putting out the garbage. She grabs the two boys by their shirt backs and walks them to the bench for a time out. She sees me and says something to the other woman. I wave. She turns away.

I walk up the pebbled concrete steps to the third landing. The door of 3C is scratched and needs paint. I ring the doorbell and when no one answers after six rings I knock, hard and loud. Still no answer. A door to my left opens a crack and then shuts. I walk over and knock. "Go away," a voice says.

"I'm looking for Darnell Taylor in 3C."

"Nobody there," the voice says. "It's empty. You want to rent. See the manager in 1A."

I most certainly do not want to rent and I feel badly for anyone who has to live here. I head back to my car in search of a piece of paper and a pen to leave a note on the door. A car comes down the street blasting music so loud I can feel the vibrations from half a block away. It pulls into the parking lot, the tires shrill against the pitted concrete surface. The music stops and just like yesterday, all four doors open at the same moment, only this time, in the daylight, I can see who I'm talking to.

"Darnell not home?" The tallest one asks. They are standing side by side as though linked together by an invisible rope. They are wearing identical gold pendants and chains around their necks, black hoodies, baggy jeans, and enormous shoes in phosphorescent colors, the laces untied.

"You his probation?" another asks.

I smile, trying to look anything but scared. "Hello again. As I explained yesterday, I'm an associate of Chester Allen, Darnell's lawyer."

"Darnell kill that lady cop?" one of them asks.

If I say yes they'll go into protective mode, do something rash to keep me away from their friend. "No," I say. "Not his style." I tried to sound as cool and confident as I can, even though I'm doing everything possible not to pee in my pants.

"He's a murdering piece of shit." The tallest one steps forward a foot. "Somebody mess with his baby mama, he'd do a beat down. Don't care if it a woman or a cop."

"Or a woman cop, she be the prize pig." This is apparently very funny because there's a lot of hand slapping and high fiving going on between the three shorter boys.

"Zip it." The tallest one says. The other three instantly fall silent. "You want to know where he works at?" he says.

"That would be helpful."

"McDonald's. 4th and Lyman Avenue."

"Thank you. I'm sorry, I didn't get your name."

He pauses for a moment. "We rap as 1704T. Darnell, sometime he our bouncer." He reaches into his pocket and my heart shudders. "Here," he says and shoves a crumpled piece of paper into my hand. I start to put it in my pocket, and the tall one tells me to read it. I flatten it out against my thigh.

It's a flyer for their next appearance. "We opening for Bad Boy Wunder. Gonna be awesome. Drop by," he says, "If you dare." Everyone laughs.

I walk to my car, slowly, pretending my legs aren't shaking. I want to look back in the worst way, see if they're following me, guns out, switchblades drawn. I risk a small peek after I lock the car doors. The parking lot is empty and all the apartment doors are closed.

* * *

The McDonald's at 4th and Lyman needs an upgrade. It's old, worn, and sits at a crazy angle to the street requiring driving customers to make a U-turn to get into the parking lot. The place is empty, save for a table of four small children. One is asleep, her head on her hands, the other three seem to be doing their homework. A woman appears behind the counter; she's young and obese. My guess is that she's been eating up the profits, feeding her little family french fries and burgers. Cheap, but filling. Fish and vegetables cost as much as steak these days, if you can find them. East Kenilworth is a food desert, nothing but bodegas and liquor stores. You have to cross the freeway to Kenilworth to find a head of lettuce or a bunch of bananas.

"May I help you?" she says, looking, not at me, but at her children, raising her two finely stenciled eyebrows as a warning to be quiet, although I can't imagine how much more quiet they need to be. I wonder if they live here, sleeping on the plastic benches, curled up next to the deep-fat fryer.

"I'm looking for Darnell. Is he here?"

She looks at me, a hard challenging look, and shakes her head. I notice for the first time how haggard she is, premature lines crisscross her face and small sacs bulge beneath her eyes.

"Do you know where he is or when he's scheduled to work?"

She shakes her head again and turns back to the kitchen area.

She's got me pegged. I'm not here to eat. I'm here to ask annoying questions.

"Perhaps someone else in the kitchen might know."

She turns back to me. "He didn't show up for work now for a week. No phone call, no nothing. For all I care, I hope the fucker's dead."

CHAPTER THIRTY-ONE

The chief looks exhausted. Even Pence seems worn down. The entire management staff looks like they could use a good night's sleep. It's been nearly a month since Randy's murder. Between the investigation and keeping an eye on the continuing public demonstrations, all leaves have been canceled and everyone is buried with work. Chester Allen is still leading the charge to rid KPD of police brutality, but without Randy as a target to consolidate public anger, the crowds are smaller and Ms. Gibbs is keeping a low profile, privately grieving and, I suspect, keeping an eye on Omari and Rashan.

There isn't much for me to do beyond a psychological debriefing, and that was preempted by the chief and Pence. I've asked several times if I can go ahead with it, and the answer is always the same—a flat "no, we're too busy to spare anyone." Hard to imagine an hour or two making that much difference, but evidently it does. I'm just a consultant here, I don't have the authority to make any decisions and it's clear that Pence, especially, wants it that way.

"Good morning, everyone," Pence says. "Time to start." Chief Reagon has been letting Pence run more and more Monday staff meetings. The chief is dressed in her usual non-uniform uniform; plain suit, nylon shell and flat shoes with no jewelry except her watch. She bends over her notes. Pence turns to Manny who is scheduled to give an update on the ongoing investigation.

"Nothing new on the ground, Captain. If there were any witnesses they're not talking to us. Chester Allen is glued to the

Gibbs kids like white on rice." Somebody chortles at the ineptness of his metaphor. The chief raises her head, clearly not amused. Manny sits down.

"That's it?" Pence says.

"Yes, sir, sorry, sir, wish I had more. We're working on it." His report finished, he starts to leave the room.

"What about Darnell Taylor?" I ask. All heads turn to look at me.

"What about Darnell Taylor?" Pence asks.

"He's missing, isn't he?"

"How do you know this?"

"He hasn't been to work in a week. And there's no one home where's he's living."

Pence steps around his side of the table and is in my face before I realize that I've just told the entire management staff that I've been nosing around a police investigation, without permission or authorization.

"How exactly do you know this?"

"A friend told me."

"What friend?"

"I can't say. It's really not a friend. It's a client. I can't talk about my clients or tell you their names."

Pence bends over me, so close I can smell his hair gel, a nauseating confection of tropical fruits.

"We are working day and night to find this kid. If you know something, you need to tell us."

"How come the newspapers haven't said anything about his disappearance?"

Pence's face turns red. "Do not talk to Jack Shiller. Not a word. Do you understand? One word and you're fired. No leaks." He stands. "That goes for everyone in this room. We want the public to think we know where he is. We want him to get sloppy. Show his face. We have a dead cop. We have to look like we're on top of this."

"That's enough, Jay. Sit down." Chief Reagon speaks for

the first time. Pence glares at me and walks back to his seat. "As of yesterday, I have negotiated with the city council to offer a $10,000 reward for information about Darnell Taylor's whereabouts. It will be in tomorrow's paper." There's a murmur of approval from the staff. "Our hope, of course, is that someone who knows Darnell will choose money over friendship."

Pence shifts in his seat. "Why don't we just put Dr. Sherlock on the case? She seems to know more about Darnell Taylor than we do."

"I doubt that," I say, "but this may help." I hand the flyer to the chief. "I can't tell you how I got this, but it is my understanding that Darnell Taylor sometimes works for this group as a bouncer. He may be at their next concert."

The room drops into silence as Chief Reagon looks at the wrinkled flyer. 1704T stares into the camera, their faces sultry and pouty, as though daring—not inviting—people to come to their show. "Who are these young men?"

I shrug my shoulders.

"Do you see adolescents in your practice?"

I shake my head no.

"If they aren't clients, then how do you know them?"

"As I said, I can't tell you." Not without admitting I've actually gone looking for Darnell. I've already thrown myself under the bus big time. No profit in making it worse than it already is.

"I'd like to keep this, if you don't mind." She studies the flyer for a minute and then passes it to Pence. He scowls as he reads, deep lines furrow his forehead. He hands it on without looking up. A murmur follows the flyer as it circulates around the table until it gets back to Pence.

"This stays in the room," he says. "Does everyone understand, and I mean everyone?" He turns to me. "Darnell Taylor is a very dangerous man. I have officers out looking for him 24/7. If you talk to anyone, you'll put my officers at risk and put yourself at risk for interfering with a police investigation, which, let me remind you, is a criminal offense. Do I make myself clear?"

The chief doesn't wait for my response. "Dr. Meyerhoff, I don't understand your motivation to get involved in something for which you are totally ill equipped. But, whatever you do and for whatever reasons, I need you to stop. For your sake and ours. My officers need to focus all their efforts on looking for Darnell Taylor. They do not need to use their time rescuing you if you find him." She turns back to the others. "Captain Pence, we'll need an organized team to attend this concert. You'll have to use mutual aid to do it. Get some officers from the county-wide task force to demographically match the concert goers. Make sure they have not had any previous contact with the criminal element in this part of the county and are in little danger of being recognized. Thank you everyone, we have a lot of work to do and not much time to do it in."

Everyone gets to their feet. Pence is first out the door.

"Chief," I say, "I need to talk to you."

She looks at me and at the door, pulled in two directions. "I have a lot to do."

"Just a minute, that's all I need." She turns back to me. Her shoulders drop slightly and she expels a long breath, as though settling in for a long, boring speech.

"I thought I was being helpful giving you information about Darnell Taylor. In no way did I mean to create trouble or make anyone's job more difficult or dangerous than it already is. I feel helpless. All of you are working so hard, and I don't seem to have a role to play."

The chief is not my friend, not even my colleague. She moves through my life like a phantom, totally opaque, unreachable, deflecting every attempt I've made to reach out to her. And yet here I am apologizing. She places her hand on my shoulder. "We all tried to help Randy. Each in our own way. None of it worked.

Sometimes, no matter how good our intentions are or how hard we try, the outcome is not what we were hoping for. It is painful to confront our own limits. And admit our own mistakes." She bends to gather her papers. "All we can do is show up to do the next right thing."

"If only," I say, "I knew what that was."

CHAPTER THIRTY-TWO

I stand outside police headquarters buffeted by a cold wind, mortified that the chief needed to console me, not the other way around. Helping people through hard times is supposed to be my job. I get into my car and drive to Fran's. The least I can do is see how she's doing.

It is lunchtime chaos. No telling which is louder, the clatter or the chatter. I take a seat at the counter, four stools away from three KPD cops. Eddie and Fran are both working behind the counter. It's a comic ballet watching these two enormous people squeezing past each other while balancing plates heaped high with hot food, never spilling a drop. The speed at which they work along with the heat from the griddle coats their faces with a greasy gloss. I envy the tangible rewards they reap from satisfying people's hunger, the most basic and simple of human needs.

Fran looks better than she did when I saw her last and gives me a big smile. She bends over, placing her palms on the counter, stretching her back like a cat and grimacing. "This is a young woman's job, Doc. I envy you: nice cushy office, not on your feet for hours, no grease under your fingernails. Education, that's the thing. I should have stayed in school."

"Not cushy lately," I say.

"Of course not. I'm sorry. You've probably been working night and day."

"And you?" I say. "How are you doing?"

"I got triggered. It happens. But I know how to deal with triggers because someone in your line of work taught me." She smiles and I feel a wave of warmth from and for her. "How are the families doing? Must scare them to death, having one of their own murdered. Same when BJ died. No one could believe it. Stuff like that happens in New York and LA but not Kenilworth."

"I've gotten a lot of phone calls from concerned families. They're all worried, of course."

"What are you doing about it?"

"Not much I can do. Listen. Reflect."

"What about a debriefing?"

"Admin doesn't want to spare the time, not until there's a suspect in custody."

"I don't mean for the cops. I mean for the families. Get them together, let them talk about their concerns. I'll come if it would help and I can get some other older wives to come with me, too. What happened to me is their greatest fear. If they can see that I survived it, maybe that will give them hope."

I want to slap my hand to my head and yell "Duh." Why didn't I think of this? Families need reassurance—they need a chance to vent, to be acknowledged for their fears and all the other challenges that come with being married to a cop: missed birthdays, canceled vacations, overtime for court, living life in a fishbowl. It's a long list. I stand up, lean over the counter, and give Fran a big hug.

"What was that for?" she asks.

"For showing me the next right thing."

* * *

Eddie chases me out to the parking lot and grabs hold of my car door before I have a chance to close it.

"Where's my hug?"

"I don't hug clients. Especially when they're all sweaty and covered in tomato sauce."

"Didn't keep you from hugging Fran." He feigns disappointment.

"You look happy, Eddie. Working with Fran seems to suit you."

His face falls into a grimace. "Are you kidding? Where'd you get your license to practice, off the back of a matchbook cover? I'm just biding my time until the chief brings me back. I'm going crazy here, Doc. Police work is not what I do, it's who I am. Look at me. I'm the fuzz that was. I can't stand it. Flipping burgers for all these young cops, listening to them talk. What do I have to say? Want your burger rare or well done? The whole fucking department is overworked looking for the creep that killed Randy. I can help. Talk to the chief. I'll work for free, I don't care. Just get me back on the job."

CHAPTER THIRTY-THREE

Fran was right. The response to my invitation to a family debriefing has been overwhelming. The chief actually volunteered to kick off the meeting and then leave so that the families would not be intimidated by her presence. Pence, on the other hand, was not nearly as gracious. The minute the invitations went out, he was on the phone to me, clearly irritated that I had reached out to families without his permission. According to him, the department has no business interfering with officers' private lives. He knows what happens when cops' wives get together—it's a gabfest. All they're going to do is gossip. I tell him, in the most polite way possible, that if I had put invitations in the officers' mailboxes, most of them would end up in the wastebasket.

"That's the officer's choice, then," he says.

"Don't their families have a choice? This job and Randy's death affects them, too."

"Then remind the chief that the vote of no confidence is still pending. This harebrained idea isn't going to help her any."

* * *

I call Rich Spelling to invite him personally. He did tell me never to call him again, but he was grieving and angry at the world. I don't want him to find out that we're offering counseling to the KPD families and that we didn't include him. I expect him to hang up on me.

"Yo, Doc," he says. "How's things in the nuthouse?"

"You sound cheerful."

"What other choice do I have? I can't just lay down and die. Randy's dead, not me."

"You've had an enormous loss. You need time to grieve."

"Not my style."

"How's work?"

"It's okay except everyone looks at me funny, and I'm taking a lot of grief off the a-hole inmates. They make these little crying noises, or they chant 'boo-hoo for the screw' every time they see me."

I tell him about the family debriefing and, as expected, he declines saying all he'll get is pity if he attends, not something he wants.

"I'm not too cool about being around people right now. Randy's family reached out a couple of times, but I don't feel comfortable being around them. They look at me like they think I'm responsible."

"How could that be?"

"I don't know, Doc. You tell me. I'm still seeing Dr. Johnson for therapy every week."

"How's that going?"

"Okay," he says. "Good."

* * *

Fran is setting up the coffee service in the cafeteria, stacking paper filters filled with coffee next to an enormous stainless steel coffee urn. There are trays of cookies, four pies, and three layer cakes. Two older women, veteran wives, are distributing tissue boxes and small vases of flowers to each table. Fran's brought enough food and coffee to feed an army. Eddie rumbles into the room pulling a dolly loaded with cold drinks and ice. He unloads the dolly, pours the ice into a cooler, and lifts it onto the counter with a theatrical grunt.

"Is that it? Anything else?" Fran shakes her head. "Then I'm out of here. If I stay any longer I'll get estrogen poisoning." He rumbles back down the hall dragging the dolly behind him.

The chief arrives first. I'm surprised to see that she's dressed in the class-A uniform usually reserved for important ceremonies and funerals. She introduces herself to Fran and Fran's friends, Irma and Lillian, as though it isn't patently obvious that she is the police chief. She thanks them for coming and for the food and flowers, but declines to eat or drink anything. Outside, the night is gloomy. Our reflections stare back at us from the windows that line the wall along the street. Headlights from passing cars illuminate a fine drizzle. We sit and wait in silence listening to the coffee urn percolate and the clock tick.

Fran looks at her watch. "Has anyone checked? Is the outside door to the lobby unlocked? I'll go." She bustles out of the room.

If no one shows up, I'm going to have egg all over my face. I've finally latched onto to something to do and it's a bust. I got fifteen "yes, I'll be there" responses. They couldn't all have changed their minds. A small movie plays in my head. The association president emailing the entire membership, telling them not to let their wives or their girlfriends come to this meeting. Warning them about gossip and God knows what else he thinks happens when a group of unsupervised women get together.

Fran comes back through the door, followed by a line of mostly young and mostly pretty women. "Someone forgot to tell the front desk people we were having an evening event." She looks at me, the suspect "someone," and I interpret her look to mean that I'm a total idiot.

Irma and Lillian jump to their feet and get to work greeting everyone. A small traffic jam builds at the doorway as each woman stops to fill out a name tag, shuffling raincoats, umbrellas, and handbags. The chief stands next to me. We shake each woman's hand as she files by. The wives I've seen in therapy avert their eyes fearful that any mutual recognition between us would be a giveaway, a clue that all was not well at home. The only woman to greet me directly is MaryAnne Forester, Tom Rutgers' girlfriend. I notice a small diamond ring on her left hand, perhaps because she's waving it in my face. I do the right thing and acknowledge it.

"Are you and Tom engaged now? Congratulations." I wonder if they have solved their problems or if Tom has simply given in to inertia. MaryAnne flashes a satisfied smile and takes a seat with three other women. It doesn't take long before she is showing them her ring and they are responding with the obligatory oohs and aaahs. I wonder how many regret the choice they made to marry into this profession because, when it comes to law enforcement, you don't just marry the man, you marry the job as well.

If I married Frank, it would be different. Contractors have problems—dissatisfied clients, clients who won't pay their bills, subcontractors who don't show up—but they don't live life in a fishbowl. Neighbors don't bang on their doors asking them to threaten unruly children with jail time if they don't behave. Realtors don't sell houses with the promise that the neighborhood is really safe because a contractor lives next door.

The chief stands and there is an instant hush. "I salute you," she says raising her hand to her head. "You are the backbone of this organization. Without you to hold down the fort while your loved ones are working, we would not be able to provide the community with the service it deserves. Your efforts, your fears, your sacrifices, and your children's sacrifices are invisible to the public. But let me reassure you, they are not invisible to me."

Someone sniffles. Several others have tears in their eyes. This kind of acknowledgement is rare.

"Our department has been through the worst thing that can happen, the death of one of our own. Healing will take time. Coming here tonight to share your grief and your fears is part of that healing. So please, take advantage of this evening. Talk openly with each other about your concerns. Don't hold back. Feel free to say whatever's on your minds. I have just a few remarks to make and then I'll leave you in Dr. Meyerhoff's hands."

She's not just being polite, she's acknowledging without saying so that most of the women present have likely been warned by their mates to be quiet and not ask any stupid questions, especially in front of the chief. She gestures to Fran and her two friends. "These three women are all seasoned veteran wives who have graciously volunteered their time to share their experiences, good and bad, with you. I want to thank them and you for coming tonight, in the rain and in the dark. I know that many of you have jobs of your own, many of you have childcare issues, and some of you have both. I want this meeting to mean something for the future. Your futures and the department's future. So please, speak openly. Get to know each other, if you don't already. Law enforcement families need each other because, as you know from recent experience, when bad things happen, your loved ones will be called into work. This is why it is so important that you have extended social support." She puts her hands together in a gesture of gratitude. "Thank you for your attention. Have a good evening." She leaves, followed by a soft round of applause.

I'm up next, mostly to introduce our panel of veteran wives. I look at the women's faces in front of me. If Rich Spelling were here, he would have been the only man in the room. There is a noise behind me. A tall, slender, blond woman in a winter-white wool suit and high heels stands at the door, as though she just stepped off the cover of Vogue. The rest of us are dressed in jeans or casual slacks. Fran is wearing a new sweatshirt.

"Excuse me, am I in the right place? I was looking for the family meeting."

Her question is disingenuous. Women make up less than ten percent of law enforcement. It would be hard to mistake this group of women for anything else.

She steps forward. "I'm Jean Pence, Jay Pence's wife."

What is it with these alliterative names? Mark, Melinda, and Milo, my ex and his new little family, Rich and Randy, now Jean and Jay. Who invited her anyway? I sent invitations to the line level only. No one in management is likely to die in the line of duty unless they're murdered by a homicidal subordinate, which would accurately describe my current state of mind. That rat fink Pence has sent his wife to spy on me.

"Fran, why don't you get the women to introduce themselves and then start the panel? I'll be back in a minute," I say over my shoulder as I muster a welcoming smile and walk toward Jean Pence.

She's like a snow queen, blond and glittery, with a sparkling smile faker than mine. She holds out her hand. The diamond in her wedding band is the size of an ice cube. I wonder if it's as phony as she appears to be.

"I am so sorry," I say, extending my hand. "I'm Dr. Dot Meyerhoff, department psychologist and the organizer of tonight's event. There must have been a misunderstanding. This meeting is for the families of line-level officers only. If we had the families of superior officers present, it would inhibit the conversation. I'm sure you understand."

She smiles even more broadly. "Actually, I don't understand. For one thing, Jay thought it would be a good idea for me to come. Managers have feelings, too, and so do their wives. For another, I thought, being married to him for so long, I could help. After all, Jay is under stress too. Officer Spelling's death has been terrible for him. All that responsibility."

She's exaggerating or Jay Pence is one of two things: a two-faced liar or the kind of man who puts on a good front at work and then collapses into a heap at home.

"I appreciate your concern and I don't mean to indicate that managers are immune to stress. They are anything but. Still, the fact remains that the young women who came here tonight would be intimidated by your presence. They would be fearful that anything they said would reflect badly on their husbands. Think back to the early days of your marriage. How do you think you would have felt if Jay, Captain Pence, was having frightening nightmares, and you wanted to talk about them, but you were sitting next to the wife of the man who sits on his promotional board or writes his performance evaluations?"

She contemplates my question. "But I can promise you and the other women that whatever they say is our secret. Zippo lippo." She draws a long, silvered fingernail across her mouth.

"I'm sure you can be trusted." I'm lying through my teeth and I hope it doesn't show. "But, sadly, I doubt anyone would take the chance. You know how it is, they've all been warned by their husbands not to talk about personal things. It's an act of courage that they've shown up tonight. I don't want to do anything to jeopardize their fragile trust. You do understand, don't you?"

She gives this some thought.

"I appreciate that you took the time to come here," I say. Not to mention whatever it cost her to get her hair and nails done for the occasion.

"I could help. I am a veteran wife, like those other women."

"Why don't we think about that? Perhaps sometime in the future. Maybe I could convene a gathering of management families."

She lights up like a Christmas tree. "I could have everyone over to my house. For cocktails and a buffet." This woman is either unclear on the concept of a debriefing—we provide food, but it's not a party—or desperate to do something with her life besides waxing, tanning, and working out at the gym. "I like that idea. Let's you and I get together soon and make a plan. We could have lunch." Whatever it is that floats her boat, this exchange is apparently enough to send her out the door on a face-saving mission.

* * *

By the time I get back in the room, the discussion is underway. Fran flashes me a thumbs up. Several women are dabbing at their faces with Kleenex while others are patting their teary friends on the back. Not the high fiving, back slapping that men do to connect with each other. More like mothers instinctively reaching out to comfort an unhappy child. These women share a lot with each other. Tonight would be a big success if they can recognize that they don't have to suffer in silence. Isolation is what damages police families.

"I have a question for the doctor," MaryAnne Forester raises her hand, the one with the ring on it, and leaves it in the air just a second or two longer than need be. "One of the things that worries me is when Tom has to work with somebody he doesn't trust, because that person doesn't know what to do in an emergency and can't be counted on. I don't mean to speak ill of the dead, but that's what happened when he worked with Randy Spelling and I'm worried it will happen again."

There's a low buzz in the room. I don't know where she's going with this and apparently no one else does either.

"Does anyone else feel this way?" She looks around. Most of the women have become deeply interested in their coffee cups.

"Well, I'm going to say it, if no one else will."

I think back to the time I visited her and Tom at their home after the incident at the creek. How she took it upon herself to tell me what Tom himself didn't want to admit—that he was having nightmares and was afraid to work with Randy Spelling. Whistle blowing seems to be MaryAnn's calling.

"Randy Spelling was not a fit officer. She got Tom hurt and got herself killed. It could happen again. What's the guarantee that it won't? Everybody knew she was a bad officer and no one did anything about it. I appreciate that the chief came here tonight, but she's part of the problem."

"How?" I say.

"She's going to hire more women. She said so. In the newspaper."

"Wait a minute," I say. Fran and her friends are looking panicked. "What is your point?" I don't like MaryAnne Forester. I didn't like her when I first met her and I don't like her now.

"Women shouldn't be police officers. Dispatchers, okay, but not police officers. Randy was way too emotional. Even her husband said she'd be a wreck after every shift."

"Rich Spelling talked to you about Randy?"

"He tried to do more than talk. And not just with me. I don't think they were getting along. Everybody knew it." She turns to the group for confirmation. Most avert their eyes.

I don't know exactly what MaryAnne's agenda is, but I doubt she's as worried about officer safety as she is about the tenuous hold she has on Tom Rutgers. If I don't get in front of her, she will have hijacked this entire evening, turned it into the gossip session that the association president, Jay Pence, and three-quarters of KPD are expecting.

"MaryAnne," I say. "This isn't appropriate. Let's talk privately later."

"No," she says. "We need to talk about this now. Everybody's worried about the same thing, even if they won't say so."

"This is malicious gossip. I don't know what you're doing or why, but if you don't stop, I will have to ask you to leave." There's an audible gasp in the room. She's forced my hand. Maneuvered me into a fight. I look like an idiot. First I sponsor a meeting for family members and then I throw two of them out.

"I'm only saying what everyone else is thinking," she says. "No one else has the nerve." And she sits down, hard, and crosses her arms over her chest, ring finger facing outward. She's going to be the kind of wife who wants to run the department from her living room, giving statements to the newspaper, writing nasty notes to the city council. Embarrassing her husband with her incessant public histrionics.

Fran jumps in: "Any other questions? Perhaps on another topic?"

* * *

We're exhausted by the time everyone leaves. Eddie arrives to help us clean up. He senses our mood and asks what happened.

"Not a complete disaster," Fran says, "but it came close. What do you think, Doc? You look a little down in the mouth."

I tell Eddie about MaryAnne Forester and her allegations. How I don't give an ounce of credence to her mean-spirited insinuations. And how tempted I was to ask the other women in the room if Rich Spelling ever made a pass at any of them. Restraint is not my strong suit, so I was pleased to have at least one thing to boast about.

Eddie drops the box of leftover food he's hefting back on the counter. "Whiskey, tango, foxtrot." He shakes his head. Fran explains what this means to Irma and Lillian who know it already because they are married to cops. "You didn't ask if Spelling put a move on anyone in the room? Don't quit your day job, Doc. You'd stink as a cop."

"What are you talking about?"

"We got a murder investigation on our hands, no time to be polite." It's so automatic for him to say "we" even though he's still on leave and not even remotely involved in the search for Randy's murderer.

"First of all, I don't trust MaryAnne Forester. Second of all, it's not my job to investigate Randy's murder, even if I thought her allegations had some bearing on it."

"If Spelling was a skirt chaser, that sheds a whole new light on the situation, don't you think?" We look at each other and say nothing. He picks up the box again. "Up to you, but if you really want to be helpful, here's what you should do. Tell Rutgers to get his fucking balls out of Forester's pocketbook and run while he still can."

CHAPTER THIRTY-FOUR

By the time I get to work the next morning there are eight messages on my voice mail. The first three are from wives thanking me for the family meeting. The fourth is from Dr. Bernstein asking me if I would be willing to test her two grandsons to see if they have the potential to murder anyone. She's convinced that psychometric testing would be mitigating evidence if her grandsons are ever formally charged with Randy's murder. I want to tell her that psychometric testing alone isn't a reliable predictor of violence. She's still desperately looking for a way to protect her grandsons from something that hasn't yet happened and may never. The chief wants to know how last night went and asks me to give a short report at Monday's staff meeting and Frank wants to know if I remember him. "I'm the tall horny guy with blue eyes, grayish hair, and a beard."

The only call I return is to Frank. "Got any plans for the weekend?" I ask. "Want to go to a concert?"

* * *

"This is not what I expected, exactly. You do take me to the most interesting places." Frank and I have just wormed our way inside the Boom Room, a rundown dance club in an equally rundown part of East Kenilworth. It's small, cramped, and smells like stale beer and the need for larger bathrooms. I'm here because one, I'm curious. Two, it can't hurt to be friendly to 1704T. It's not like I'm developing informants, but who knows, someday, I just might need their help. And three, I want to get another glimpse of Darnell Taylor. He seems a cipher, a lost boy with no home, no obvious family, and no job. As far as I can tell, the only things he does have are a lousy reputation and the tattoo of a dead girl on his chest.

Frank is looking around, his eyes wider than usual.

"You were expecting maybe Brahms, Bach, and Beethoven?"

I grab his hand and we squeeze through the crowd, trying to get closer to the stage. I'm not exactly sure how I'm going to explain this to the chief at Monday's staff meeting. I can hardly explain to myself why I'm disregarding her instructions to stay out of the way. I rationalize that 1704T is only the opening act and as soon as they finish, we'll leave. If we can. There must be three hundred people jammed in a club designed for 150. All of them looking at us. No chairs, no tables, no fire exits that I can see. Just a multicolored sea of teenagers taking pictures of each other with their cell phones. We're not the only white people in the room, but we sure are the oldest.

"When is this thing going to start?" Frank yells in my ear over the noise. "I need a beer."

"There must be a bar in here somewhere. I can smell it."

"Nobody here looks old enough to drink. But I bet we could score a little pot without a problem. Maybe even something stronger."

Suddenly, we are standing in the dark. Light beams flash across the ceiling. There is a blast of sound like the beating of a rusty metal drum as 1704T bursts onto the stage as though they're being chased from behind. They're wearing oversized football jerseys, baggy pants, baseball caps turned to the back or the side, and those enormous sneakers. Their thick gold chains and pendants bounce and flash on their chests as they skip, or something that looks like skipping on bad knees, and scatter across the stage. The tallest boy yells into his microphone, "We 1704T," and the crowd roars back. Colored lights sweep over us. If there are undercover cops in the room, and I have no doubt there are, I don't know how they could spot Darnell in this crowd.

There is something compelling about the group's relentless

pounding of words. Something about it connects to our earliest experiences of primitive human rhythms; it is like a pulse, a heartbeat, an endless exchange of breath in and out of our lungs. The crowd moves in sync, mouthing every word of what sounds like an endless rant, although neither Frank nor I can understand anything but the word "fuck" which accents every beat. The group alternates between rapping and rhythmically twisting their bodies in ways that defy belief, spinning on their heads without regard for their young spinal cords. I flash on a rehab center where I once interned in grad school. The spinal cord patients strapped into wheelchairs, their heads and limbs flopping uselessly.

The tall boy jumps from the stage onto the dance floor, followed by the rest of the group. They push through the crowd, leading their cheering fans forward in a raucous conga line. This is Mardi Gras, Chinese New Year, and Macy's Thanksgiving Day parade rolled into one. The leader spots me, raises his eyebrows in surprise and flashes a thumbs up before pushing Frank and me in front of him right into the moving spotlight.

* * *

"That was fun. I think." Frank says as we settle in his living room with a glass of wine. "So, what was it this time?"

"I told you. I thought it would be a hoot. Something different."

He raises an eyebrow. "That's all, just something different? I don't think so." He eyes me again. "Out with it."

"KPD has got their eyes on these kinds of clubs. You know, underage drinking violations. Sounded interesting. I don't know anything about the hip hop culture, so I thought we'd tag along. Watch the action. Maybe learn something."

"All that to catch underage drinkers? Sounds like a poor use of my taxes." He leans forward and looks me in the eye. "My guess is that our little outing has something to do with Randy Spelling's murder."

I take a sip of wine. Hold my breath and then take another.

"Well, does it?" Frank is getting red in the face.

"They were looking for the missing homicide suspect."

"And you could help how?"

"I'm an extra pair of eyes. Nothing more. I've seen him before at headquarters. If I had told you ahead of time, you wouldn't have gone with me and you would have been mad at me if I went by myself."

"Now I'm mad at you for lying."

"I didn't lie, I just didn't give you the whole picture."

"Now I'm mad because you manipulated me."

"It was perfectly safe. The place was full of undercover cops. You said so yourself, we had a good time. If I had told you beforehand, you'd have been worried the whole evening."

"You miss my point."

"I really appreciate your going with me. Don't be such a worrywart. Think of it as a little adventure. Nothing bad happened because we went and, I promise you, nothing will."

CHAPTER THIRTY-FIVE

The projection screen in the staff room is pulled down and Pence is fiddling with a laptop as I take my seat.

"Well," he says, "if it isn't the famous Dr. Meyerhoff, our very own celebrity shrink. And, coincidentally, the first item on our agenda. Too bad the chief is going to miss this meeting. She's taking a few hours of personal leave. Never fear, I'll fill her in the minute she gets back." He flips off the overhead lights. The computer hums softly as it wakes up.

"Buckle your seat belts," Pence says. He aims the remote and clicks. "I hope everybody here is over eighteen, because this is an R-rated performance." A lopsided video splays across the screen. "KPD presents Dr. Dot Meyerhoff shaking her booty at the Boom Room." The camera moves haphazardly from floor to ceiling. The soundtrack is a blurry mix of metal on metal mixed with shouts and grunts. "Not only is she shaking her booty, she's leading the line. And now we see her grinding her booty against a juvenile male identified as the leader of 1704T."

"Stop it." I jump to my feet. "Where did you get this?"

"Facebook. You've gone viral."

"I don't look at Facebook."

"Well, my wife does. She loves this stuff, Facebook, Twitter, Instagram. You remember my wife don't you, Doctor? Jean Pence? The blond-haired woman you kicked out of the family meeting."

"I didn't kick her out. I asked her to leave because the meeting was for line-level families. She was only there because you sent her to spy on me. No one would have talked in front of her."

"You are confused, Doctor. All in a snit about privacy one day and flaunting your booty all over Facebook the next." He loves using the word booty, letting every letter roll off his tongue.

"I did not flaunt myself. I didn't even know anyone was taking pictures of me."

"What century do you live in? That's all kids do anymore. Take pictures of themselves and each other and put them on the Internet."

"Is that why you're humiliating me? Because I asked your wife to leave a meeting she wasn't invited to?"

"I don't need to humiliate you, Doctor. You're doing a bang-up job of it yourself."

"That's enough." The chief has been standing quietly in back of the room. She looks at me. "What were you doing at the concert?"

"Looking for Darnell Taylor."

"Did you find him?"

"No, and apparently neither did anyone else."

Pence's lips are puckered with rage. "We need to address this now," he says. "The entire community and the police association are going to demand that you do something about her." He points at me although next to the chief I'm the only other woman in the room. "She sent us on a wild-goose chase. Thousands of dollars wasted on overtime. We put officers in danger based on her bogus informants."

"Then why didn't you send someone who knows what they're doing to interview them?"

"We didn't know who they were. Remember? You couldn't tell us. Wouldn't tell us."

"If you had, they would have told Darnell and scared him off."

"Enough," says the chief. "This is my responsibility. I made the decision to go with Dr. Meyerhoff's information. And I made the decision to deploy officers to the concert. Second guessing my decisions, Captain Pence, is not helpful unless you're trying to amass evidence about my incompetence."

* * *

If no good deed goes unpunished, where's my punishment? I wait three days to be summoned to chief's office and fired. I'm not sleeping and I'm eating everything that isn't nailed down. Now I know, or think I know, how Randy must have felt getting off with what seemed to her like a slap on the wrist. When the punishment doesn't fit the crime, all a person is left with is self-punishment.

Nothing happens, no phone call, no letter, no email. It's Thursday. I don't think I can make it through the weekend without talking to the chief. I need to apologize again. Plead for my job. I put cops in jeopardy, I put the investigation in jeopardy, and I put Frank and myself in harm's way.

When I can't stand it any longer, I call her. She thanks me for calling and professes to understand that my intentions were well meaning if not well reasoned. She's not going to punish me or fire me. All she asks is that I observe boundaries and never again interfere with police business. I've been going nuts with worry and her affect is so flat, it's like talking to a carp. She wishes me a good weekend and we hang up. I sit in my office staring at my blank computer screen. I was expecting to be fired, but what I got was a slap on the wrist.

CHAPTER THIRTY-SIX

Frank and I are going to have dinner at my house Friday night. As usual, I have nothing in the refrigerator and at week's end I'm too brain-dead to think about cooking, unlike Frank who's always whipping up some last-minute fabulous meal from leftovers. The only leftovers in my refrigerator have long since passed the expiration date. I call Fran from my office and order one of her meatloaves, with mashed potatoes, salad, and pie. A perfect counterpoint to the dreary winter weather and the never-ending rain.

"I'll pick it up on my way home from the office," I say.

"Hold on a minute. Eddie wants to talk to you, but first he has to dry his hands."

"Yo, Doc," he says. "I'll deliver this for you. My treat."

"No need. I drive right past Fran's on my way home."

"You may not have a need, Doc," he says, "but I do."

* * *

Frank lights a fire in my fireplace using some pressed-wood logs I bought at Home Depot.

"Why don't you let me bring you some wood? I'm a remodeling contractor, remember? I have tons of scrap wood to burn. It's not beautiful to look at, but neither are these phony things." He pours me a glass of the pinot noir he brought and because he knows me, he's also supplied cheese, crackers, and a bowl of olives. "Nothing fancy," he says. "But we shouldn't drink on an empty stomach." By the time Eddie knocks on my door, we're halfway through the bottle of wine and I'm no longer hungry.

Eddie's carrying enough food for six people. Frank takes the boxes into the kitchen. Eddie hangs his wet rain gear on a hook in the hallway and walks into the living in his stocking feet.

"Great night for a fire." He sits down. "That your boyfriend?"

"Haven't you met?"

"I don't remember, but then I don't remember a lot of stuff."

Frank comes back into the room with a wine glass. He and Eddie shake hands and Frank starts to pour him some wine.

"Not for me, thanks," Eddie says. "I'm off the sauce. Better for all of us if I stay that way. Okay to talk?" Eddie tilts his head toward Frank.

"Depends. What's going on?"

"Maybe Rutgers' girlfriend is on to something. I got friends at the sheriff's department, so I asked them a few questions about this Rich Spelling."

"You didn't," I say. "You're going to get in trouble."

"I'm already in trouble. I told you, I'm going bug nuts slinging burgers. People think I'm washed up. I'm not washed up. I still got what it takes. I just need to prove it to that damn chief."

"And you think disregarding the terms of your administrative leave will put you on her good side?"

Frank pours Eddie a glass of water. "Do you guys need some privacy?"

"Yes," I say.

"No," Eddie says at the same time. "I talk so loud you could hear me all the way to Timbuktu. So sit down, enjoy your wine. Sorry to interrupt." He turns back to me. "Here's what I know. Spelling has a temper. That's no news. You saw what he did to Darnell Taylor. He said he didn't do it; I say bullshit. Taylor just offed his wife. What do you expect?" He looks at Frank for some kind of confirmation, as though any man would understand Rich's behavior. Frank's face is hard to read. "Rumor has it that Spelling's a skirt chaser. Either that or he blows a lot of steam in the locker room. Hard to tell. Guys lie to each other all the time." He turns to Frank again and winks. "Fits half the COs I know."

"What's a CO?" Frank asks.

"Correctional officer, jailer, new jack, screw."

"You're talking about the same man I saw at the funeral? You think he murdered his wife?" Frank shakes his head. "That can't be. He was devastated, falling apart."

"You took your boyfriend to the funeral? What is that, your idea of date night?" Eddie shifts to face Frank. "Listen, buddy. The doc here is a BWB, but sometimes she's unclear on the concept."

"What's a BWB?" I ask.

"Babe with brains. But just so you know, Frank, better be on your good behavior. The Doc swings a mean ten-pound weight."

Frank looks at me. "Later," I say.

He turns to Eddie. "Let me get this straight. Just because the man lost his temper with the person who killed his wife, and may or may not be unfaithful, doesn't prove anything. Like you said, that description fits a lot of men." I make note of this. Frank's never given me reason to be afraid of him or worry that he would cheat behind my back. My girlfriends think he's a real catch, but they also thought my ex was a catch and look how that turned out.

"What'll I do next?" Eddie stands. "Darnell's in the wind. You probably chased him off with that caper at the Boom Room. The video went viral."

Frank's eyebrows go way up and his eyes nearly pop out of their sockets.

"What video?"

"Later for that, too," I say.

"Doc, I need to get back on the job. Help me out here. Find me something to do before I lose my mind. What's left of it."

* * *

The minute Eddie leaves, Frank tells me to sit down. "What the hell is going on?"

"Something came up at the family night. Something that may indicate that maybe Rich Spelling played around."

"That's not what I'm talking about. I want to know about the video."

I sigh. "Pour me another glass of wine first, please." He does and I tell him about the video.

"Once again, you're sticking your nose in where it doesn't belong. Only this time, you've dragged me into it. What if something bad had happened at that club? What if you actually ran into that Darnell guy who's running from the police because he's accused of murder?" Frank is almost shouting. "What if one of my clients saw me in that video?"

I try to say something and he tells me to shut up. Frank has never spoken to me like that before. I don't like it. My first impulse is to fight back; my second impulse is to burst into tears.

"What if we got into a fight and I had to protect you? Look at me. How well do you think I'd do fighting a bunch of teen aged ninjas, probably all armed."

"I told you," I say. "There were undercover cops everywhere, they would have helped us. I felt safe."

"Bullshit. That place was so crowded we would've been dead before they got to us."

"Second of all, Randy Spelling was my client. The police aren't getting anywhere. I want to know what happened to her."

"It would be nice if you cared as much about the living as you do about the dead." We sit silently for a moment breathing heavily. Arguing can be aerobic. Outside the wind and the rain slap against the living room window.

"As for the video, you're not in it. Just me. I've seen it twice now."

"You don't know that. There were a dozen kids, maybe more, with their cell phones out. All of them taking pictures and videos. I have a business and a reputation to uphold. Do you think my clients would trust me after seeing me on Facebook hanging out with a bunch of juvenile hip hoppers? How comfortable would they be letting me have the keys to their houses, allowing me to be there when their teenage daughters come home from school?"

"But you weren't in the video."

"I could have been and that's my point. You only think about yourself and your goddamn cops. I don't even come up on your radar."

"That's not true, Frank. I love you. I don't want to hurt you. I'm sorry."

"The next time. If there is one. Think first, then maybe you won't have anything to be sorry for." He stands up. "I'm going home."

"But we have meatloaf."

"I'm not hungry anymore."

CHAPTER THIRTY-SEVEN

The county jail is a testimony to eyesore architecture. It looks more like an air conditioner than a building designed to house human beings. Once it was surrounded by walnut orchards and citrus groves. Now it's the crown jewel of a dizzying sprawl of cheesy sub-developments and strip malls. A public bus stops in front, transporting school children and sex offenders to their destinations. I park behind the bus stop and watch as a small group of weary women slowly dismount, carefully breaching the gap between the bus and the sidewalk. They heft shopping bags over their shoulders and, without looking up, turn toward the well-worn front walk.

I line up at security and wait impatiently to pass through the metal detector. Bright red signs posted on the wall warn me that I am subject to being searched and not permitted to bring weapons beyond this point. There's an argument at the head of the line between a guard and a gray-haired woman who appears to be someone's mother. A second guard intervenes, speaking Spanish, and pulls the woman aside. As I pass he is emptying the contents of her parcel on top of a steel table, shaking his head and pointing to a sign that says inmates may not receive food, packages, or reading material from visitors. The woman starts to cry.

We move slowly forward, me, the sorry women beside me, and an occasional briefcase-carrying attorney. I show the deadpan guard at the end of the line my KPD security badge and ask if I might have a tour of the facility. He looks at me like I've just landed from Mars, points to a wooden chair that's shoved up against the wall and picks up the phone. "Wait here," he says and goes back to stand at his station.

Jail tours are evidently low priority. I wait twenty minutes before a door to my left opens and a uniformed guard steps out into the hall. "Tour bus starting now, tickets please," she says. I stand up. "Welcome to the fun house." She presses a large black button that is anchored to a metal wall plaque and turns to face one of the many cameras that are mounted on the ceiling. The nearest camera rotates with a low buzz until it fixes on us. "Central control wants to see my smiling face before they let us in."

"I thought people want to break out of the jail, not in," I say.

There's a loud click and she pulls open a heavy metal door that leads into a long hallway. Once on the other side of the door she turns and shakes my hand. Her name tag reads Foster, but she prefers to be called Jackie. She's an enormous woman with short, blunt-cut gray hair, sixty extra pounds straining the seams of her uniform and bulging over the top of her duty belt. She looks mannish, despite a beautiful face that's all dimples. I wonder what it's like to be a woman working in a man's jail. Maybe she wants to be as big as her charges. No doubt safety trumps fashion and skinny women with long hair are at risk for being grabbed and overpowered.

"So, what brings you here today and what do you want to see?"

I explain who I am and that even though I've been consulting with KPD for over a year I've never had the opportunity to visit the jail. Since booking suspects into jail is a routine part of everyday life at KPD, I thought I'd benefit from getting to know what the place was like.

We walk down the long hall to yet another locked door. The concrete block walls are painted a sunny yellow and there are office doors on either side. "Mahogany row," she says using the familiar slang for the administrative wing.

Once again we go through the ritual buzzing and security clearing. "Central control is on the second floor. Staffed two at a time, always. They got two cameras aimed at every door. We can go there first if you want. It's pretty interesting."

"Randy Spelling worked at KPD," I say. "I understand her husband works here at the jail." She stops, turns, and looks at me over the top of her glasses.

"Yeah, so?"

"Do you know him?"

"Not really. He works another shift on a different floor from mine. Why are you asking?"

I can hear people yelling in the distance. Now that we've passed over the border between administration and detention, the air smells of sweat, disinfectant, and human waste.

"I did know Randy though. We were in WIES together." She pronounces the word "wise." "She was a cute kid. Wet behind the ears, but she tried hard."

WIES, Women in Emergency Services, is an organization for women cops, fire fighters, and EMTs. We meet every other month to help each other prepare for promotions, deal with harassment, EEO complaints, and all the many hurdles women in law enforcement face.

"Did she ever talk about her shooting?"

Jackie gives me the once over. "Are you a reporter?"

"I told you. I'm the KPD psychologist."

"She told us she saw some shrink after the shooting. Told us the shrink was making goo-goo eyes at Rich. Was that you?"

"Absolutely not. I hardly knew Rich. There was another therapist involved. For couples' counseling."

Jackie adjusts something on her duty belt. Correctional officers used to carry a pound of keys and jingle whenever they moved. Electronics has replaced all that. "I went to her funeral. We all did. That SOB Darnell Taylor killed her. He's been in here a dozen times. I'm surprised he got out with only a beating."

"Do you have any idea why Randy would put herself in harm's way? Not take someone with her when she went to talk to Lakeisha Gibbs' family?"

"Is that what she did? I just knew she was murdered, I never knew the details."

"It's almost like she was asking to be hurt." I'm playing this like Columbo. Stupid. Naïve. Innocent. It worked for him, every episode.

Jackie motions me through a side door into a small room with a coffeepot, a vending machine, a sink, three tables, and a bulletin board. She leans against the Formica counter.

"After the shooting, Randy was not a happy camper. I'm not saying she was suicidal. Nothing like that. Never crossed my mind. But she was mixed up."

"How?"

"She felt like crap for killing that kid. Who wouldn't? But there was more. She and Rich weren't getting along. I told her to see a marriage counselor. That's probably when she found Dr. Goo-Goo Eyes."

CHAPTER THIRTY-EIGHT

"This is the confidential voice mail for Dr. Marvel Johnson. I'm so glad you called and sorry I can't come to the phone right now. Please leave a message and your phone number, slow and clear, and I'll call you back as soon as I'm able. Have a great day and be safe." I hang up and call back again. She picks up.

"Screening your calls, Dr. Johnson?"

"No, not at all. I just couldn't get to the phone in time." Her voice changes to a twitter. "How have you been? How is everything?"

"I want to talk to you."

She loses the twitter. "About what?"

"I'd prefer to talk in person. How's five this afternoon?"

"I have a client. Sorry."

"Six?"

"That won't work either. I have appointments booked through the evening."

"Are you seeing anyone at ten p.m.?"

"You're not serious."

"Good, I'll be there at ten." She starts to protest, and I hang up, planning to be in her waiting room long before that, just in case she has an opportunistically scheduled last-minute cancellation.

* * *

Dr. Johnson's office is located in one of Kenilworth's few high-rise office buildings, all copper-tinted glass and steel. Her waiting room is furnished with antique rugs and custom-designed chairs.

Beautiful prints and Japanese textiles hang on the wall. Frank tells me Midwestern taste runs to pheasant motifs and Native American paraphernalia. No wonder the marvelous Marvel Johnson is overjoyed that her caseload is full to the brim. She's probably up to her ears in debt for the furnishings as well as the services of the decorator who chose them.

"So nice to see you again, Dr. Meyerhoff." She strides across the waiting room, her hand extended toward me. A streak of pettiness keeps me from shaking it. I reach for my purse instead. "Come in," she says, unfazed. "Would you like something? Water, tea, cappuccino? I just bought one of those machines with the little capsules. You can have caffeine, decaf, flavored—"

"Shut up and sit down," I say.

I am more startled than she is at the tone of my voice.

"Is there something going on between you and Rich Spelling?"

Her mouth drops open and then closes. "What do you mean? I was his therapist. You know that."

"Was? You're not his therapist anymore?"

Her face tightens just slightly. "No, not anymore. We terminated our work."

"Why?"

"How is that your concern?"

"The average period of mourning for the death of a spouse is about three years. Randy dies and Rich terminates therapy barely a month later? I know you don't believe in prolonged terminations, but that seems pretty abrupt."

She hesitates. Bites her lower lip. "Sorry to say, but I wasn't able to help him any further. Sometimes you just get to a point with a client when you don't seem to be making any progress. It's unethical to continue taking their money. You know, like how it was with you and Randy."

An unrestrained flood of rage urges me out of my chair and across the room so that I can slap Marvel Johnson's face until she spins uncontrollably in her pricey Herman Miller Aeron chair. I take a deep breath, and then another until the urge passes.

"Randy and I were working well together until you interfered."

"You were stalled. Therapy wasn't working. Randy told me so."

"And you believed her? She was manipulating you. She wanted to apologize to Ms. Gibbs, a very dangerous, possibly suicidal thing to do, as we both now know all too well." I watch her face for something, signs of remorse, fear, whatever. I get nothing.

"You actually encouraged her with your ten steps to healing PTSD crap. Making amends. That's what got her killed. Plus you padded your therapy hours with the world's longest fitness-for-duty evaluation and then you violated every ethical guideline in the book for patient transfer."

She backs up a little in her chair. "What do you want?"

"The truth." Her mouth settles into a grim line.

"I don't know what you're talking about."

"Then figure it out, Dr. Goo-Goo eyes."

A small tic begins pulsing under her left eye.

"Dr. Goo Who? I don't know what you mean."

"Don't you now? Are you, were you having an affair with Rich Spelling?"

"Who told you that?"

"The same person that Randy told."

"Randy was a very disturbed woman."

"I see. You believed her when she told you that therapy with me was going nowhere. But when she told someone you were making eyes at her husband, then you accuse her of lying. How convenient. Randy had PTSD. She wasn't psychotic. I think she lied to you and told the truth to her friend."

"Get out of my office." Marvel stands. "Now." Her voice tilts up at the edges, with just the hint of a whine. Next she'll start pouting and stamp her foot.

Silence is a therapeutic strategy that works the same with Marvel as it does with my clients. The longer I hold my tongue and stay in my seat, the more ridiculous she looks standing up, pointing at the door. I focus on my breathing. She focuses on me, as if glaring at me would shock me into speaking. Finally she sits again, primly, with her legs crossed at the ankles and her hands cupped in her lap. She sighs loudly, getting ready to patronize me with some little crumb of information.

"I'm going to assume that this is a confidential consultation between peers and for this reason only, I will present some aspects of my clinical work."

She is not my peer, not even close. It irritates me, not only that she thinks she is, but that I even care what she thinks.

"Rich was very lonely; Randy was caught up in her own problems. She didn't have any time for him. He felt abandoned and this activated memories of childhood neglect. His father worked all the time and his mother was so depressed she couldn't get out of bed. She never cooked and sometimes forgot to pick him up after school. So he transferred his feelings to me. I was a surrogate for the love and attention he wasn't getting at home."

"His wife didn't understand him? What a novel reason to begin an affair. So tell me, what step in your ten-point plan to eternal happiness is fucking your therapist?"

"It is not necessary for you to be crude." She glares at me. "We did not have an affair. I wouldn't consider it. Rich was hard to work with, very concrete in his thinking. You must have seen that."

"Rich wasn't my client, Randy was." If he had been, maybe I would have seen through the veneer of aggrieved husband to the needy little boy underneath who couldn't stand not having Randy's full attention.

"Rich needed a distraction, something to do to keep busy." She sits straight in her chair like she's giving a book report to the teacher. "His department doesn't have a peer-support team. After Randy's shooting, he realized how much he and Randy could have used one. So he was going to start a team, and I was helping him. That's why I saw him extra times. At no charge. If Randy thought something else was going on, she was wrong. I'm surprised she even noticed."

"Let me make sure I understand. You were using Rich to help worm your way into his department."

"It was a survivor's mission. Making something positive out of something bad is a well-regarded therapeutic strategy. Part of his healing."

"Congratulations. Of all the self-serving rationalizations I've heard, this one takes the cake. The Board of Psychology will be fascinated."

"Do what you need to do. This is no longer my problem. I'm surrendering my California license to practice psychology and moving back to Nebraska."

"And why is that?"

She takes a large draft of air. "He tried to kiss me. I was shocked, believe me." I don't, of course. "That's when I realized what was happening. I didn't wait a minute. I told him that I couldn't be his therapist anymore. Or Randy's either. I told him that the ethical guidelines for psychotherapists are very clear about this, psychotherapy never includes sex."

"And then what happened?" Her face mottles.

"He asked what would happen if a therapist and patient fell in love?"

"What did you say?"

"I told him that if a therapist and client fall in love, guidelines say they have to wait a year after termination to see each other again and the therapist has to refer the client to an independent and objective clinician who has been recommended by a third-party therapist."

I wonder how Rich understood this potentially enticing bit of information. Given the special attention Marvel had already showered on him, my bet is that he took it as a barely disguised promise of things to come.

"You see, don't you? I was in complete accordance with all the ethical principles for psychologists."

"What I see is that you seem to have memorized the code of ethics."

"Adultery is wrong," she says. "Even if there were no guidelines, I have principles beyond those of earthly authorities." She refolds her hands. "Is there anything else?"

"Yes. Why are you moving back to Nebraska?" She takes another deep breath.

"After I explained everything, Rich still persisted. He wouldn't stop coming here or calling me. Even after Randy died, he'd just show up. I'd have another patient and there he'd be sitting in the waiting room. He wouldn't leave me alone. I felt like I was being stalked. I finally told him that if he didn't stop, I'd get a restraining order against him and that's when—" She stops. Closes her eyes. Her breathing is shallow.

"When what?"

"That's when he said, 'After what I've done so that we could be together?'"

My heart bangs in my chest and I have to force myself to keep breathing normally.

"What did you think he meant by that?"

"I was too scared to ask."

"You need to go to the police and tell them this."

"I can't break confidentiality."

"He may have been telling you that he killed Randy."

"If he did kill her, then he's already committed a crime. I'm not legally obligated to report a past crime."

"The police are convinced that a man named Darnell Taylor killed Randy, or that someone in the Gibbs family was responsible. You need to step forward and stop this. If you don't, somebody innocent could go to prison."

"It won't go that far."

"How do you know? At the very least the stain of the accusation will follow them and ruin any chances they have for a decent future."

"He'll kill me. If he killed Randy, he could kill me too. I've given notice to my landlord."

"He'll follow you."

"Oh, God," she says, her bravado dissolving into tears. "I'm scared, I don't know what to do." Her hands are shaking and for the first time she looks like what she really is and always has been—frightened, confused, and in over her head.

CHAPTER THIRTY-NINE

First thing in the morning I call the chief. Her secretary tells me she's taking some personal time off this week and won't be back until Monday, five days away. She's been taking more and more time away from the office. My bet is that she is wearing down from fighting off memories of her own incident. When traumatic memories come back, they come back with a wallop, dragging all the attached emotions with them. Then there's the strain of investigating Randy's death and the pending vote of no confidence. I tell the secretary that my call is urgent and ask if the chief has left an emergency number where she can be reached. "Sorry," she says, "but my instructions are to direct all calls to Captain Pence."

Frankly, I don't know a chief who wouldn't leave an emergency number unless they were out of the country. Even then they'd have email or texting or some other inescapable electronic chain to tether them to the job.

"If she calls in for messages, please ask her to get in touch with me. This is urgent."

"Did you hear the news?" the secretary says. "They've just arrested Darnell Taylor. He was hiding in the basement of a friend's house. Excuse me a minute." She puts me on hold. I can only hope that this time someone has the good sense to incarcerate Darnell someplace where Rich can't get to him.

"Captain Pence just came in. I'll transfer you."

I contemplate for a minute whether I should talk to Pence and tell him what I know or wait until the chief returns.

"Acting Chief Pence, how can I help you?" What a pompous ass. The chief is out for a few days of personal business and he announces himself as though he's already been anointed as her successor. When he realizes it's me on the phone, he drops his public-servant voice and reverts back to normal.

"I hear you have Darnell Taylor in custody," I say.

"So?"

"I have some information that may cast doubt on his guilt. I was going to talk with the chief, but since she's not available I can tell you."

"Do you have a hearing problem, Doctor? I told you once before, interfering with a police investigation is a criminal offense. If I were chief, I'd be seriously considering charging you."

"So you don't want to hear what I have to say?"

"Get a hearing aid," he says and hangs up.

That turned out the way I expected. Now what? Something Eddie Rimbauer once said to me floats into my mind. "Have a plan," he said. "Then have a backup plan because your first plan won't work."

* * *

I call Marvel. This time she picks up the minute she hears my voice. "This is what we're going to do," I tell her. "You don't get to vote on this. If you don't cooperate, I'm telling the police, the Board of Psychology, the newspapers, and anyone else I can think of that you were sexually involved with a client. I'll also write to the Board of Psychology in Nebraska so you won't be able to get a license there either."

"You have no right to threaten me. I thought we had a confidential patient consultation. If you say anything to anyone, you're guilty of violating confidentiality."

"Reread your Psychology Code of Ethics, Standard 1.05. I would be in violation if I failed to report you knowing that you've had an inappropriate relationship that harmed one client and may have led to the death of a second."

"We did not have sex. Why won't you believe me?"

"You led him on, intimating that you might be available in a year. Why else would he do something so that—and I'm quoting you—the two of you could be together?"

"Just because he said that doesn't mean I led him on or that he killed Randy."

"You were ethically obligated to terminate your relationship with Rich and Randy the minute you recognized he had romantic feelings for you. And you were ethically responsible for referring them both to another therapist to repair the damage."

"I told you. I stopped therapy the minute I realized—"

"Baloney. You stopped seeing Rich when he scared you. Up until then you encouraged him, for your own benefit." She starts to protest. "In case you were wondering, the person Randy confided in, the one who told me what Randy said, is a law enforcement professional. Very credible and comfortable testifying in court."

"What do you want me to do?" Her voice is a petulant whine.

"I wanted you to go to the police, but since you've refused, we'll have to take an indirect route."

"What do you mean, an indirect route?"

"Call Rich, tell him you miss him, and that you want to work things out. Invite him to your apartment and get him to confess."

"You don't believe a word I say. Why would you trust me to do this?"

"Because I'll be there, listening to every word and recording everything he says." There's a moment of silence. I can hear her breathing.

"Is that legal?"

"I don't know and, frankly, I don't care. My goal is to get KPD to broaden the focus of their investigation. Look beyond their current suspects. As far as I know, Rich is not even on their radar."

"What if I refuse?"

"Not a good idea. Evidently, I'm the only person who knows what you've been going through. If you need a restraining order to get away from Rich, you need me to back you up. Cops look out for each other. They won't take your word over his without some corroboration."

"What if he attacks me? He has a gun." I can hear her breathing over the phone in short, shallow little breaths. "Do it in my office. In the middle of the day when there's people around."

"I've been to your office. There's no place to hide."

"No way am I meeting him in my apartment unless you bring a police officer with you, someone who could protect us both." Actually, not until this very second has it occurred to me that either one of us might get hurt.

"Good idea," I say. "And I know just the person to ask."

CHAPTER FORTY

I head to Fran's and tell Eddie that I have a job for him. He is so anxious to dive in I have to stop him from ripping off his apron and abandoning Fran in the middle of the breakfast rush. I tell him to wait until there's a break in the action and join me at a back table for a cup of coffee.

"So, what up, Doc? Gimme the scoop."

Fran, coffee in hand, walks over. "Can I join you?"

"No," Eddie says. "Don't mean to be rude but the doc and me have some private business."

"Do what you can, Doc," she says as she walks back to the counter, "This boy needs a tune-up."

I tell Eddie about Marvel and Rich. He gives a low whistle. "The husband. Just like on *Law & Order*."

"I don't know for sure—that's the point of getting him to talk."

"So why are you doing this and asking me for help? Why isn't the PD crawling all over him?"

"Good question. The chief's missing in action and can't be reached and Pence won't give me the time of day."

"Smart guy," Eddie rolls his eyes. "Just kidding. When do we get started?"

"Marvel's going to ask Rich to come to her apartment on Saturday night at eight. If we get there at seven that should give us enough time to set up the recorder and find a place to hide."

"Excellent. That'll give me a couple of days to hit the range. I need a little practice. I haven't fired a gun in a while. Fran doesn't approve of shooting people who don't like how she cooked their eggs."

"You don't need a gun. We have a voice recorder."

"So what am I doing there?"

"Protecting us."

"With what? This guy's twenty years younger and in a lot better shape. Plus, you think he killed his wife, which, in my book, means he's capable of doing some serious shit. My motto has always been be polite and professional, but have a plan to kill everyone you meet."

"Bring pepper spray instead."

"This is a CQB situation. Close-quarter battle. I spray him and we all start crying."

"What about a taser?"

"Taser is health insurance. A gun is life insurance."

"I think bringing a gun will just escalate the situation."

"So if I go in unarmed, nothing will happen, is that your theory? That's like expecting a bull not to charge you because you're a vegetarian. Look, you want my help, you got to let me do it my way."

"What if you get into a fight? What if he takes your gun away? You already said he's younger and more fit."

"If he does, he'll have to beat me to death with it because it'll be empty."

"I don't know. This takes everything to a different level."

"Trust me on this, Doc. I may be frequently wrong, but I'm never in doubt."

CHAPTER FORTY-ONE

Whatever money Marvel has to her name these days must go into furnishing her office, not her apartment. Multicolored afghans conceal the wear on every secondhand chair in her small living room. Her bedroom is a virtual zoo of stuffed animals. A framed cross-stitched rendition of the Lord's Prayer hangs over the bed. The woman who sleeps here is homesick and lonely.

"I'd have a helluva time getting it up in here," Eddie says. "That Rich has weird taste in women."

We find a hiding place for the recording device on a bookshelf in the hall, behind a collection of delicate china teacups, each of which comes with its own provenance. For some reason Marvel thinks it's important that we know which cup belonged to what relative. When she picks them up, her hands are shaking so hard, they clatter in their saucers.

"Sit down for a minute," I say. "How did Rich react when you called him?"

"Surprised. Happy. Wanted to come over right away, but I told him he had to wait until tonight." She looks at her watch. "What time is it?"

"Not to worry, you've got time." She's gnawing at her fingernails. I need to find something to distract her. Given how many teacups she owns, I ask if she can make us some tea while Eddie and I pick a place to hide ourselves.

We don't have many choices. This is a small apartment. The living room, kitchen, and dining counter make up one room. The one bedroom has a closet and a tiny deck, and there's a bathroom and a closet in the hall. We eliminate the deck, Rich would spot us as he came up the outer stairs and Eddie's too fat to squeeze into either closet.

Eddie walks to the kitchen counter and perches on a stool while Marvel fixes us tea. He looks right at home leaning on a bar. "So, what's his habit? Single ready to mingle the minute he gets in the door, or does he like a little floor action before he hits the bedroom?"

Marvel turns scarlet. "I told her, we never had sex."

"That leaves the bedroom and the bathroom. I don't want to be in the bathroom if he has to take a leak. I draw the line somewhere. The doc can sit on the floor of your closet, and I'll take the bed and hope I don't fall asleep because it's so comfy in there."

"You can't sleep..." Marvel says, looking panicky.

"Just kidding, sweetheart." He opens his windbreaker enough so that she sees his shoulder holster and gun. "Not to worry." He walks back to the bedroom. There's a mirror on the back of the closet door and one attached to an old chest of drawers that probably belonged to the same relatives who gave Marvel the teacups. He adjusts the door, tilts the mirror, and steps back to check the angle. "Brilliant. The Rimbauer periscope."

Marvel announces that tea is ready. She pours me a cup and offers one to Eddie. "Never touch the stuff," he says and looks at his watch. "I'm going to get set up. Make sure you clean these cups so Richy doesn't think you've got company."

When he leaves the room, she looks at me. Her face is as white as the proverbial sheet. "I feel like I'm going to faint." She sets her teacup down, puts her elbows on the table, clasps her hands together, and bends her head in prayer. "May the strength of God pilot me, the power of God uphold me, the wisdom of God guide me. May the eye of God look before me, the ear of God hear me, the Word of God speak for me. May the hand of God protect me, the way of God lie before me, the shield of God defend me, the host of God save me."

Eddie steps back into the living room. "Just in case God's got something else to do—" He pats his weapon, "Me and Dr. Glock are just around the corner."

* * *

Rich is right on time.

"You look great," he says. "I've missed you."

"Me too," she says. Somehow, in the last few minutes, she's managed to get the tremor out of her voice. "These are lovely," she says. "Thank you."

Eddie places his hands over his heart, gives me a simpering smile, and mimes the word "sweet." We are in Marvel's bedroom. I'm sitting on the floor, my back against the wall. Eddie is sitting on the bed, his gun out of the holster, lying next to him.

Rich and Marvel move into the kitchen. I hear water running. I'm guessing flower-arranging activity. There's a pop. Flowers and champagne. Who would have guessed that Rich was such a traditionalist? The champagne popping is followed by the business of setting out some snacks, opening and closing the refrigerator, pulling out drawers. I hear the clink of silverware and dishes better than I can hear what they're saying. I can only hope the recorder in the living room is picking up more than I am. Twenty minutes of domesticity pass. Eddie's starting to squirm, making hurry-up, get-going motions with his hands, and tapping the face of his watch.

They move back into the living room. More small talk. "This is good, did you make it?"

"Want some more?"

By now we've been here for forty-five minutes with no progress, and my fifty-minute bladder is giving me fits. Stupid me for drinking that tea. And then Marvel makes her move.

"One of the reasons I wanted us to talk is that I need you to clarify something."

"Anything," he says.

"Remember when I said I couldn't see you anymore. That we'd have to stop?"

"Worst day of my life," he says. Is that possible? Worse than the day he murdered his wife?

"You said something to me. You said I couldn't stop seeing you after what you'd done so that we could be together. What did you mean by what you'd done?"

There's a pause.

"I need to know, Rich. What did you mean?"

"I don't remember. I was upset. I didn't mean anything."

Ask him, I think, quit beating around the bush.

"Did you kill Randy?"

"Is that what you think? That I could do something like that?"

"I don't know. Did you?"

He gets up. I can hear him walking around the small room.

"You know better than anyone that being married to Randy was hell. I used to sit in your office, watching the two of you and wishing I was married to you, not her. All consumed with herself. Nothing and no one mattered but her. All that drama. I finally told her, 'You want to apologize to Ms. Gibbs, then apologize, but get it over with. Stop talking about it.' She wouldn't listen." He stops pacing. "I couldn't take it any longer. I asked her for a divorce. I felt like a shit, leaving her in that state. But I could tell it was never going to end—it would never be any different between us."

"So what did you do?"

"I said fuck it. You want to apologize? I'll drive you there. So I did."

"And then what happened?"

"I don't know."

There's silence. Rich starts pacing again.

I catch Eddie's eye and mouth the words 'I really need to pee.' He leans over and points to the closet, tilting the mattress as he shifts forward. His gun slides off the bed and clatters to the floor.

I hear Rich say "Who's in there?" and in a nano-second he's on top of Eddie and they're struggling for the gun. Marvel's screaming. Maybe I am too. There's a lot of grunting and banging. I duck down, push back into the corner with my hands over my head to avoid getting hit by a barrage of legs and arms. It occurs to me that I'll be a lousy witness if this ever goes to court.

"Motherfucker," Eddie screams. They are both on their feet now, Eddie panting and sweating. Rich is holding Eddie's gun, pointing it right at him. His hands and the gun are larger than life. Then there is the loudest noise I've ever heard. I watch Eddie crumple to the bed, slide off, and lay motionless on the floor before someone whacks me on the head and everything goes dark.

CHAPTER FORTY-TWO

Something soft rubs against my face. Whatever's beneath me rumbles like a clothes dryer. A giant bump—first up, then down—jolts me forward, followed by the screech of tires. A voice says "Goddamn it," and I'm awake, tied up in the back of my own car with the chenille belt from Marvel's bathrobe. It has to be hers. I never wear pink. I push myself up far enough to see the front seat. Rich Spelling is driving my car.

"Where are you taking me? Where's Eddie?"

"Shut up," he says. I can see his reflection in the rearview mirror. He is sweating or crying. Maybe both.

"Is Eddie dead?" I try to squirm into a sitting position. My neck is killing me and my head weighs a ton. "Where's Marvel?"

"Behind us. Driving my car."

"Why? Where are we going?"

"I should have left you in the apartment. Shot you, put the gun in Eddie's hand. Made it look like he killed you and then shot himself."

Foggy as I am, I'm pretty sure the inevitable has only been postponed. I don't want to appear ungrateful, but I have to ask, "Why didn't you?"

"Marvel begged me not to. Said we'd go to Hell for breaking God's commandment against killing."

Thank God for Marvel, I say to myself, before I remember I'm an atheist.

There's another screech. The car swerves and bumps over a curb. Rich hits the steering wheel with both hands. "Fuck," he says. Then he brakes, backs up, and does a U-turn. I roll forward and almost fall off the back seat onto the floor.

"Watch how you're driving," I blurt before I realize that the more erratic his driving, the better the chances that he'll get pulled over by a cop and I'll be rescued. I roll back against the seat.

"Shut up. I can't think when you talk." He makes a sharp turn to the right and I slide down the seat towards the passenger door. Streetlights whiz by. I can see parts of buildings from my prone position, but nothing looks familiar. Wherever we are, it's very dark. He turns another corner and I slide back in the other direction bumping my head on the door handle.

"Why is Marvel following us? Is she helping you?"

He's slowing at every corner, craning his neck at street signs.

"Listen to me, Rich. You're in a terrible state. You're too agitated to think clearly. Pull over, let's talk this through." He jams his foot on the accelerator and speeds up.

"Marvel set this whole thing up, didn't she? Told you I'd be in the apartment by myself, listening. She'd ask you if you killed Randy, you'd say no and that would be the end of it. I'd be off your back and everyone would go on thinking Randy was killed by Lakeisha Gibbs' family or Darnell Taylor."

"Darnell Taylor is a piece of shit."

"That may be so, but one day you're going to have to explain why you shot Eddie and why you did whatever you're planning to do to me." Several deadly options run through my mind. Rich brakes hard, stops a second, and speeds forward. "Marvel didn't tell you that Eddie was going to be in her apartment with a gun, did she? You're just a fling for her. She doesn't intend to stick with you, she's going back to Nebraska. She told me so." Divide and conquer. Worked for Julius Caesar.

He makes a wild turn and slams on the brakes.

"Are you going to kill me?"

"I told you to shut up."

"You killed Randy. Tell me. I'm dead anyway."

"You're just like her. It's all about you." My mother would say this was a perfect example of the pot calling the kettle black. "Randy was violent. You didn't know that, did you? She threw stuff at me, hit me. Why do people always think only men are violent?" I decide to overlook the obvious irony of his question.

"I didn't know, Rich, because you didn't tell me. This makes everything different, don't you see? I can back you up. Be a character witness. I can testify that Randy was suicidal, out of control. If you kill me, you lose the one person who can help you."

He turns in his seat and looks at me. "And why would you want to help me? You hated me from the beginning. Took her side all the time. Randy needs this, Randy needs that. What about what I needed?"

"I'll help you because I want to live." The realization that this is the truest thing I've ever said is so astonishing that after I say it I go mute. I want to live so much it hurts. My heart aches with it. I can taste it. Feel it vibrating in my body.

People who are about to die are supposed to see their entire lives flashing before their eyes. What plays out in front of me is the life I won't get to live, the pain I'm causing my mother by dying first, the grief I feel for Eddie blindly following me to his death. And Frank, dear Frank, all that love squandered, wasted, because I don't know when to give up.

Rich opens the door and drags me out of the backseat onto the ground. Pebbles dig into my backside. I try to focus. Marvel is several yards away standing next to Rich's car, staring at me, frozen with fright.

My eyes adjust to the dark. An apartment building looms in the shadows. It is three stories high with outside passages. I've been here twice before and this is the first time there is a light on in 3C.

With one hand Rich jerks me into a sitting position. He has Eddie's gun in his other hand.

"Where are we? What are we doing here?" Marvel says and takes a few steps towards us.

"Stay back, " Rich says. "You don't want to see this."

"You told me we were going to the police so you could turn yourself in. I begged you."

His face crumples. For just a moment I think he's going to cry. "I'm sorry. I have to do this. I don't have a choice."

"No," Marvel says. "Stop, please."

"I killed a cop. I'll go to jail."

"Two wrongs don't make a right." She takes another step forward.

"Get back in the car, please."

"Pray with me, Rich. Ask God for forgiveness and guidance."

"Get in the car."

"No." She screams it this time. Her voice is a mix of fear and fury. Rich looks wild, his eyes popping, sweat pouring off him in the chilly wind. He looks from her to me and back again.

"I killed a cop."

"It was self-defense. You said so yourself."

"No one's going to believe me. I could've stopped that fat bastard with one hand."

"Marvel's right. Eddie had a gun," I say. "I saw it."

"And you're going to defend me? Bullshit. You think I killed Randy. You can't wait to tell someone." He gestures with his gun. "Darnell's out on bail, up there in that apartment. He knows you've been snooping around. That's why he kills you. Perfectly believable. He's the number-one suspect."

"I've been in the incident room. Your name is up there with his. On the list of potential suspects." I haven't a clue if this is true, but at this point I don't think it matters.

Rich pulls me to my feet. "Untie yourself," he says, holding me by the back of my shirt, his gun hand in the air. I can't see Marvel, but I can hear her crying. And praying. I don't move. "Do it. Now." He's in full cop mode, shouting so loudly that I can't believe people aren't coming outside to see what's going on. Then I remember where I am. In this neighborhood angry voices make people turn out the lights and move away from their windows.

Marvel turns toward her car. I can hear her footsteps moving away, first loudly, then softer, all my senses sharpened by impending death. She's my only witness, my only advocate, and she's abandoning me. I hear the car door slam and the motor start. Rich shoves me toward Darnell's building. I hobble forward and stumble. There is an explosion of sound, tires screeching and spitting gravel. The air is perfumed with the smell of burning rubber. Rich pushes me down and runs toward the noise.

"Marvel," he screams into the night, "Come back. Don't leave me here." He raises his gun to firing position, holds it there for a moment and then buckles forward, his hands on his knees, gasping. It takes several seconds before he uncurls his body and turns back to me, his face twisted in rage. I'm still there, completely frozen by fear.

"Don't you see? Marvel is using you."

Something flashes in his eyes like he just woke up.

"There's more. Did you know that Tom Rutgers' girlfriend told a room full of women that you were a womanizer?"

He responds with a blank stare, like I'm speaking some language he doesn't understand.

"Did you know Randy told several women that she was unhappy at home? I've met them. They're going to testify that she was planning to leave you."

He's staring at me, but his eyes are unfocused.

"Do you understand what I'm saying? All this makes you the perfect suspect for Randy's murder. I'm your only defense."

My feet and hands are going numb from lack of blood flow. My head is still throbbing and my bloodied mouth tastes like the inside of a rusty can.

"Here's what you say: Randy was determined to kill herself. Self-sacrifice. An act of atonement for killing Lakeisha Gibbs. You tried to stop her, you fought, grabbed her gun, and it went off. It was an accident. And then you were scared that no one would be-

lieve you, so you wiped the gun clean, kept quiet, and let everyone think it was Darnell or the Gibbs boys. It's a lesser crime than
murder."

A cold wind whips through the parking lot. Rich is still
sweating profusely.

"I'm all you have. Marvel doesn't care about you. She was using you."

He shifts the gun back and forth between his hands like a
hot potato. "I just killed a cop."

"Eddie attacked you. Came out of nowhere. I was there. I
saw it. I'll tell them. Give yourself up, plead self-defense, and get
yourself a good lawyer."

"I'll go to prison. Do you know what it's like for a cop in
prison? It's a death sentence." He starts to lift the gun towards his
head.

"No, Rich. Please." He looks to his right where Marvel had
parked his car. There is no one there. "Listen to me. Think about
what you're doing."

His face crumples and for a split second I see a hopeless,
lonely little boy, waiting for someone who will never show up. I
change tactics.

"Marvel will come back. Of course she will. Forget what I
said, I think she loves you. You scared her. Now you need to bring
her back. Think how devastated she'll be if you kill yourself. Or
me."

His hand wavers back and forth, towards his head, towards
me, towards his head, towards the ground. Then his shoulders sag
and his gun hand falls back against his thigh. "What do you care
if I kill myself?"

Under the circumstances, it's a fair question. Better him than
me. But then I'd have Eddie's death and the blood from Rich and
Ben's suicides on my hands, not to mention an indelible image
of Rich's shattered skull to live with. He raises his gun again and
points it at me. Suddenly, all the adrenaline I've been churning
loses its force. I sink back to the pavement and close my eyes. I

have nothing more to say. He's going to shoot me or shoot himself. I don't want to see either one.

The air fills with a soft thrumming. I open my eyes. The sound grows increasingly louder. Rich is looking around wildly. His face splits into a grin. "Marvel, Marvel? Over here. I'm over here." Lights sweep across the parking lot. A car pulls into the space next to where I'm lying. It stops with a jerk as though someone has slammed on the brakes. All four doors open at once.

What happens next happens so fast I can't take it in. It doesn't help that I'm curled in a fetal position with my eyes closed. I've never been in a physical fight, let alone a melee, unless you count the time I hit my ex on the head with a wine bottle and he slammed me to the floor. And now I've been in two fights in as many hours. There's a lot of grunting and cursing. I can hear feet scraping the pavement.

"Piece!" someone shouts.

"Pop him!" another hollers.

In the distance, I hear the long whine of a cop car.

"What up?" someone yells from the apartment house.

"Get gone, Darnell. This ain't your business. Best you stay in your crib."

The tallest boy pulls me to my feet and cuts me free with a knife. The other boys have Rich on the ground. He's struggling to break away. "What you doing, white boy, messing with my fan club?" Tall Boy says over his shoulder. He looks at me. "You beat down. You need a doctor."

"He's a cop," I say.

"I know. Works the jail. I seen him before. He be looking for Darnell."

A line of police cars, lights flashing, sirens blaring, turns the corner.

Rich shouts at me. "Help me. You promised."

My legs start to fold again. The tall boy puts his arm around my shoulder to steady me.

"If you hadn't come along, I'd be dead now. Thank you."

"1704T at your service," he smiles broadly. "Not every day we get to pound a cop and get thanked for it."

* * *

Tom Rutgers puts me in the front seat of Manny's patrol car and tells me to relax, Manny's going to drive me back to the station. 1704 Travis looks like the parking lot at police headquarters. Every patrol car in Kenilworth and three surrounding communities is there, light bars flashing like Christmas gone wild. Now that I no longer need them, the residents are hanging over the balconies in their nightclothes watching the spectacle. Only in 3C is the window dark and the front door closed. I grab Tom's arm before he closes the door.

"Eddie Rimbauer is at Marvel Johnson's apartment. Rich Spelling shot him. He needs an ambulance."

"We're on it," he says.

"I think he's dead."

"Medics are on their way."

"Who sent medics?"

Rutgers looks at me. "Dr. Johnson. As soon as she escaped, she called 911, told us about Eddie and where to find you."

"Where is she now?"

"Back at the station."

"Those four boys over there—"

Rutgers turns his head in the direction I'm pointing.

"They are a rap group called 1704T. They helped me, saved my life. Don't you dare arrest them or treat them like suspects."

Rutgers wheels around. "I don't take orders from you."

"I'm telling you what happened. If it wasn't for them I'd be dead."

"We found a gun on one of them."

"The gun belongs to Eddie Rimbauer. Rich used it to shoot him. Those boys took it away from him. If they hadn't, he might have shot me."

"I'll be sure to check that out," he says with a small smirk.

"If any of those boys has so much as a scratch on him, I'll be checking that out, too. Count on it."

* * *

I tell Manny that I want to go to the police station first. I need to see for myself that Rich Spelling is locked up and can't hurt me. Then I want to talk to Marvel, actually, I want to strangle her, but then I don't because she saved my life. She and 1704T. On the other hand, I want to see Eddie before I do anything else. I hope Manny knows where he is, what hospital or, God forbid, what morgue. But that's not right either, the first thing I should do is call my mother and Frank before they hear on the news that I've been kidnapped and nearly killed.

Manny looks at me. "You okay, Doc? You're talking to yourself."

"I don't know what to do first."

"Not to worry," he says. "I'm driving. You're going to the emergency room. That's an order."

* * *

The ER doc seems a little perplexed at my status. First he asks me if I need to speak privately with a domestic abuse victim advocate. When Chief Reagon arrives with news that Eddie is waiting to go into surgery and that Fran is with him, the doctor asks me if I'm a cop because I'm clearly getting the VIP treatment. When Frank arrives, I burst into tears and cry so hard the doctor asks if I want to talk to the on-duty psychiatrist. In all the confusion, he forgets to ask me if I lost consciousness after being hit on the head. I decide not to tell him I did because I haven't got any of the classic symptoms of concussion and I don't want the doctor or anyone else to keep me from going home with Frank.

CHAPTER FORTY-THREE

Frank watches me like a hawk, asks me every other hour how I'm feeling, won't let me have a glass of wine and, worst of all, he won't let me watch the news. "Doctor's orders," he says. "You're supposed to rest and take these." Whatever "these" are knock me out almost instantly. I wake up with a headache, a bruised cheek, a swollen lip, road rash on my butt, and a bald patch where the doctor shaved my head to suture my scalp. Frank hears me moving around and opens the bedroom door.

"Hey, sleeping beauty. Finally decided to get up?"

"How long have I been asleep?"

"A little over ten hours. Hungry?"

"I have to go to the hospital. I need to see Eddie."

"You're not going anywhere. First of all, I don't know where your car is, and if I did, I'd hide the keys."

* * *

I wake again in another four hours and this time I'm starving. Frank makes me breakfast although I haven't a clue if it's morning or night. My headache is gone and I need a shower. Frank warns me not to get my bandage wet and tells me my bald spot makes me look like a cross between a Chinese Crested hairless dog and a punk rocker. When I get out of the shower, he tells me to come into the living room, that he has something to show me.

"I recorded this for you while you were sleeping," he says. "And, the chief called. Twice." He clicks the TV remote.

Chief Reagon is standing in front of a phalanx of reporters in the large conference room. Chaplain Barnes and Jay Pence are standing next to her, one on either side. Cameras are whirring and clicking. Jack Shiller is sitting in the front row.

Chief Reagon thanks the reporters for showing up at such an early hour. She's being gratuitous. There isn't a reporter in the room who would have missed this just to get some extra sleep. Shiller is so excited he's wiggling in his seat. Then I remind myself that it's better to live in a country with a free, albeit blood-lusting, press, than to live where the press is censored or a tool of government.

"Let's get started," the chief says. "I am happy to report that Officer Eddie Rimbauer has come through surgery and will recover from his gunshot wound." There is a smattering of applause from the back of the room. I join in from my perch on Frank's sofa.

"Dr. Dot Meyerhoff, our department psychologist, sustained some non-life-threatening injuries and is at home recuperating. As you know Deputy Rich Spelling from the Sheriff's department is in our custody."

Shiller's on his feet. "Is he a suspect in his wife's murder?"

"We're just beginning our investigation. I can't divulge any details, other than to say that he was one of several prime suspects."

"Prime suspect? What are you saying? That I almost got myself killed for nothing?"

Frank puts his hand on my shoulder. "You're talking to the television, Dot. The chief can't hear you. I recorded this hours ago."

"Dr. Marvel Johnson is a psychologist who has had a clinical relationship with both Officer Spelling and Deputy Spelling. The exact nature of her involvement won't be clear until we complete our investigation. We do know that she was present at the scene on Travis Avenue, that she escaped and telephoned the police to inform us that Dr. Meyerhoff was being held against her will and that Officer Rimbauer had been wounded and was in her apartment. Had she not done so, the outcome for both Officer Rimbauer and Dr. Meyerhoff could have been disastrous."

"Why was Johnson at the scene? Why was Rimbauer in her apartment?"

Pence steps forward. "As the chief has said, we are just beginning our investigation. When we have answers to those questions, the press will be the first to know. If there is nothing further, we need to conclude this briefing. We have a lot of work ahead of us." He and the chief turn toward the door.

Shiller won't be dismissed. "Why did Spelling kidnap Meyerhoff?"

The chief stops, thinks for a moment and then turns back to the microphone.

"We don't know, yet. What I can say is that Dr. Meyerhoff, using her skills as a psychologist, was able to..." She pauses. I imagine her groping for the right words to describe how an unauthorized civilian jumped into the middle of a murder case, almost got herself and one, maybe two, other people killed, and was rescued by a rap group. "...help us in our investigation. We are grateful for her assistance and wish her Godspeed in her recovery."

Everyone but Shiller begins to pack up their laptops and notebooks. "The POA has given you a vote of no confidence. Will you be staying?"

Once again, the chief turns back to the microphone, a slight redness in her cheeks. "A vote of no confidence is not a mandate for me to leave my position but rather a directive to improve my leadership and my relations with the rank and file. Under the circumstances, with an ongoing investigation of this magnitude, it is inadvisable for me to make any hasty decisions about the future."

CHAPTER FORTY-FOUR

Frank gives me the dreaded "we need to talk" speech and only releases me from his custody when I promise to come back that night. He drives me to the PD where my car has been towed.

"Don't forget," he says again as he lets me out. "We need to talk. Try not to get killed in the meantime."

I head straight for the hospital. Eddie is sleeping and Fran is sitting outside his room reading a magazine.

"I don't know if I should hit you or hug you," she says when she sees me.

"How is he?"

"What were you thinking, asking him to help you? That boy has pickled his brain with alcohol. He has no sense at all, and you don't seem to have any more sense than he does. The blind leading the lame, that's the two of you." She wraps her arms around me and kisses me on the cheek.

"Who's out there?" Eddie calls from his bed.

"Go on, he's been asking about you constantly," Fran says, dabbing at her eyes with a handkerchief. "And he's not the only one. The chief has called here twice looking for you. She needs you at headquarters. ASAP."

I duck under a bouquet of balloons. There are flowers everywhere and greeting cards. I give Eddie a hug and he doesn't let go for the longest time.

"Smells like a fucking funeral parlor, don't it? I may be stupid, but I'm hard to kill."

"Looks like you still have a lot of friends," I say.

"Too bad I had to get shot to know it. The chief came to

visit me. I begged her, could I get my job back, and she blew me off. Said we shouldn't talk about it until I'm better. Not a word of thanks, nothing, for me helping out with the investigation. Pence was with her. Told me he hoped my worker's comp would pay for the hospital because I was not on official police business. If getting shot isn't police business, I don't know what is." He pulls up his shirt. There is a large bandage covering much of his immense stomach. "One good thing about being fat is that the bullet stuck in my gut and didn't get to my heart." He turns his head toward the doorway and yells. "And yes, Fran, I do have a heart."

He turns back to me. "The bad thing is that they found a lot of other shit wrong with me. Doc said if I didn't lose weight and get my blood pressure down, I was killing myself on the installment plan."

A nurse arrives with Eddie's lunch tray. He looks at the tiny portions. "Fucking A, first lover boy tries to kill me and now the hospital wants to starve me to death." He shouts to Fran. "Bring me something from the restaurant. I can't eat this crap."

She stands in the doorway, hands on hips. "Stop whining and do as you're told. They'll take it away, whether you eat it or not. And you won't get anything until dinner." Eddie looks at me and rolls his eyes.

"So, how'd you get away from Spelling?"

I tell him the story.

"Gangbangers and that lunatic shrink saved your ass? Maybe my doc is right, if I had a life, I should retire. If I had a life."

CHAPTER FORTY-FIVE

My next stop is headquarters. The door to the chief's office opens and Chaplain Barnes walks out. He greets me and takes my hand in both of his. He has a winning smile and warm hands.

"Good to see you. I'm thankful that you weren't more badly hurt than you were. If there is any way I can be of help, please call me. Those of us who counsel others are not above needing a little counseling ourselves." He gives my hands a conspiratorial squeeze.

"How is the chief doing?" I say.

He is as constrained as I am by confidentiality. "You can ask her yourself. I'm sure she'll be relieved to see you in person. And now I'm off to visit Darnell Taylor." He smiles broadly. "I get to work both sides of the aisle. Darnell Taylor is a lost boy. Falling through the cracks, heading for serious trouble. Someone needs to look after him. I'm blessed that my church has a program to help such troubled young men."

* * *

The chief stands to greet me. "I've been concerned. I hope you know I've called you several times and left messages."

"All over town, apparently."

"How are you?"

"Physically I'm fine. Emotionally, it's a different story."

"Always is," she says.

"Why didn't you tell me Rich Spelling was a suspect? It would have saved Eddie and me a lot of trouble." I want to bend my head down and show her the itchy bald spot that I've tried to cover with a badly teased comb-over.

"I'm sorry that you and Eddie got hurt. But I need to remind you that no one asked either of you to involve yourselves or put yourselves at risk." She lets out a long sigh. There are new lines on her face. She looks as if she's aged years in just the last few weeks.

There's a knock on the door. "I've invited Captain Pence and District Attorney Herter to join us. I hope you don't mind."

It's a rhetorical question. The two of them are in the room before I have a chance to object, sputtering about how nice it is to see me looking well. I don't know what they want or why whatever they want has anything to do with me.

The chief pushes four chairs together, offers us coffee, and acts as though she's hosting a friendly meeting between old colleagues. Herter is still as sallow and pinch faced as he was the night he interviewed Randy after her shooting. He's a particularly unpleasant man and his efforts to be sociable are a transparent failure. He'd be better off if he didn't try.

The chief begins. "Rich Spelling is claiming that Randy was determined to kill herself in front of Lakeisha Gibbs' apartment. Some ritual of self sacrifice or atonement." I flash back to our struggle in the parking lot. Those are the very words I told him to say.

"He says that he drove Randy to Ms. Gibbs' apartment complex, thinking that once they arrived, Randy would change her mind. She didn't and when he attempted to wrestle her weapon away, it went off and killed her. Accidentally. He panicked and wiped off his and Randy's fingerprints, hoping to implicate one of our other suspects. He says you will testify to this."

"I can't do that. I wasn't even there."

"In addition, he claims you will testify that he shot Eddie Rimbauer in self-defense."

"I couldn't possibly. I was curled up on the floor with my arms over my head. I didn't see anything."

"Here's the problem." Herter glances at the chief, clearly impatient with her methodical delivery. He leans so close to me that I can smell his sour breath. "We don't believe his story. But without a confession, we have a murder with no witnesses and very little physical evidence. Will you help us?"

"First I get reprimanded for sticking my nose into police business and now you want me to get Rich Spelling to confess to killing his wife? This is crazy. You can't have it both ways."

Jay Pence moves forward in his chair. "He hasn't asked for a lawyer yet. He's waiting to talk to you first."

"I'm a psychologist, not a cop, as you, Captain Pence, have reminded me on several occasions. Interviewing suspects is your job. Not mine."

"He says you promised to help him."

"Of course I did. I would have said anything to save my life. He was going to kill me. I don't want to talk to him, I hate him. He killed Randy." So much for therapist neutrality.

Herter looks at his watch and stands up. "This is getting us nowhere. I need to file charges. Same for Johnson."

"Marvel Johnson is here, in the station?"

The chief nods affirmatively.

"Why don't you ask her to persuade Rich Spelling to confess?"

Herter walks behind my chair. His suit reeks of moldy cheese. "As I understand it, you tried that little scenario and it didn't work."

"It didn't work because Eddie's gun fell on the floor and everything went to hell before Rich said anything to Marvel about killing Randy."

"Marvel Johnson is terrified of Rich Spelling. I doubt we can persuade her to help us," the chief says.

"I'm terrified of Rich Spelling, too. I was the one he was going to kill. Not Marvel. He loves Marvel."

Herter keeps pacing. Pence examines the ends of his fingertips.

"Why should I help you? What's in it for me?"

"Maybe you'd like to keep your job?" Pence says.

"Are you ordering me to do this? Because I'm a consultant. I don't take orders from you."

One corner of his mouth arches toward a sneer and stops. He needs my help. Fighting his own instincts, he's going to have to be nice to me to get it.

"Whatever we do, we do it because we owe it to Randy," the chief says. "I let her down once, as Dr. Meyerhoff has made abundantly clear. I don't want to let her down twice."

A cold prickle runs across my neck and shoulders. The chief isn't to blame for Randy's death. If anyone beside Rich is to blame, it's me. I was wrong not to have paid more attention to him. I was so invested in Randy's problems, I didn't see this coming and I should have. Rich was fine when the attention was on him and what he needed. But when Randy was the one in need, he couldn't go the distance. And now it's me refusing to go the distance.

CHAPTER FORTY-SIX

Psychotherapy is more art than science, more intuition than deductive reasoning. Evidence-based treatment has its place, but it will never replace my gut feelings or the images that float up out of my subconscious. The image forming in front of me now is Rich Spelling in the parking lot on Travis Street, the look of desperation on his face as Marvel drove away. The image shifts like a curtain blowing in the breeze. This time he's a little boy, waiting by himself in a dark schoolyard. All the other kids have long gone home. He's cold and hungry. Once again his mother has forgotten to pick him up.

"Let's go, Doc," Pence says. "We haven't got all day. Can you help us or not?" This is beyond ironic, three highly ranked law enforcement professionals are waiting for me, the organization's stepchild, alternately appreciated and ignored, to help them get a confession.

Intermittent reinforcement. It's what keeps people coming back to Las Vegas. Because sometimes you win and sometimes you lose. It's never the same and it's never predictable. Intermittent reinforcement is what kept Rich waiting for his mother in the dark. It's what keeps him tethered to Marvel. And it's what is keeping me from walking out of the room.

"Sit down," I say. "I have something that might work."

* * *

The sky outside is as dark as the mood in our little brainstorming session.

"Here's what I suggest. Tell Marvel that you'll drop all charges against her if she will get Rich Spelling to confess. Give her a detailed description of what her life will be like in prison, with an emphasis on the bad parts. Tell her what to say. I'll write the script."

"I doubt she's going to prison. Maybe we can charge her for withholding information, interfering with a police investigation, but not much more." Pence looks from me to Herter for confirmation.

"Too bad being manipulative, ambitious, naïve and biting off more than you can chew is not considered a crime," I say.

"Do you think she helped murder Randy?" The chief looks incredulous.

"No," I say. "If she didn't have the guts to find Randy unfit for duty, I doubt she had the guts to murder her."

Herter gives me a look. "So how am I supposed to convince her she'll go to prison if she doesn't cooperate?"

"I'm just a psychologist. What do I know? But isn't it legal for a cop to lie to a suspect to get a confession? I doubt Dr. Johnson knows anything about criminal law. You could tell her the punishment for withholding information from the police was the electric chair and she'd probably believe you."

CHAPTER FORTY-SEVEN

We're standing on the viewing side of a one-way mirror watching Rich Spelling pace around the room under the watchful eye of the largest correctional officer I've ever seen. He's a newly hired lateral from another county with no ties to Rich. Rich is wearing an orange jumpsuit. His feet and hands are shackled causing him to shuffle like an old man.

It took Marvel forty-five minutes to recover from the shock that someone was actually going to hold her accountable for her behavior. She was two offices away and we could hear her crying and pleading with Herter. By the time she walked out, clutching her Bible and the script I wrote for her, her eyes and cheeks were scorched red from crying.

Rich is expecting me, not Marvel. A little shock and awe to destabilize him. He's a jailhouse cop; he knows someone is on the other side of this window observing him. My hope is that once he sees Marvel, nothing else will matter.

As soon as she enters the interview room, he lets out a howl of joy and pain, pushes out of his seat and stumbles toward her. The CO steps in front of him and warns him that there is no touching allowed. Marvel is shaking. The CO directs her to a chair at the opposite end of the table. She and Rich sit face to face, six feet apart, staring at each other.

"Why did you leave me in the parking lot?"

"You were going to kill Dr. Meyerhoff. I'm a Christian. Killing is wrong."

"I wanted to scare her. I wouldn't have killed her."

"How can I be sure? You killed Randy, didn't you?"

Pence gives Herter an elbow in the ribs. The chief scowls. Rich is now shuffling in front of the one-way window. Looking at us.

"They're watching me. Recording everything I say."

"If our relationship is going to work, we need to be honest with each other," Marvel turns her head in our direction. "They want to send me to jail."

"It's me they're going to lock up. Not you," he says.

"Pray with me, please," she bows her head and places both hands on her Bible. "Dear Lord, help us to redeem ourselves. Give us the courage to go forward, no matter how dark or uncertain the future. Help us in our hour of need." She lifts her face. There are tears streaming down her cheeks. "They think I helped you kill Randy because I wanted to be with you. They're going to send me to prison. Tell them I had nothing to do with it. Please." Now she's sobbing between words. "I'll wait for you. I'll write to you. I promise."

Pence and Herter are wiping mock tears from their faces.

Rich walks back to his seat. "Why should I believe you? You set me up, tried to entrap me. And then you left me." He is wailing now. His eyes are glossy and the ends of his mouth quiver in an effort to keep back his tears.

"I didn't want to. They made me. Told me if I didn't cooperate I'd go to jail."

"Swear on your Bible. Swear you love me, that you'll wait for me."

"Will you accept Christ and confess?" Marvel shoves the Bible across the table. The CO grabs it before Rich does.

"Sorry, ma'am. You cannot give the prisoner any reading material." He points to a sign on the wall listing all the things a prisoner may not receive.

"It's a Bible. A Bible," Marvel says.

"Sorry, that's the rule," he says and hands it back.

"You do it," Rich says. "I don't want to hide our relationship anymore. If we have to hide it, it's not worth having. Swear on the Bible that you love me. "

"And then you'll confess? A Christian man would never let a woman be punished for something she didn't do."

"Then swear on the Bible that you love me."

Marvel swallows hard, sets her Bible on the table and gently pushes it aside. "I'll do something even better."

She stands and walks to the one-way window, positioning herself right in the middle, her nose up against the glass. I step back. Herter chuckles. Pence lifts his eyebrows. "Not to worry," the chief says, "she can't hear us or see us."

Marvel is standing ramrod straight. One hand dangling at her side, out of Rich's view. Her fingers are crossed. "Whoever you are. I love Rich Spelling. Record that." She scuttles back to her seat.

Rich rises from his chair. "I knew it," he says, "You love me. I knew it."

Marvel gives him a weak smile and reaches for her Bible.

"Now?" she says. "Now will you tell the truth?"

Rich struggles to his feet and turns towards us. He raises his hands. The metal shackles wink in the overhead light. "My name is Rich Spelling," he announces. "I killed my wife, Randy Spelling. No one else was involved."

"Why?" Marvel says. "Tell them why."

Now tears pour down Rich's face. "I didn't matter. All that mattered was her and her troubles. I wanted a divorce, she wouldn't listen, didn't have the time. I felt trapped. I didn't want to kill her. I felt sorry for her, she was so miserable. But I didn't have another choice." He goes back to his seat. Marvel gets up and heads for the door. "I did it for you," Rich calls after her. "Not for me. Never for me."

Pence and Herter do a few high-fives.

"Thanks for your help," they say, almost in unison. "Couldn't have done it without you." It's not an Academy Award, but it feels good.

* * *

The chief is quiet on the way back from the jail. "I lost the vote of no confidence, did you know that? I'm going to give it another day or two, but I'm fairly certain I'm going to retire. I've got more

than twenty years on the job. I could collect my retirement today."
We pull into the parking lot at police headquarters. "I thought I
had worked through all of my issues about my own incident, but
Lakeisha Gibbs' death brought it all back. I can't face another incident of this magnitude. I don't want to face another incident
of this magnitude. That's not the attitude a police chief should
have."

"That's the nature of PTSD," I say. "It bites you in the butt
when you least expect it. And it's hard to avoid." I think of something my father used to say, "If you want to get hit by a golf ball,
baby girl, stand on the golf course." No way the chief can stay in
police work and not continually run into herself over and over.
She can try to compartmentalize her feelings, but, like Rich Spelling, it's inevitable that they will catch up to her.

"KPD deserves a chief who can give 100 percent of his or
her attention and energy to this job. I think Jay Pence can do that.
He's ready. He's been loyal to me, despite all his anger and misgiv-
ings. None of us know what lies in the future. Rich Spelling could
recant his confession. Chester Allen is mounting a campaign for a
citizens' review board. I don't have what it takes to see any of that
through. "

"You wanted to bring more women into the force. Pence
hates women. He hates me."

"If I've learned anything in this business it's to take the good
with the bad. Jay Pence has more good qualities than bad. At any
rate, there's no guarantee he'll get the job. The city council will
have to launch another national search. National searches are ex-
pensive; they'll no doubt need to wait until another budget cycle."

"Great," I say. "That gives him plenty of time to fire me first."

CHAPTER FORTY-EIGHT

My next-to-final stop for the day is the Gibbs household. I asked my mother about Charla Bernstein, but all she could remember was a tall, graceful woman of color who wound up marrying a Jewish doctor. And then she said she had to hang up or she'd be late for water aerobics. I couldn't bear to press her on the subject, but I have no such reservations about confronting Dr. Bernstein.

Bernstein opens the door, barefoot and wearing a loose caftan, her hair flying around her shoulders. No jewelry, no makeup. Her jaw drops slightly in surprise.

"May I come in?"

She steps back, opens the door wider, and gestures me toward the living room. The apartment is as it was the last time I was here. The dining table set for four, everything neat as a pin and looking untouched.

"My daughter is at work and the boys are at football practice. What can I do for you?"

"Were you telling the truth about your relationship with my father?"

"I wouldn't worry about that if I were you. What's past is past."

"You're not me."

"If you've come here to get me to promise never to approach your mother you've wasted your time. I'm not a cruel woman. I'm a grieving grandmother who would do anything to protect my remaining grandchildren."

"That's what worries me."

We're standing in the hall, not more than a few feet from the front door. It's clear she's not going to ask me to sit down.

"I should be thankful," she says. "The police surveillance has been removed from the parking lot and my grandsons have stopped complaining that they are being followed around school by plainclothes officers. Evidently you were instrumental in exposing the real murderer." She shakes her head. Her hair lifts and settles like smoke. "And I understand Darnell Taylor is back in jail. He's a troubled young man. He needs help and he won't find it in jail."

I'm not buying her concern. She would have thrown Darnell Taylor to the wolves if it would have saved her grandsons.

"My grandsons may be off the hook, but nothing else has changed. Didn't you see how easy it was for everyone—the police, the newspapers, the community—to assume that the person responsible for Officer Spelling's death was a black male?"

"Isn't it logical to assume that whoever killed Randy was related to Lakeisha?"

"Not to me." She looks at her watch and walks to the front door. "You'd better leave before my daughter comes home from work. She is still very angry."

"And you're not?"

"I lost my granddaughter. You're the psychologist. You tell me."

CHAPTER FORTY-NINE

By the time I get back to Frank's house, the sky is dark. A cold breeze bends the bare branches on the trees lining his street. It's been nearly two weeks since our big fight. He was very angry with me then and I expect he still is.

I ring the bell even though I have a key. He opens the door and looks surprised that it's me.

"I wasn't sure you'd show up," he says. "Come in, make yourself at home." He has a fire going and there's a bottle of wine on the coffee table with one glass, half-full. He gets another and pours me a drink.

"So," I say. "This morning you said you wanted to talk about something."

He frowns. A tense line spreads across his forehead. He stares into his glass for two, maybe three minutes before he looks up.

"Sure," he says. "Let's do it." He rearranges himself in the chair. "The only reason I knew you were in the hospital was because I heard on the evening news that an off-duty KPD officer had been shot and the department psychologist was kidnapped and wounded. Would you have called me if I hadn't shown up?"

"You were very angry with me just before that happened. Remember? Would you have come if I'd called?"

"You didn't call and I came anyway. What do you think?"

Now it's my turn to stare into my wine. A cracking noise in the fireplace startles me as the pyramid of logs fall into an ashy heap. Frank excuses himself and goes outside to get another log. My heart is banging against my ribs, and I have an urge to run out of the room before he comes back. It's now or never, I say to myself. And then I tell myself not to be such a drama queen. He comes back into the room, fixes the fire, and sits down again. His face is a neutral screen.

I take a deep breath. "When I thought that I was going to die, that Rich Spelling would kill me, a lot of things went through my mind." The memory rushes me, stinging my eyes with tears. "But the worst thing, the thing that broke my heart, was the thought that I had squandered your love and would never see you again." I take a deep breath and let the tears roll freely down my face.

Frank doesn't move for a very long minute. Just sits there, watching me digging in my sleeve, hunting for a tissue. "Then marry me," he says.

I don't think I've heard him right.

"Marry me. I'm tired of waiting to ask you."

"Two weeks ago you told me that I'm stubborn, self-involved, headstrong, a workaholic, plus I talk back to the TV, and I'm too damn old to change."

"I didn't tell you about the 85 percent rule though, did I?" He smiles.

I shake my head. "Never heard of it."

"After my divorce, I figured that if I ever again found a woman I could love, it would be foolish to expect perfection, so I'd just have to settle for 85 percent and ignore the 15 percent I don't like, because I can't change it and it would annoy you if I tried." He takes a sip of wine, his eyes on my face. "So I'm just going to ignore the 15 percent. Although with you, it won't be easy. What do you think? Deal or no deal?"

The chief's words float up in front of me. About no one dying without remorse for something they did or didn't do. I'm going to die, like everyone else, with a duffel bag of regrets. But this is one regret I can stop before it starts. "Deal," I say, "but at 85 percent I think your standards are too low."